PARADISE INHERITED

BY

KATHY BROCK BOYLL

Let them give glory to the LORD and declare His
praise in the islands…
Isaiah 42:12

Copyright © 2010 by Kathy Brock Boyll

Paradise Inherited
by Kathy Brock Boyll

Printed in the United States of America

ISBN 9781609575311

All rights reserved solely by the author. The author guarantees all contents are original and do not infringe upon the legal rights of any other person or work. No part of this book may be reproduced in any form without the permission of the author. The views expressed in this book are not necessarily those of the publisher.

Unless otherwise indicated, Bible quotations are taken from The Amplified Version of the Bible. Copyright © 1987 by The Zondervan Corporation and the Lockman Foundation.

www.xulonpress.com

Dedicated to Pauline Hatfield Brock
Thank you mommy for sharing your love
of reading.

With love and appreciation to my husband, Patrick, who encouraged me to keep writing when I wanted to give up. To Joe Spencer, my beloved cousin, who first told me I should write. To Sinjen Lawson, for countless hours of reading, rereading, and awesome suggestions. To Pam Huber Perry, girlfriends forever, for taking the time to read and encourage. To Terry Lowen for being the comma police. Your help and prayers were greatly appreciated. To Lani Ababon deGuzman, my Hawaii sister, for her prayer support and for including me as member of the Ababon Ohana. And to my father, God, who gave me the story, page by page.

Chapter One

December, 1959

The wedding rehearsal was over. All participants knew when to walk down the aisle and where to stand at the front of the sanctuary, which was decorated for Christmas as well as the wedding. Everyone was in good spirits - everyone that is, except the bride and groom.

Katherine Hampton had noticed looks passing between the couple all afternoon and evening looks that were far from loving. There seemed to be a lot of tension between Tom Tyne and his bride, Susanne, Katherine's older sister by six minutes. Susanne, usually the belle of any ball, was subdued and had abruptly burst into tears and run out of the room several times that day. As for Tom, usually comfortable, funny and friendly in any situation and a friend since childhood to both sisters seemed much quieter than usual as well.

Katherine hoped that she and Susanne could enjoy one last, late night chat as single sisters before they went to bed. For years on Saturday nights, when their parents thought them fast asleep, the girls would huddle in the walk-through closet between their individual bedrooms and talk and giggle until the wee hours of the morning. Chewing on her bottom lip, Katherine realized those chats had stopped when Susanne had become engaged to Tom.

As Katherine slowly walked toward the staircase, her thoughts turned toward Tom and how she had always thought one day she herself would be his bride. Even her mother and father had thought they would marry. She recalled overhearing her parents talking late in the night after Susanne and Tom had come home and announced their engagement. They had been quite surprised.

Her father had spoken loud enough for Katherine to hear as she listened through the door. "Ever since the girls and Tom were children it was always Tom and Katherine who shared the same interests, liked the same books, the same movies. They could talk for hours on just about any subject, even argue, and still walk away best friends. They have been inseparable since kindergarten."

With a tremor in her voice, Katherine's mother had added, "She was there when he broke his leg falling out of the tree-fort they spent the summer building when they were ten years old. Remember when Tom carried her home when she sprained her ankle from a slide into home plate that won the church league softball team the championship? They had measles and chickenpox at the same time, even had their tonsils removed on the same day.

"They were even baptized on the same day," she said as she sniffled.

With a slight laugh that sounded strained, her father said, "Remember how they argued over who would keep the trophy they won at the jitter bug dance contest in high school? Tom and Katherine have been a team from the beginning!"

The sound of what must have been her father's hand slamming against the top of his desk caused Katherine to jump, but she still heard him say, "Sarah, the boy has made his choice! I just never saw this coming!"

Shaking her head to clear away these memories, Katherine quietly climbed the stairs that lead to her bedroom, as she had that night six months ago. For several weeks she had struggled with her feelings about this situation, but eventually she decided to accept, at least on the surface, that Tom had chosen Susanne to be his bride. Because she loved her sister and her best friend, Tom, Katherine had hidden her feelings and put on a happy face for both of them, secretly crying into her pillow at night.

As she brushed her hair, Katherine's thoughts went back to Susanne's behavior when they had arrived back at the house after the rehearsal dinner. She had been surprised when Susanne asked Tom not to walk her to the door, had not kissed him goodnight, and had stomped up the stairs in a fury. Although when she thought about it, Susanne had been behaving oddly, even for Susanne, for the last month. Giddy one moment, and brooding the next.

Katherine's first thought was that Susanne hadn't gotten something she wanted, since that's what usually caused that sort of behavior. Susanne could be a very tender and loving young woman, but first and foremost she was a 'what's mine is mine and what's yours is mine' kind of girl.

"What was that all about?" Samuel Hampton, the girl's father, asked his wife.

"Did the kids have a fight or something?"

Mrs. Hampton stopped in mid-stroke of the embroidery piece she was working on and gave her husband a quizzical look. It was quite odd for him to notice much of anything about her or his daughters. His head was usually into the operation of his hardware store. For the twenty-two years of their life, anything to do with the twins he had typically left to Sarah. She had often wondered if his involvement in their lives would have been different if the twins had been boys.

"Honestly dear, I don't know," Sarah replied timidly. "Everything seemed fine while we were decorating the church this afternoon. Susanne was a bit moody, as she has been for several weeks now. I think it's just nerves."

Having just returned to the den to kiss her parents good night, Katherine had heard her mother's last statement just as she entered the room.

Nerves! That is mother's answer for everything that doesn't go well, Katherine thought. Sarah Hampton had been born and raised in the South. She was soft spoken, Victorian in manner, a real southern belle. The running of the house and children were her responsibility. She also had a tendency to faint under pressure, real or imagined, which enabled her to avoid difficult situations.

"Katherine, do you know what this is about?" Sarah asked.

"No, mother, but I can try to find out if you'd like."

"No, no, let's just give Susanne some time to herself. She'll tell us when she is ready."

With that said, Sarah went into the parlor, as she called it, Samuel headed to the den, and Katherine shrugged her shoulders and started up the stairs to see if Susanne would open her door and talk. She was about half way up when someone knocked on the front door.

"I'll get it," Katherine said to no one in particular.

A second knock came just as Katherine reached for the door knob. Opening it quickly, she was surprised to see Tom standing on the other side of the door. Katherine laughed and said out of an old teasing habit, "Oh, it's you, what do you want?"

Noticing Tom didn't smile or tease back as he used to, Katherine stepped back and opened the door so Tom could come in.

"Actually I need to talk to your father," Tom said sadly.

Hearing Tom's voice Samuel stepped out of the den.

"Tom, lad, I didn't expect to see you until tomorrow afternoon."

"Yes sir, I know, but something has come up and I need to speak with you. It is rather important."

Samuel's bushy brows lifted in surprise then quickly lowered in concern. He obviously couldn't imagine what his soon-to-be son-in-law would need to talk about so solemnly the night before the wedding.

"Very well. Let's step into the den." Samuel motioned Tom ahead of him then followed, closing the door firmly behind him leaving Katherine standing in the entry way.

Her first instinct was to tip toe over and place her ear on the door to listen in on the conversation as she and Susanne had done many times over the years. Just as she stepped in that direction her mother came out of the parlor and Susanne appeared at the top of the landing. Each spoke at the same time.

"Was that Tom?" Both women asked.

Katherine nodded her head and looked from the closed door to her sister and back again.

The women waited, hearing muffled voices from beyond the door, the Grandfather clock in the entry way ticking off several minutes. Then they heard only the clock. Another long moment passed before the door opened.

Samuel motioned for his wife to join him in the den and then looked at his daughters. In his 'no nonsense voice' he ordered, "Susanne come down here, this concerns you. And Katherine, I know you'll have your ear to the wall, so you might as well come in too"

A brief smile flashed across Katherine's face. Biting her bottom lip to keep a laugh from erupting, she put her head down and walked quickly past her father into the room.

At the same moment, out of learned obedience to her father's rules, Suzanne took one step toward the stairs, then stopped, stomped her foot and screamed, "No father, I will not be a farmer's wife and go grubbing in the dirt on some island, and leave my friends and family. As for you Tom Tyne, how dare you go behind my back and try to get my family to support your ridiculous plans? Or are you trying to weasel out of marrying me? Well let me save you the trouble. I won't marry you now or ever! It's over Tom!"

She turned and stormed back to her room, slamming the door for emphasis.

Katherine stood there in total confusion with her mouth hanging open. Who was a farmer? Tom had worked at father's hardware store since he was fifteen and was next in line for promotion to Shipping Manager. What island? What was this all about?

"Katherine, close your mouth," her father snapped.

Sarah looked through the doorway and stared at the empty staircase for a moment, then asked her husband, "What was she talking about? She can't just call off the wedding the night before. What will people say?"

"You and Katherine need to sit down. Tom will explain it." Samuel replied as he directed them to the couch.

"I assume you have a good reason for upsetting my sister on the night before the wedding," Katherine spoke up in her sister's defense.

Clearing his throat and running his fingers through his hair, Tom looked at each off the Hamptons briefly and said, "There is no easy way to say this. I must leave within the next two hours to catch a train that will take me to San Francisco, where I am to board a ship bound for Hawaii."

"Hawaii! Wow that is exciting!" Katherine smiled and then checked herself when she saw the panic appear on her mother's face.

"Whatever for?" Sarah said just barely above a whisper.

"Because he has inherited some land, a farm or coffee plantation or something, he doesn't really know, and must leave immediately," came the answer from Susanne who had crept down the stairs and now stood quietly behind them in the doorway.

"He expects me to drop all our wedding plans and leave in the middle of the night with no way of knowing when, or at least how long it would be until we'd come back. He doesn't even know if there is a house or a grass hut!"

Samuel looked from Tom to Susanne, then toward the couch where his wife lay, having apparently fainted during or just after Susanne's statement. He sighed and scratched the back of his neck. "Two hours you say. Well, my boy, it seems you have some decisions to make. Stay here and marry Susanne as planned or call off the wedding, making a laughing stock of my poor daughter, and go off on a grand adventure."

"Father!" Susanne screeched. "Didn't you hear me, don't you listen? I just called off the wedding! I refuse to marry him now or ever!"

At the same moment, as if not hearing her sister, Katherine spoke - "Hawaii! What an adventure! Oh, Tom, how exciting."

Susanne hissed between clinched teeth. "Exciting? Adventure? Katherine are you crazy? If you think it's so grand, so exciting, you marry Tom. You go!"

Susanne stomped out of the room and up the stairs and slammed her bedroom door.

This is going to work out perfectly, Susanne said quietly to her reflection in the dressing table mirror. She did a little jig as she spun around and placed her brush and comb in the open suitcase on her bed.

After Susanne's abrupt departure, Tom sighed, realizing he felt relieved by her rejection. He winced at the sound of the slamming door, but continued with his story.

"You see sir, I haven't told you everything. There is a part of the plan that does cause quite a dilemma for me. In order to receive my inheritance I have to arrive in Honolulu by Christmas morning, which is the end of this week, and I have to have a wife. I have to live in the islands for five years before I can officially inherit whatever is there for me.

"Just how and when did you come to know of this information?" Samuel asked.

"I received a telegram this morning. Apparently I have, or had, an uncle on my mother's side and they were both Hawaiians. I am listed as the heir in his will and all his earthly possessions including some land go to me if I meet the specified requirements."

Tom could tell by everyone's expressions that the news that he was part Hawaiian had come as a surprise. Actually it had been quite a surprise to Tom as well. His parents had died when he was very young and his father's sister had raised him, never mentioning his mother's heritage. But it certainly did explain the permanent tan he'd been teased about all of his life.

"So what are you going to do?" Katherine asked.

He looked at Katherine but addressed Samuel. "Well sir, its apparent Susanne won't have me now, and I do feel this is my only chance to make something of myself. I guess I'll just go in hopes they'll give in and allow me to stay single a while longer."

Samuel shook his head and said, "Did the telegram explain why you had to have a wife?" Or why you have to be there by Christmas Day?"

"No sir. I suppose they just assumed I'd be married by now. Their only other instructions were to take the taxi that would arrive to take us to the train station. The telegram did mention that other instructions would follow."

"That's quite a chance you are taking, Tom. Considering Susanne's stance on this matter, however, it seems you have no other choice," Samuel replied.

"That's not entirely true, Father," Katherine spoke softly.

Quickly stepping between the two men and looking deeply into Tom's eyes she continued. "I'll go with you."

Surprised at the statement, both men looked at Katherine.

Seeing the confusion on their faces she plunged ahead. "Listen to me. It's a reasonable idea. Tom and I have been friends, since kindergarten. Good friends. What better way to start a marriage? Tom, I know you don't love me like a sweetheart, but it could work."

She looked from Tom to her father, then back at Tom. Her heart raced as she waited to see if Tom would agree to this suggestion. She chewed her bottom lip and didn't realize she was holding her breath until she heard her father speak.

Looking at his daughter with a mixture of sadness and amazement, he said to Tom, "Well, son, it seems you have yet another decision to make, and quickly. Your two- hour time limit is now down to one hour and a half."

Tom took Katherine's hands in his and looked deeply into her eyes.

"Are you sure Kate?" he whispered. "This isn't a game. It's a lifetime decision. If we marry it's for life, not until supper, like when we were kids and you wanted to play house."

"I know the difference, and I know I'm not your first choice, but if you'll have me, I'll go with you," she whispered back.

A smile crept slowly over Tom's face and then his eyes.

"Alright!" He whispered.

He then looked over Katherine's head at her father, and spoke boldly, yet respectfully, to Samuel. "I know this is quite unusual sir, but with your permission, may I have Katherine's hand in marriage?"

Her father didn't say anything for several moments. Then he looked at his daughter rather oddly, like he was suddenly seeing her for the first time and just realizing *she wasn't just his little tomboy anymore. When had she become such a beauty*? He thought to himself.

Katherine had moved to sit on the couch next to her mother during her father's silence. Hands clenched tightly, she nodded her head when her father's eyes asked the question that words did not say. Samuel sighed. "Alright my boy, but I've run out of daughters so you'd better stick with this one!"

Katherine could barely keep herself from leaping up and throwing her arms around her father's neck. Both her heart and head were spinning at the sudden turn of events.

"Thanks for everything sir. I'll take care of her I promise," Tom said as he eagerly pumped Samuel's hand.

"Now I've got to go get my things!" He bolted for the door and called over his shoulder, "I'll be back in an hour!"

Katherine nodded, and when the door closed she ran as fast as she could up the stairs. She had much to do in so little time.

"I'll be right up to get the trunk Katherine," her father called from the den.

"Trunk? Why does Katherine need a trunk? Where is she going?" asked Sarah, who had just regained her senses.

"Well dearest, it seems our Katherine is to marry Tom and go to Hawaii for five years."

Sarah blinked once then promptly fainted again, managing to land squarely on the softest of the throw pillows. Samuel sighed with exasperation, then went to retrieve the steamer trunk from the attic.

Several thoughts whirled around in her head as Katherine waited for her father. *Was this really happening?* In less than an hour she would be off on the adventure of a lifetime. *How was this possible?* Only two hours ago she had stood next to her twin sister preparing to be the maid-of-honor, and suddenly she was to be the bride. She had accepted the fact that Susanne had somehow managed to land Tom, the man she had always dreamed would be hers. Now, by default, he would be hers, after all.

The thoughts were confusing, but she knew there was no time to spend hashing this out.

"I'll worry about it tomorrow. Right now I've a train to catch." She chuckled to herself as she realized how often she had thought of Susanne as the Scarlet O'Hara type, yet here she was *putting off thinking until tomorrow*. Again she chuckled, feeling a bit giddy at the thought of what was before her.

"What's so funny?" her father asked when he walked in with her trunk just as the giggle erupted from Katherine's throat.

"Nothing really, I suppose it is nervous laughter."

"Well, humor is a good way to relieve stress, but you'd best get moving. You only have about forty-five minutes left until Tom returns," he said as he left the bedroom to go downstairs to check on his wife.

If he returns, Katherine's inner voice said. *Maybe he'll suddenly realize he's making a big mistake and just head off to Hawaii alone.*

She gave her head a tiny shake to clear those thoughts. Father was right- time was slipping by very quickly.

"You'd better get moving" a soft voice spoke from the closet doorway.

Katherine's head popped up and she made instant eye contact with her twin. Rushing to her, she threw her arms around Susanne and hugged her tight. "Oh Sus, are you sure you won't change your mind?"

"No Kat, I won't change my mind" Susanne replied. "It should have been you marrying Tom all along. I never really wanted to marry him, it was just my jealousy over the friendship the two of you have had all these years. It's just, well, things got out of hand. I'm ashamed to say I tricked him into thinking he'd proposed when in fact he hadn't really. But being a gentleman, he didn't know how to back away once I'd started telling everyone we were engaged."

Stunned, Katherine stepped back then slowly lowered herself to the floor. "Oh Sus how could you do this to him?"

Fighting back tears Susanne sat on the closet floor in front of her sister and tried to explain. "It was awful and mean of me I know, and I tried to tell mother, honest I did, but she just wouldn't listen.

Fortunately it's really turning out for the best. You'll see. I meant what I said. I'm not cut out to be a farmer's wife. Adventure is almost too large a word for me to spell, much less live out."

The girls sat there a moment longer, and then Susanne stood up, took Katherine's hand and pulled her up after her.

"Can you ever forgive me?" Susanne asked in a whisper.

Katherine had never been able to stay mad at her twin for long, so she just smiled and hugged her sister once more. "Come on, help me pack" she said.

The trunk wasn't large, but there wasn't really time to pack much anyway. She'd have her mother send the rest of her personal belongings once she and Tom knew their address. The girls whirled around the room gathering things that each thought should go. Katherine reasoned that the weather in Hawaii was much the same as California and was relieved that she had the necessary clothing. After rejecting some items and running around hunting a few more things, the girls had the trunk nearly full in an amazing twenty minutes.

"Don't close it. I'll be right back," Susanne said as she hurried through the closet passage.

Katherine took one final review of what she had packed. Blouses, peddle-pushers, two skirts, one dress for church, jeans, sneakers, sandals, bathing suit, the family picture taken last Easter that had sat on her dresser, and most importantly her Bible. Of course there were the personal grooming items, nightgown and bathrobe. Seeing those items made

Katherine blush as she realized she would soon be Tom's wife. Just as Susanne came back into her bedroom carrying a carefully wrapped package and an envelope, Katherine heard her father call. She glanced toward the door but quickly turned back to ask about the package.

"What's that?"

"Oh just a little something I bought for you a while ago," Susanne said with a sneaky smile, and a twinkle in her eye. "It's a surprise, and I don't want you to open it until after you are on board the ship, but definitely before the wedding."

The twinkle then appeared in Katherine's eyes, "Oh no way, let me open it now."

Susanne shook her head and hid the package behind her back. "Nope, it's my way or I take it back."

"Katherine" her father called again.

"Coming father," she shouted, then stuck her tongue out at Susanne as they had done as children. She left the room laughing and hurried down the stairs.

Susanne sighed and turned with her package and placed it lovingly in the trunk. This is as it should be, she thought. We'll all be happier. Closing the trunk and fixing the lock she turned and walked back to her bedroom, gently closing the closet door behind her. She wouldn't see her sister off, she was too embarrassed at her behavior toward Tom and besides, she had some things she needed to take care of quickly.

Samuel stood in his den looking out the window into the night sky. The stars were shining brightly with the moon casting just enough light to make the world look peaceful.

I should be upset, he thought, *but strangely, I'm more at peace about this situation than I ever was at the idea of Susanne marrying Tom. He's a good man, a hard worker, honest and most importantly, he has a strong relationship with Jesus. Call me crazy, but I just never could see him and Susanne as a successful match. I should have stopped the courtship months ago; I don't know why I didn't. I only hope I'm not making another mistake by letting Katherine go like this.* He sighed just as Katherine entered the room.

"Sorry father, Susanne and I were saying good-bye."

"How is she taking this change of plans?" he asked.

"Quite well, actually, she says it's for the best." Katherine knew it wasn't her place to share her sister's confession with their father; she would let Susanne explain if and when she was ready.

Samuel took his daughter's hands in his. "Are you sure about this Kitten? Is this really what you want to do?"

Hearing her father use the pet name he'd called her when she was a small child, she looked at him for only a moment then flew into his arms, tears filling her eyes. He suddenly looked older to her. She felt him sigh as she clung to him. "Oh yes father, if Tom comes back and if he still wants me to go with him, nothing could stop me."

Samuel kissed her forehead and said, "Alright then, you go with my blessing. If it were any other man besides Tom there would be no way I'd allow this, but you two have spent years developing a solid relationship. I do believe you'll make a good match."

Father and daughter stood quietly with their arms around each other for several minutes. Seeing the lights of the taxi pull into the driveway, Katherine took a deep breath, and hugged her father tightly once more.

True to his word Tom had returned. *Did he still want her to go?* She quickly kissed her father's cheek, and then with strong purposeful steps, answered the door as she had earlier, but this time with butterflies dancing in her stomach.

Tom stood in the doorway not speaking for just a moment, staring at the young woman who was so familiar to him. The top of her head barely reached the middle of his chest. As children he'd realized she had a wonderful sense of humor and infectious laughter. In their teens he'd been mesmerized by her shining black hair that waved halfway down her back when it wasn't in a ponytail. He had gotten lost in her dark piercing eyes more times than he would admit.

"Tom," Katherine finally spoke his name timidly, breaking into his thoughts. "Are we going or what?"

He wrinkled his nose like he did when he was caught daydreaming and answered, "Yes, if you still want to go. It's now or never."

"It's now," Katherine smiled brightly. "Of course I still want to go. You can't seriously believe I'd miss the opportunity for our grandest adventure yet?

Swinging from vines, with monkeys and elephants for pets?"

Tom laughed and shook his head as he took her hand. "Me Tarzan, you Jane, let's get moving."

A movement on the stairs caused Tom to pull his gaze away from Katherine to find Samuel standing nearby, holding Katherine's trunk.

Tom took the trunk from him and softly said, "Thank you sir."

Samuel nodded. Clearing his throat he turned to Katherine and suggested she go to the parlor to say good-bye to her mother.

"I'll be just a moment," she said to Tom, as she turned and walked quickly down the hall. The door leading into the parlor stood slightly ajar. The lights were dim.

"Mother," Katherine called softly as she entered the room.

"Come in dear." Her mother spoke with a slight quiver in her voice.

Katherine saw her mother standing by the window watching the night sky just as her father had done moments before. "It's time for me to leave and..."

Her mother stopped her from speaking by placing two fingers over Katherine's lips just like she used to do when Katherine was little and would be interrupting her mother's conversation.

"Katherine, I don't quite understand what has happened. I'm confused actually, but your father tells me it's probably the best possible situation. We've always loved Tom like a part of the family; it's just you girls' suddenly switching places!"

Katherine took her mother's hands in her own and gently rubbed them with her thumbs. "It will be fine I promise," She said. "And maybe you and Susanne should have a heart-to-heart tomorrow, or at least very soon."

Katherine's mother looked at her quizzically, "Why?'

"Oh, mother, now you know you raised us not to story on each other. Go directly to the source, that's what you've always said." Katherine chuckled. Standing up she held onto her mother's hand and said, "I need to go now. Tom and the taxi are waiting."

"You will write, won't you dear?" her mother asked.

"Of course I'll write." Katherine bent down again and kissed her mother. "I love you Mommy." Blinking back a tear, she turned and walked to Tom who waited by the taxi holding the door open for her.

As the taxi pulled away, Katherine turned and looked back at her childhood home. So many happy memories; it was suddenly harder to leave than she had expected. She saw three different window curtains drawn back and lifted her hand and waved. Three waves came back at her and before she could turn around each of the curtains dropped, signaling the end of this chapter of her life. A single tear slipped down her cheek.

"Are you alright?" Tom asked gently.

She took his hand and squeezed it lightly as she looked into his worried eyes and said, "I'm alright."

As they settled in for the ride, both silently prayed, *Please Jesus go with us.*

Chapter Two

Tom and Katherine were quiet for several minutes. For the first time in their years of being friends neither knew quite what to say. Finally Tom turned to her and said, "It's been quite a day."

Katherine nodded while continuing to look out the window.

"Are you sure this is what you want to do, Kate?" Tom asked.

With a deep sigh she turned away from the window. "It's not really what I want to do that is important to me at the moment. Are you sure this is what you want? I mean, you were engaged to Susanne, not me, and well, we've been friends too long not to be honest with each other now."

Tom looked into her eyes and saw hurt and hope in them. "To be honest, I'm not even sure how I got engaged to Susanne. We were walking home from the church picnic, you know, the day you were down with the flu and didn't get to go."

She nodded again.

Paradise Inherited

"We got to talking about marriage and I was asking her opinion on a few things and the next thing I knew she threw her arms around me and said yes. Like a dope I said, 'yes what'?" She started laughing and then hollering to everyone within listening distance that we were engaged. People started clapping and waving. Kate, I didn't know what to do. I didn't want to embarrass her. I really thought she was joking, but when we reached your house she ran screaming for your parents, announcing our engagement."

"I remember," Kate replied, as she recalled the moment, and could again feel the way her chest had hurt and how for a few minutes she hadn't been able to catch her breath.

Now, knowing both sides of the story, great relief flooded her heart. "Oh Tom, Susanne set you up."

"What? How? Why? What do you mean?" he asked, confused.

She took his hand. "Susanne confessed to me while I was packing that she has been jealous of our friendship for years. And well, we'd had a sisterly fight the morning of the picnic and she decided it was a good way to get even. She told me she didn't expect it to go so far. She really wanted to call it off, but mother got to planning and she didn't have the nerve to tell the truth. And she just couldn't resist being the center of attention and envy for awhile. She told me to tell you she is so truly sorry for the putting you through this."

Tom sat stunned for several seconds and then started to laugh. Katherine watched him for just a moment and then started laughing too.

"It's not really funny, Tom said finally. "I guess I was too intimidated by your father to put a stop to it."

"Don't get me wrong," he continued seriously. "I love Susanne, like a sister." He then reached for Katherine's face and gently took her chin in his hand and lifted her face so that their eyes met. "I'm not 'in love' with her now, nor have I ever been 'in love' with her."

Before Katherine could reply the taxi pulled into the train station. They were distracted by the lights and the need to pay the driver, collect their trunks and get their tickets.

When the man behind the counter handed Tom the train tickets, Katherine noticed he also handed him an envelope.

"What's that?" she asked, pointing to it.

"Secret instructions, nosey britches," he teased as Katherine grabbed the envelope from his hands.

"Hey, it's addressed to Mr. and Mrs. Tyne!" Katherine said in astonishment.

"Well, yes, remember-I am supposed to be with my wife."

"Oh, right," Katherine said, and felt herself beginning to blush.

"Wow! I've never seen you blush before!" Tom grinned. "It's cute."

Katherine gave him a goofy grin in return, and slugged him playfully in the arm.

Tom smiled while rubbing his arm and said, "Come on, let's go find a place to open *'our'* envelope and catch a train."

The train station was old and small having been built when the trains first started traveling the California coast. It was nearly deserted, but this was to be expected at one-thirty in the morning; so finding a private place to open the envelope wasn't a problem. Inside was a letter from the attorney they would meet in Honolulu. Tom held the letter so that Katherine could read at the same time.

Aloha Mr. Tyne,

Enclosed you will find your tickets for the ship. During the voyage, should you need additional funds for incidentals, my office has advised the ship's bank to extend you whatever amount you need.

I am looking forward to doing business with you. Please be at my office on the first Monday in January at 9:00 a.m. A driver will be at the front of your hotel to provide transportation. The desk clerk can assist in identifying him for you.

Respectfully,
Jonathan M. Murphy
Attorney at Law

"That's it?" Katherine cried.

Tom looked at the letter again, examining both sides. "Yep. Nothing has been added," he teased.

Still perplexed, Katherine continued. "So how is it you never knew about this Uncle? Didn't your Aunt say anything about him?

Tom gazed out the window and quietly responded, "No, she rarely spoke of my father, and never mentioned my mother. When I'd ask she'd always change the subject. I gleaned over the years that she wasn't thrilled that her only brother had become a missionary, and his sudden death was something she couldn't or wouldn't talk about. I'm hoping by next week at this time we'll both know a great deal more about my history."

Tom looked at Katherine for a moment and said, "You might want to wait to marry me until we find out who I am or rather who my family was."

"Nah," Katherine waved away the suggestion, "I know you well enough not to have any doubts. Anything we find out will just be icing for the cake. Besides, we always said we wanted to go on a grand adventure, on a road that never ends. It seems to me we're getting our dream." She leaned over and kissed Tom's cheek.

His hand went to his face and gently touched the spot where her lips had just been. It was the first time she had ever kissed him and as she blushed again Tom's eyes twinkled. Before he could say anything she again punched his arm and smiled.

"Hey, stop punching me! Husband- beating is not allowed! That is house rule Number One," he said, as they both laughed.

With a teasing tone in her voice and a twinkle in her eye Katherine asked, "Does that apply to the wife as well?"

Tom reached over and playfully punched her arm, and replied, "Maybe."

They both laughed again.

After the brief moment of playfulness, both calmed down and sat quietly waiting for their train. Suddenly Katherine popped up. "Hey, what did that letter say about extra funds?

Before Tom could answer, the station master walked up to them.

"Mr. and Mrs. Tyne? He asked.

Tom and Katherine looked at each other and smiled. Tom nodded and stood up to greet the man. "Yes, I'm Tom Tyne."

"Your train should be arriving shortly. Follow me please!"

Shortly after two o'clock the train pulled out of the station. Tom was able to find seats for himself and Katherine, as there weren't many travelers in the coach. They quickly made themselves comfortable for the three-hour train ride.

Despite the excitement she felt over the beginning of the great adventure, the start of the next chapter of her life, it wasn't long before Katherine's head rested on Tom's shoulder and she was fast asleep.

Even though he was tired, Tom had too many things spinning around in his head to sleep. But he did close his eyes and tried to relax. There would be four and a half days of ocean travel with time to sleep; right now he just wanted to sort out the happenings of this day and what it had brought so unexpectedly into his life. How he came close to marrying one sister, and by a miracle, ended up with the other sister, the one he'd wanted to marry since he was five years old.

Yes, it was a miracle, and Tom suddenly realized he's been walking and planning in his own strength the last several months instead of turning to the strength and wisdom he should have relied on. *"Oh Father,"* Tom whispered his prayer.

"Forgive me."

Tom had a silent a prayer conversation with his first best friend, Jesus. They had much to talk about.

No, Tom thought, *I have much to listen to.*

The train swayed back and forth, clacking over the rails. Katherine slept peacefully, confident in Tom, and firmly believing that wherever she went, God went with her.

Despite his intention of staying awake, Tom realized he had drifted off when he was startled by someone gently tapping his shoulder.

The conductor stood over him, his lips moving. Tom blinked a couple of times to clear his head and asked the man to repeat himself.

"We'll be arriving in San Francisco shortly," he said.

"When you depart the train, go to the main terminal entrance. A driver will be waiting to take you to the pier."

The conductor's voice had also awakened Katherine. After he walked away she stretched and yawned, "Are we there yet?"

"Yes, we'll be pulling in shortly." Tom replied. "Did you sleep well?"

"Not bad for sitting up. The pillow was a little hard, however," she said and laughed as Tom pointed to the drool spot on his shoulder.

"Nice," he laughed.

As instructed by the conductor, the couple made their way to the terminal entrance. Tom let go with a soft whistle when he spotted a chauffeur in traditional black jacket and cap, holding a sign with 'Tyne' written on it. Their trunks arrived and were quickly loaded into the slick black limousine.

It was still early, five thirty in the morning, but already the city was coming to life. After a short ride to the pier Tom and Katherine emerged from the limo just steps from the most beautiful ship either of them had ever seen.

A man in a white uniform stepped forward. "Good Morning Mr. Tyne," he said, and then tipped his hat to Katherine. "My name is Phillip. I will be your steward for this voyage. Please follow me and we'll get you settled."

Oh my, Katherine said to herself, *I must be dreaming*.

Noting that no one else seemed to be around besides crew members scurrying here and there, Tom stopped their guide and asked, "Are we the only ones on this ship, besides the crew?"

"For the moment, yes," answered the steward. "The other passengers will be arriving and boarding in a few hours. It is our pleasure to get you and your wife settled early. Perhaps you can get a bit of rest before the ship gets underway."

At the word 'wife' Tom's head snapped up and his eyes widened.

"Oh!" he said as he looked at Katherine. "Tell me, Phillip, would it be possible for me to speak to the Captain? There is a matter I must discuss with him as soon as possible."

"Of course, Mr. Tyne, I'll notify the captain of your request and get back to you as soon as I can. Would you like me to take you to your cabin first or do you wish to wait here?" Phillip asked. He was obviously curious, but too professional to ask any personal questions.

Tom noted that Katherine had taken a seat on one of the lovely couches in the lounge area, so he took that as a signal. "We'll wait here if that is alright."

With a nod the man turned and headed for the bridge.

Tom took a seat next to Katherine and explained. "I know this has been very sudden Kate, but I feel we must be married as soon as possible. I won't make you uncomfortable or tarnish your reputation by not taking this important step as quickly as possible."

Katherine didn't say anything immediately, and Tom began to wonder if she had changed her mind. "Kate, are you sure?"

She looked into his eyes then and smiled. "Yes Tom, I'm sure. We'll make a great team."

He took her hand, smiled, and softly said. "We always have."

It's what I've always wanted, she thought.

It wasn't long before Phillip was walking back into the lounge. "The captain is most pleased you are aboard sir, and will gladly meet with you. He asks if you will join him for breakfast in an hour."

Tom and Katherine thanked Phillip for his efforts and then proceeded to follow him to their cabin to freshen up. When Phillip opened the door to their cabin Tom let out a low whistle. Katherine's eyes were shining as she looked about the room.

Their suite was beautifully decorated in a Polynesian theme. The room was filled with the fragrance of the gardenias that floated in a bowl on the side-board. A bowl of fresh fruit including guava, bananas, and a whole pineapple awaited them, as well as an ample supply of macadamia nuts.

"Are you sure this is our cabin?" Tom asked. It reminded him of a small apartment. "This looks like first class!"

"Ah, yes," Phillip replied. "We are proud to offer first-class accommodations to all of our guests. As you can see, you have a sitting room, bedroom and full bath, and a private patio-or as it's called in Hawaii-a lanai.

Phillip then left stating he'd be back in an hour to direct them to the captain.

Katherine noted that their trunks were already in the bedroom, but felt a little uncomfortable going in there just yet. Instead, she opened the curtains and discovered that their room faced the pier, which was already coming to life. Dock workers were moving crates and luggage, and people were slowly beginning to fill the lobby behind the gate that would eventually be opened to allow them to board the big ship.

She turned to say something to Tom, and saw he was sprawled out on the couch, sound asleep.

"An hour isn't much, but better than nothing," she thought, as she quietly slipped past him and went to open her trunk. She had just remembered

that Susanne had given her instructions to open the package as soon as possible after boarding and before the wedding. Curious now, Katherine searched her purse for the keys to the trunk, and after unlocking the container, opened it as quietly as she was able.

The first thing she noticed was an envelope with her name on it. Also written on the envelope was the directive '*Open First*. Katherine loved surprises, and even though she was tempted to open the package Susanne had placed there, she didn't. Inside the envelope were three short notes. There was one note from Susanne, one from her mother, and one from her father. Odd, I don't remember mother being away from the parlor to put this note together with Susanne's, she thought. Then she decided her father must have included them before he brought the trunk downstairs after she had packed. Holding the letters for just a moment Katherine gently placed them back in her trunk. *I'm just not ready yet; I'll read them after we leave port.*

But before the wedding, she heard Susanne's voice in her head.

Katherine smiled and softly answered her twin, Yes, *Susanne, before the wedding.*

Being twins, they had always been able to know when one was thinking of the other, good or bad. When one was sick or hurt, the other knew before being officially told. About the time they reached junior high their mother had finally stopped dressing them alike, much to their great delight. They were, after all, as different as night and day- Susanne blond and blue-eyed like their mother and Katherine with dark eyes and hair like their father. Their temperaments and personalities were completely different, too. Still many mornings they'd step out of their respective rooms wearing if not the same outfit, at least the same color. They never planned it or even discussed their clothing choices for the next day. It just happened. It felt a bit strange to Katherine that she was soon to wed Tom Tyne, her sister's fiancé until last night, and yet more strange that her sister wouldn't be her maid-of-honor as the girls had always planned.

"God works in mysterious ways," her Granny had always said.

"And He has quite a sense of humor too," Grandpop would chime in.

Yes indeed He does, Katherine said as she closed the trunk and walked softly back into the sitting room where Tom was still reclining and snoring softly.

Katherine stood quietly in the doorway and observed this man who was soon to be her husband. He had been a scrawny, short five-year-old when she first met him. She remembered being head and shoulders taller than him through junior high. In high school Tom began to grow, and with weight training and sports had developed into a muscular six foot hunk. He had wavy black hair, and the darkest brown eyes she had ever seen. The 'Gentle Giant' he'd been nicknamed in school, and soon he would be hers for real. A chill of excitement ran through her.

As promised, Phillip returned within the hour and escorted Tom and Katherine to the captain's cabin. They were greeted warmly by the captain and a little gray-haired lady who turned out to be the captain's mother. She insisted that the young couple call her Martha.

"Some old folks go to retirement homes-I cruise," Martha said, matter of factly.

You meet the most interesting people aboard this ship. Why, a couple of years ago we had the pleasure of having Elvis on board. Sweet boy that Elvis. I don't quite understand 'rocks-n-roll,' but he sure is mighty pretty to look at." She added the last part with a big grin on her face, which caused everyone to laugh as they sat down to breakfast.

Most of the conversation during the meal centered around the history of the ship. The captain explained that the first ship in the cruise line had been a three-masted schooner, which carried tons of food, plantation supplies and general merchandise to Hawaii. It had all started back in the 1800's.

"Our ships have served our country proudly," the captain continued. During both world wars the military requisitioned the company's ships to become troopships and military cargo carriers. It took millions of dollars to restore them to carry tourists. Several of the ships were sold to make this reconstruction possible. This vessel alone carries 761 passengers, all in first class accommodations."

"That's why all the movie stars travel with us." Martha said.

"Movie stars? Will we see movie stars?" Katherine asked with a hint of excitement in her voice.

"You just never know," the Captain said with a twinkle in his eye.

As the meal came to a close, the Captain said, "Mother, how about you take the young lady on a tour before our other passengers arrive. Tom and I will have the talk he requested and we'll meet you in the main reception hall shortly."

Martha looked thrilled to have been given this responsibility, and took Katherine's arm to escort her to the door. Katherine gave Tom a flash of a smile and then walked out behind Martha, who was already delivering a well-rehearsed tour-guide lecture.

"Now then-what can I do for you?" the Captain asked.

Tom didn't hesitate for a moment. "Sir, I'd like to ask you to perform a wedding ceremony as quickly as possible."

A startled look crossed the captain's face for just a moment, but he recovered quickly. "I thought you and Katherine were already married."

"No sir," Tom continued. "We had to leave quickly last night in order to catch the ship on time. Our wedding was scheduled for this afternoon" He didn't think he should mention that there was a different bride involved.

"Ah, I see," the Captain said, as he nodded his head. "Well, it would be my pleasure."

Tom sighed with relief.

"Did you bring your license?"

"License? Oh no sir, we didn't." Tom hadn't given that a single thought.

"We can take care of that," the Captain assured them. "We'll have the ship's doctor re-do your blood tests, wire for the license, and everything should be in order to get you two hitched on our last night at sea before reaching Honolulu." With that the Captain reached out to shake Tom's hand.

Noting that Tom wasn't reaching back the Captain asked, "Is there a problem with that plan?"

Tom felt like a school boy. "Well sir, there is one problem. You see, our cabin has one bedroom."

"Ah yes, well, we'll have Mother stay with Katherine in your cabin, and you can bunk with your steward, Phillip. His cabin partner is not with us this voyage, and I'm sure he won't mind."

Speaking with almost an apologetic tone in his voice the Captain said, "I'd give you another cabin, but we are booked solid this trip, it being Christmas week and all."

Tom looked relieved as he shook the Captain's hand and told him those arrangements would be fine.

Chapter Three

Tom gave Katherine a thumbs-up sign as he walked toward her. She gave him a smile and nod in return. Since passengers were starting to board and the railing where Katherine had been waiting was filling up fast, there wasn't time for the couple to talk privately. Besides, Martha was still talking a mile a minute.

"Can't get a word in edgewise," Katherine whispered to Tom, who just chuckled. Eventually even Martha became interested in the passengers who were boarding and politely excused herself to greet some return guests that she spotted.

Tom took this opportunity to direct Katherine to a more private spot inside the lounge and gave her the news about the delay of their wedding and the cabin arrangements.

The launch was indeed festive, complete with streamers, confetti, balloons, horns and people waving and yelling. For just a moment Katherine and Tom felt a pang of disappointment that no one was down there to wish them bon voyage, but the excitement was contagious never the less. Martha had given them streamers and confetti of their own to throw, and they couldn't let it go to waste!

The ship's horns blasted as it started to slowly move. It was amazing to watch those tiny tugs move the huge ship. After several minutes, people started leaving the railing, heading off to begin making vacation memories.

Martha, Tom and Katherine also started to leave, but when Katherine took one last look at the receding pier she let out a squeal.

"Mother," she yelled and started waved frantically.

"Where?" Tom quickly moved to where she was standing and saw them too. "Mr. H, "Tom hollered and he began to wave his arms over his head.

When Katherine's mother spotted her daughter and Tom, she began to jump up and down and waved back.

"Good luck children, we love you," the wind carried the words over to Tom and Katherine.

Tears fell down the cheeks of the young couples faces.

They must have driven all night to have gotten here in time, Katherine thought. *God bless you both*, Katherine sent up a quick prayer for her parents, and then blew kisses and gave them 'long distance hugs,' which her mother returned.

"What are you doing?" Tom asked. "I've seen you guys do that for years and never was quite sure what it meant."

Katherine smiled and explained that when she and Susanne had started kindergarten their mother had come up with the idea of 'long distance hugs.'

"You stretch your arms out in front of you and pretend to hug the person you are missing or can't actually hug at that moment. Susanne and I both loved this idea and have many times talked about teaching it to our children."

When the Hampton's could no longer be seen, Tom threw an arm around Katherine's shoulder and started walking in the direction of music that was coming from the lounge. It was a comfortable buddy moment, one they had shared many times over the years. Still there was something different about it this time. This time each felt a tingle, like a tiny electric shock, running through their bodies.

The first day aboard ship the two discovered there was plenty to keep them entertained. Everyone was in a jolly Christmas mood. There were crafts to make, tons of sugar cookies to decorate and eat, and even some trees to be decorated. Christmas carols were sung by crew and passengers alike. Someone had even said they had seen Santa in a bathing suit and straw hat at the pool. There was shuffleboard, checkers, card games of every variety and plenty of books and magazines to read. People who had only just met became instant friends, though it was unlikely that most of them would ever see or hear from each other again after the end of the voyage. Nighttime brought moonlight strolls, dancing, and more Christmas carol singing. Best of all, according to Tom, was the food. It was everywhere, at any time day or night, and really good.

It was quite late when Tom and Katherine decided to call it a day. Many continued to party, but the lack of sleep from the night before was beginning to take its toll on both of them. Katherine found Martha and told her she was leaving.

"Good night, Dear. Don't wait up. I've met a nice gentleman who has promised to take me dancing." Martha's eyes twinkled as she leaned in and gave Katherine a quick hug and a pat on the shoulder.

"For an 86 year-old woman, she is amazing," Katherine said to Tom as he walked her back to their cabin.

Before parting for the night Tom and Katherine bowed their heads and Tom prayed. Praying together was another of those things they had done forever, usually with the youth group on Sunday evening. This was the first time they had prayed as an official couple.

Tom thanked God for the blessings of the day, seen and unseen, and asked for guidance and wisdom for them to walk wisely before men, and to be a light to those around them. Finally thanking God for Kate and asking protection for her, he closed his prayer seeking these things in Jesus name.

Neither spoke after that, they just looked deeply into each other's eyes and smiled. Their relationship was taking on new dimensions fast, and even though they didn't speak of it, each was thrilled with the new feelings and emotions that had begun to stir.

Katherine had turned off the light next to her bed and was just starting to fall asleep when she remembered the letters and package she had yet to open. She was just about to get out of bed when she heard the door open and knew it was Martha coming in. Laying back down she pulled up the covers and closed her eyes. It wasn't that she didn't want Martha to know about the package and letters, but something just told her to wait and open them privately.

Before turning off the bathroom light Martha looked over at Katherine and softly sighed at the sight of the sleeping young woman.

Her life is just beginning, Martha said to herself. *I envy her, such a nice young man, he reminds me of my Peter, God Rest his soul.*

The ocean crossing was smooth and neither Tom nor Katherine suffered from seasickness. They participated, at least once, in every activity available on the ship. At dinner, the first night at sea, Tom and Katherine met Ellen and Stafford Lansing, a young couple on their honeymoon. A special friendship between the two couples began and they each promised not to let time or distance bring an end to it.

When alone, Tom and Katherine talked about any and every subject, except the wedding. As comfortable as they were with each other, their coming nuptials made both of them a bit nervous.

This is so silly, but I need him to bring it up, Katherine thought, as she realized she was still unsure of Tom's feelings about marrying her.

Men gathered around the pool or at the bar and discussed sports and cars. Many argued over the win by the Los Angeles Dodgers in the World Series over the Chicago White Sox. Opinions also flew regarding the 1960 Lark by Studebaker and the Rambler Custom 4-door hardtop that was being advertised.

The ladies talked about the latest fashions and the newest movies starring Rock Hudson, Frank Sinatra, and Sandra Dee. Everyone who had not previously been to Hawaii speculated on what awaited them in the Islands. Nearly all the ladies had purchased and brought along James Michener's novel, 'Hawaii.' Several of them found it boring and hard to get into. Others were scandalized by conditions discovered by the first missionaries. Katherine and several others thought the book was wonderful and not only discussed the story but also expressed their opinion that it was exciting that Hawaii had become the 50th state just that past August.

On the second night of the cruise Tom and Katherine felt well-rested and were able to let loose and kick up their heels. It was Big Band Night and the ship's orchestra was doing an excellent job playing the tunes of Benny Goodman, Tommy Dorcey and Glenn Miller.

"They're playing our song, Kate. Should we show them how's it's done?" Tom asked as he stood and reached for Katherine's hand.

Katherine wiggled her eyebrows and gave Tom a mischievous grin.

On purpose they started out off beat and struggling to do the steps, just as they had done at the high school dance contest. People around politely smiled and encouraged them to keep dancing. The couple suddenly stopped moving then began to clap to the beat of the song. When the cymbals crashed Tom reached for Katherine, lifted her up and spun her over his back. She landed and flew through his legs and they were off

The crowd let out a cheer and moved back to allow the couple to swing to their hearts content. It didn't take long for the spotlight to be turned on the dancing couple. The orchestra played one song right into another and Tom and Katherine kept right in step. When the music stopped, a thunderous applause greeted the couple's performance. The couple, slightly out of breath, smiled, bowed and laughed as they ran out of the room into the cool night air.

"We've still got it," Tom said, as they strolled along the deck.

Katherine laughed again. "How long has it been since we danced like that?

"We've been out of high school for four years, so I'd say four and a half years at least."

They walked in silence for a few moments and then Katherine spoke. "Can you believe tomorrow night is Christmas Eve?"

"I know," Tom replied, without saying another word.

It wasn't normal for Tom to be so quiet. Katherine guessed something was on his mind and he'd tell her when he was ready, so she kept quiet, trying not to let any fears or worries take over her thoughts as the two continued their evening stroll in the moonlight. Finally, upon reaching a private, quiet place far away from the activity of the dining room and the music of the ship's orchestra, Tom stopped and turned toward Katherine and looked into her eyes for several minutes. Just as Katherine started to ask if something from dinner was on her face, Tom spoke, softly and with emotion in his voice. "Kate, you are so lovely in this light."

Katherine was thankful it was dark enough that Tom could not see her blush again and gave him a shy smile. He had never said anything like that to her. They had always been pals, buds, best friends. She liked it. These were the type of words she had always dreamed she would hear him say, but had doubted she ever would.

"Kate, did you hear me?" Tom broke through her thoughts.

"Yes, I heard you. I'm just enjoying the moment," she said through a smile. "A girl doesn't hear things like this every day. Let me savor it for a while."

Tom stepped from foot to foot, nervously shifting like the ground was too hot. Then as if remembering something important he said, "Oh. Wait," and reaching into his coat pocket he withdraw a tiny black box.

He bent down on one knee and then raised the tiny box toward Katherine. Tears appeared in her eyes as she watched him. Then she heard the words she had longed to hear.

"Katherine Francis Hampton, I've loved you since we were five years old, I can't imagine my life without you in it. Will you marry me?"

A huge smile erupted on Katherine's face. She leaned down and threw her arms around his neck and squealed with delight.

"I'll take that for a yes," Tom teased.

"Yes! Yes! Yes!" she cried, as happy tears fell down her face. "I love you too."

Suddenly a thunderous applause and cheering broke out behind them. Half the ship's passengers, including Ellen and Stafford, had quietly followed to watch and listen to the romantic moment.

Tom looked back at Katherine and said, "Boy I'm glad you didn't say no. This crowd might have thrown us overboard."

"And this time there will be no question that you proposed. We have witnesses." Katherine laughed.

"Several of them in fact," Tom replied and then he too laughed as he hugged Katherine with one arm and shook hands with Stafford and anyone else who took his hand.

As the men congratulated Tom, the ladies surrounded Katherine to see the ring. It was a simple diamond solitaire, which gleamed and sparkled in the light of the moon. On Katherine's finger it looked perfect. Not too big and not too small.

Back in the lounge, while taking a break from dancing, Tom led Katherine to a table back in the shadows where they could be alone for a few minutes. Reaching for her left hand he kissed the ring and softly spoke.

"This ring belonged to my mother. When my Aunt died I found a couple small boxes with my parent's names on them in the attic. Inside one of the boxes were my mother's journal, the ring and some letters. I haven't read the letters or the journal, but I remembered the ring just before I took the taxi the night we left California. I thought I might need it."

"Thank you," Katherine whispered. "I'm honored to wear it."

In truth, Katherine was deeply touched that he would give her this ring, especially since Susanne had never had an engagement ring, telling everyone she preferred just a plain gold band. That had often puzzled Katherine because Susanne had always loved big, flashy, gaudy pieces of jewelry, whereas she preferred simple, smaller pieces, such as this dainty diamond ring. It was perfect and more than she had expected when she first suggested going with Tom to Hawaii. Even better was the fact that Tom loved her, not just as a friend, but as a sweetheart, a woman he wanted to share this adventure and his life with.

Everyone who had followed Ellen and Stafford to watch the romantic proposal went back to the dining room, so the dancing continued. It seemed every passenger stayed up late into the night to dance and enjoy the celebration with the couple. Everyone was in love that night. Everyone on board was a friend. It was amazing what a bit of romance could do to liven up a party, and it was one great party for the bride and groom-to-be.

Finally, near dawn, the Orchestra stopped playing and the remaining passengers went to their cabins to get a little rest before making the most of their last full day aboard ship.

At her cabin door Tom and Katherine again stopped to pray and give praise to their Heavenly Father before they parted.

"It's been quite a week, Miss Kate," Tom said.

"Indeed it has." she replied, her eyes glistening with happy tears.

He leaned in to kiss her cheek, and then turned and whistled as he walked down the passageway to the cabin he would share with Phillip, only one more night.

Martha let Katherine sleep in the next morning and returned just after nine o'clock with a plate of fresh fruit, bagels and cream cheese and coffee.

"It's time to get up dear," Martha said when she opened the bedroom door and saw Katherine lying there looking out the window at the blue sky.

"Good morning Martha. How thoughtful of you."

"Well, dear, it is your big day and we have a few things to finish this morning."

Katherine felt a sweet tenderness toward Martha, who was filling the role of the bride's adopted grandmother perfectly.

"You have an appointment to get your hair and nails done at the salon, and we really should get your wedding dress out and have the cleaners freshen it for you."

"Dress! Oh my gosh! Martha, I don't have a dress. I mean, I have a Sunday church dress, and the evening gown that I've worn at dinner." Katherine started to panic as she realized she hadn't even thought about a wedding dress. Well, at least not since the day she had gone shopping with her mother and sister for Susanne's gown.

While Susanne had been moody, picking out the most awful dresses and finally selecting one that made her look like Scarlet O'Hara with all the hoops and ruffles, Katherine had admired a simple A-line, empire waist, satin and lace gown. She had held it up to herself in a mirror, but quickly put it away when she heard Susanne and mother headed her way.

Martha gave her a sweet smile and said, "Never mind then Dear. I'm sure your Sunday dress will be lovely."

Martha left the cabin telling Katherine she had some things to check on, and reminded her again of her salon appointment.

Katherine threw back the covers to get up and take a shower. While taking her things from the trunk she realized that she still had not opened the letters and the package Susanne had placed there.

"Now Sis, before the wedding," Susanne's voice echoed in her head.

"Okay, okay. Gee, thousands of miles away and tons of water apart and you are still bossy." Katherine laughed and spoke out loud, as if Susanne were there and could hear her.

She picked up the envelope with Susanne's handwriting on it marked 'Open First.'

Dear Kat,

Again I ask your forgiveness for the dirty trick I played on you and Tom. I realized almost too late that I would have messed up the perfect couple. You and Tom. I do wish you both every happiness and will always keep you both in my thoughts. I hope you find great pleasure in the gift I have for you.

God's Blessings to you on your wedding day.
Love always,
Sus

It was a sweet, touching note, the first and hopefully not the last one she would receive from her sister. Turning to the package, Katherine discovered it was slightly heavier than it appeared. She opened it carefully, almost afraid to know what was inside. With a gasp, she quickly tore off the paper when she spotted what the package contained.

It was the gown, the very gown she had held up to the mirror in the bridal shop. *How is this possible?* Katherine asked herself as tears began streaming down her face. When she took the dress out of the box another note fell out of the folds.

Gotcha,

Mother and I saw you admiring this dress while we were shopping. We decided to buy it and save it for you, never realizing you would use it so soon. We both knew no matter how you tried you'd never find a dress more perfect for you. We wish we could be with you. Know we are there in our hearts.

Love always, Sus.

Along with the dress were all the necessities. White lace stocking, long white slip, new undergarments, and satin ballet slippers just like she and Susanne had always said they wanted to wear when they got married.

The next letter, addressed in her mother's handwriting, was labeled with the directive, 'Open After The Package.'

A locket fell out of the envelope as Katherine removed the letter. Quick reflexes enabled her to catch it just before it hit the ground. Katherine recognized the locket. It had been her Granny's. She clutched it to her heart as she read mother's note.

My Darling Katherine,

Always remember I love you. There have been times when I sensed you doubted my love. Those were times I was caught up in my own growing up and I am sorry if you ever felt my love for you was less than it should have or could have been. Wear this locket as a reminder that your heart is never far away from mine, though we are an ocean apart.

God Bless You on your wedding day and always,
Love, Mother

This brought Katherine to full blown sobs, causing great big tears to splash onto her letter. It was in this condition that Martha found her when she returned from her errands.

"Oh my dear, what has happened?" a distressed Martha asked.

Katherine was able to compose herself long enough to point at the beautiful gown and hand Martha the two letters she had read moments before.

"Ah," Martha replied after reading them. "So you see, your family will be here in spirit after all."

Katherine smiled through her tears, and between gulps asked Martha if she would take the dress to be pressed, as she needed to hurry to get ready or she would miss her salon appointment.

Martha was thrilled at this chance to be helpful and hurried off on the next errand.

It was while showering that Katherine remembered she had not opened the third letter, the one her father had written to her.

Oh I don't think I can do it emotionally right now. Besides the instructions were only to open the box before the wedding, Katherine reasoned. "Later, yes I will read it later."

"Yes, Miss Scarlet," she said out loud, laughing at her own silliness.

Tom spent his day trying to find ways to be useful. The main dining room was being decorated for the wedding. He asked if he could help, but was told everything had been taken care of. After several laps around the deck, he plopped into a chair and tried to relax. This lasted only minutes, then he was up and pacing again.

Why am I so nervous? It's not like I haven't thought of this day many times. It feels so natural, so right. Come on Tom old boy, get a grip.

Shaking his head to clear his thoughts Tom decided to go to the barber shop and get the works. A good hot towel on his face would surely calm his nerves.

If I were a drinking man a good stiff drink might be called for. Laughing, he entered the barber shop for his last shave and hair cut as a single man.

The day passed quickly, but not quickly enough for Katherine. She wondered what Tom was doing, and allowed herself to think of her parents and sister and wished they could be with her for the wedding.

If wishes were pennies we'd all be rich, Katherine thought to herself.

All curled and polished, Katherine paced nervously, occasionally stopping to study herself in the mirror. She was hardly able to believe the vision was her. A single tear of joy had just slid down her cheek when her attention was interrupted by a tap on her cabin door.

Martha opened it to admit Ellen. Ellen, dressed in a simple but stylish red cocktail dress, was to be Katherine's matron-of-honor, and Phillip had agreed to walk Katherine down the aisle.

"I'd be most honored," he had replied to Katherine's request the night before. She guessed Phillip to be nearly the same age as her father, and since her father wouldn't be there, she had decided he would make the perfect stand-in.

"You look beautiful!" Ellen exclaimed as she rushed over to give Katherine a hug.

"If I'd had a daughter, Phillip said, "I'd hope she would have been just as beautiful and sweet a girl as you."

Martha held out the bridal bouquet of gardenias, tuberose and yellow roses.

"Oh Martha, these are beautiful! Thank you so much!" Katherine exclaimed. She knew there were fresh flowers on the dinner tables every evening, yet had not considered flowers for her wedding.

"I'm so pleased you like them, my dear." Martha smiled warmly. "Now, I do believe it's time to go.

After quick hugs and a heartfelt thank you to Ellen, Phillip and Martha, Katherine softly asked, "Can I have just a moment alone?"

Everyone stepped out in the hall. When the door closed behind them, Katherine closed her eyes and took a moment to enjoy the lovely fragrance of her flowers, and then said a quick prayer. She couldn't imagine the biggest event of her life without asking her Heavenly Father to be there and to guide, direct and help her be the wife Tom needed.

Nearly everyone on board- passengers and crew- filled the dining room, waiting for the bride to arrive.

The room, normally decorated beautifully, was over-the-top, in Tom's opinion. The crew had gone above and beyond to make this Christmas Eve wedding extra special. The crystal chandeliers were turned down low, allowing the candles and Christmas lights to fill the room with a peaceful, gentle glow. An archway filled with fragrant flowers stood at the end of the isle Katherine would walk down. A big window allowed the glorious setting sun, just reaching the horizon, to provide the exact amount of light to make the tinsel sparkle on the Christmas trees.

Tom kept blowing little puffs of air as nerves began to take hold of his body. He looked from the captain to Stafford and said, "It is a good thing I'm standing between you guys, in case I fall over," he joked.

Just when he didn't think he could bear even one more minute of waiting, the doors opened. The orchestra began to play, and Ellen began a slow step down the aisle.

As the music swelled, a vision stood in the doorway. Tom grinned from ear to ear at the sight of his bride. He knew at that moment that he was seeing an angel.

Katherine slowly walked toward him, a sweet, peaceful smile on her face.

Phillip held her hand on his arm and wore the look of a 'proud papa' on his face. Tom was sure his heart was going to burst from happiness. Then she stood next to him, took his hand and smiled. Together they turned to face the captain and the ceremony began.

When asked, "Who gives this woman to be married to this man," everyone in the room hollered, "We do," which of course brought laughter to one and all.

Tom surprised Katherine again when he placed a beautiful gold band with three tiny diamonds alongside her solitaire engagement ring. Now the set was complete and it fit perfectly.

He wished his mother could see how lovely Katherine looked wearing her rings.

Finally the words, "I now pronounce you man and wife," were spoken.

"Tom, you may kiss your bride," The captain encouraged, as he smiled at the young couple.

For the first time in her life, since meeting Tom, Katherine suddenly felt shy. She had dreamed of this moment more times than she could remember. Then Tom smiled, silently mouthed the words, "I love you," and pulled her gently into his arms.

Katherine's shyness immediately lifted, replaced by an overwhelming sense of contentment such as she had never known. Lifting her face toward Tom's they leaned into each other, sweetly, tenderly allowing their lips to meet for the very first time. Katherine's first thought was how soft Tom's lips were. The kiss only lasted a second, but was pure and wonderful.

At that moment someone in the room yelled, "Hey Tom, you can do better than that"

Tom winked at Katherine who laughed and before she knew it, Tom had bent her back over his arm and kissed her soundly, just like Rhett Butler had kissed Scarlet, in '*Gone With The Wind.*' This brought the entire room of attendees to their feet, hoots and applause filling the room.

After the simple ceremony everyone was invited to a special buffet dinner to be served out on the deck. It was a lovely evening. The stars were shining brightly and a warm breeze gently blew, as the ship sailed smoothly into the night.

While everyone ate, the crew performed their magic and turned the dining room from a chapel into a beautiful ballroom. A table had been set up, and to Tom and Katherine's surprise, gifts surrounded a three tier wedding cake. The reception began and everyone danced until midnight. At the stroke of midnight everyone shouted "Merry Christmas!" then broke into a sweet rendition of 'Silent Night.'

Just before saying their prayers that night for the first time as husband and wife, Katherine suddenly realized it was Christmas and she had no gift for Tom. Tom took her into his arms and told her he was receiving the greatest Christmas gift ever.

"I have you! What more could I possibly want?" he whispered into her ear.

She smiled shyly, and then with a gleam in her eye she said, "Yes, well maybe this year it's okay, but let's be clear. Just because our anniversary will fall on Christmas, that doesn't mean you can get away with only one gift!"

"Yes, Dear," Tom said with a laugh and a huge smile from Katherine.

Chapter Four

Almost all of the passengers including Tom and Katherine were on deck bright and early the next morning. The sun was warm on their faces as they stood and watched the ship get closer and closer to their destination.

"Hey, we're stopping! Why aren't we going on in?"asked a man standing at the railing next to Tom.

Martha, who had just arrived with two cups of coffee for the newlyweds, spoke up and shared her wealth of experience and knowledge about this particular cruise ship, and some of what she'd learned about Hawaii.

"The captain slows the ship to a stop at the entrance to the harbor to ask permission to enter. Listen. In just a moment you'll hear the request."

Just then three long blasts sounded from the ship's massive horn. Moments later a return trumpet could be heard from a conch shell that was being blown by a young man at the end of the pier.

"As this was once the land in which a King and Queen reigned, this simple ceremony is in their honor and is also given to honor the gods of the island. The return trumpet of the conch shell is their issue of welcome."

"What do you mean by the gods of the island? I thought the missionaries changed all that years ago?" Katherine asked.

"Yes, the coming of the missionaries in the early 1800's brought many changes to the islands. And even though the one true God is worshiped by many, there is still a strong desire in the people to cling to and respect the beliefs held by their ancestors. Religion permeates the everyday life of the Hawaiian peoples. Nature plays an important role. Patterns and symbols in nature and also certain plants are said to have spiritual power. It is a common belief among many that even the natural events such as volcanic eruptions or tsunamis are caused by the moods of the gods."

As Martha talked a small crowd gathered around her to listen.

"There were some forty-thousand gods and demigods worshiped by the early Hawaiians. For every daily event there was a god, with men and women having different gods. They took the form of idols, normally carved of wood. Some were also made from feathers, straw or stone with human hair covering the heads. Today most do not worship in this way, but the traditions are still respected and during your visit to the islands you will have many opportunities to see evidence of this."

Everyone became excited as they listened to Martha speak and all began asking questions at the same time. Martha chuckled then held up her hand for silence. "We could talk all day about this subject as it is fascinating, but we are about to dock, so I'll answer just a few more questions."

A woman wearing large sunglasses and an even larger straw hat asked, "What is that tall building with the clock on it?

"Ah." Martha smiled. "That's the Aloha Tower. It was built in 1921. The tower stands nine stories high and is Honolulu's tallest building. On Boat Day that tower is almost always the first thing people who sail to Honolulu look for."

"Sort of like the Statue of Liberty," piped up a young boy standing next to Martha. "We learned about her in school." He beamed at the adults standing around him.

"Good example," Martha said, as she ruffled his curly blond hair.

"What do you mean Boat Day?" someone else asked.

Martha laughed out loud. "My dear, today is Boat Day. Anytime a ship sails into the harbor bringing its newest visitors to the island it's Boat Day. It's always full of fun and energy. People even take off from work to go down to the pier and watch the ship come in."

Several more questions were directed at Martha, who glowed in the importance of her job as Unofficial Ship's Tour Guide.

It wasn't long until the huge ship gently bobbed against the pier in Honolulu. Katherine and Tom again threw streamers to the waiting crowd while the

Royal Hawaiian Band, who met each arriving ship, played wonderful Hawaiian music.

Martha was quick to point out that many of the tunes had been written by the last reigning monarch, Queen Liliuokalani. Lovely brown-skinned maidens in grass skirts swayed a hula of greeting. The couple watched as each departing passenger was given a kiss on the cheek, and a lovely flower lei was placed around their neck.

As Katherine watched this arrival ceremony she recalled the lei making class on board ship that she had attended. There she had learned that the lei were more than just a decorative necklace of flowers, shells, or kukui nuts. It was also the nicest way to say 'hello,' 'goodbye,' 'congratulations,' 'my sympathies are with you' and best of all; 'I Love You.' The instructor had gone on to explain that according to Hawaiian chants, the first lei was given by Hiiaka, the sister of the volcano goddess Pele. In ancient times leis were given to "alii," which means 'high-ranking chiefs.'

Another lady taking the class shared that she had heard a modern-day tale which told of an entertainer who kissed an officer on a dare, and then quickly presented him with a lei, saying it was an old Hawaiian custom to cover her embarrassment.

Katherine noticed that Tom seemed much more interested in the hip swaying hula dancer than in the information being exchanged. She was a bit miffed about where his attention was focused, so she gave him a firm poke in the arm and then pointed out the luxury automobiles being unloaded below them.

Paradise Inherited

"Hey!" Tom yelped. "What was that for?" he asked with a sheepish grin on his face.

A few moments later she chuckled to herself over her moment of jealousy. *Where did that come from? I've never felt jealousy before. Of course, he's never been all mine before either,* she thought to herself.

Looking at her husband, Katherine smiled at him and squeezed his arm, allowing the physical contact with him to bring fresh the sweet memories of their first coming together as man and wife. In the early morning light they had whispered words of love to each other and gave thanks to God for protecting them and keeping each one pure for the other.

On the deck, Tom gave her hand a gentle squeeze in return and turned to face her. He reached up and gently swept some hair off her face that the warm tropical breezes were tossing around. "Shall we begin our newest adventure, Mrs. Tyne?" he said, as he leaned down to kiss her.

"Oh I do love the sound of that," Katherine sweetly answered him as she leaned into his arms one more time.

Their trunks had been taken from their cabin earlier, so Tom and Katherine walked hand in hand toward the exit ramp. However, just before they reached the ramp, Martha and the captain came toward them with a package.

"We thought you'd like this souvenir," said the captain, smiling brightly as he handed the package to Katherine.

"Don't open it now dear," Martha whispered. "Wait until you are settled in your hotel."

The couple exchanged puzzled glances, but agreed to Martha's directions.

"Your driver has arrived and is waiting curbside to take you to your hotel," the captain said. "It's truly been a pleasure having you on board."

The men shook hands and Martha and Katherine hugged each other, promising to keep in touch.

"Oh Captain," Katherine asked, "Did the wire get sent to my parents last evening notifying them of our wedding?"

"Yes, although there has been no reply. Perhaps you should try wiring again when you arrive at your hotel."

Katherine thanked the captain again, then followed Tom off the ship.

Just like at the train station, their driver again held a sign that read: "Tyne." Once settled into the comfortable seats, feeling as excited as children at Christmas, the couple watched the passing scenery. Tom noted all the fishing and pleasure boats in the harbor and Katherine enjoyed the flowers blooming everywhere.

As the car drove away, the captain reached for a telephone from a desk located in the lobby of the pier terminal shipping office. "They've arrived and are on their way to the hotel." "Yes sir." "Thank you sir." "It's been a pleasure sir," he said, then smiled as he put down the phone.

After a few moments Katherine turned to Tom and asked, "Do you know where we are going?"

"No, he replied, but apparently the driver does, so let's sit back and enjoy this ride."

Katherine agreed, although she felt a little nervous about not knowing where they were headed.

It's all part of the adventure, she reminded herself as she turned back to watching the palm tree lined streets and admiring the colorful shirts and dresses worn by people walking on the sidewalks. *I must get one of those dresses*, she thought. Seeing a particularly bright dress she also determined to get one like it to send to Susanne. *It's flashy. Susanne would love it.*

The trip turned out to be quite short, for only minutes later they pulled up to the Royal Hawaiian Hotel.

"It's pink," Katherine squealed through giggles.

Tom was just as amazed as Katherine, but managed to remain calm. "Yep, it's pink alright. A whole lot of pink," he replied as the car stopped at the main entrance of the elegant building.

Entering the lobby, Katherine stopped to admire the black terrazzo marble flooring and the highly-polished brass banisters on the stairways, while Tom checked in at the registration desk.

"Aloha, Mr. Tyne." "Your suite is ready." announced the desk clerk as he handed Tom the room keys and a letter with the attorney's name on it. "We hope you enjoy your stay."

"Thank you," Tom said as he turned to look for Katherine, who was busy gathering brochures with details about the hotel and suggested tourist sites.

On the way to their suite both took notice of the exquisite floor rugs, pictures of the former Kings and Queens on the walls, the magnificent china vases and the carved wooden doors that led to the rooms. Upon entering their room, Katherine's jaw dropped and her eyes opened wide as she scanned the interior. The room was elegantly decorated with Hawaiian-print flowered wallpaper and furniture from the 1920's that included the most beautiful four-poster canopy bed either of them had ever seen.

As soon as the door closed behind the porter, Tom let out a hearty whoop of joy, picked Katherine up and swung her around the room. "Oh, Kate, this is more than I could ever have dreamed giving you for a Honeymoon."

She hugged his neck and kissed his cheek. "Just so you know, I'd have been content with a trip to Carmel, but this works," she replied, as laughter and love filled the room.

Taking a few minutes to relax, Tom sat down to read the letter from the attorney while Katherine read the hotel's brochure.

"Tom, listen to this," Katherine said. "The Flamingo Pink Palace opened in 1927. It was built on the same spot where Queen Ka..ahu..man.u had her summer palace. This hotel is the destination of the rich and famous. After its doors opened, the Pink Palace became a second home to many of the world's influential statesmen and early Hollywood stars. The palace cost four million in US dollars, and took one and a half years to build. The architecture was influenced by Hollywood legend Rudolph Valentino and his Arabian movies."

Tom set down his letter giving Katherine his full attention as she continued to read.

"The first official registered guest was Princess Abigail Ka...wa..na..na..koa."

Katherine giggled at her attempt to pronounce the Hawaiian name.

Continuing, she read, "The Princess would have eventually been queen of the Kingdom of Hawaii had the monarchy survived. Duke Ka..ha..na..moku, the legendary Olympic swimmer and popularizer of the sport of surfing, spent a lot of time at the hotel restaurant and private beachfront. During World War II, the Royal Hawaiian became the "White House" of the Pacific. It was surrounded by barbed wire and heavily-armed guards. U.S. President Franklin D. Roosevelt used it as his Hawaiian residence. During the war it was closed to tourists, and instead was used as a place of rest and restoration leave.

"Can you imagine!" Katherine exclaimed. "President Roosevelt may have stayed in this very room."

"Maybe." Tom replied. "You do realize this brochure is outdated now."

"Outdated?" "How?" Katherine asked.

"Well," Tom said as, he stretched and locked his hands behind his head. "Don't you think if it were current it would include 'the honeymoon destination of Mr. and Mrs. Tom Tyne.'

"Ah, yes." Katherine agreed, as she sank down onto her husband's lap. "Most definitely the honeymoon destination." She lowered her face to kiss him.

Later that evening she noticed Tom was reading, once again, the letter from the attorney.

"What does it say?" she asked softly.

"You can read it for yourself. But basically he says that because I am reading the letter it means we have met the first two requirements: arrive by Christmas Day, which is today, and have a wife with me, which is you."

"Is there any explanation as to why you needed a wife?

"Nope." Tom shrugged. "I just hope I haven't made a foolish decision giving up my job and bringing you half-way around the world not knowing what to expect."

He then continued. "It seems we are to take the next two weeks to just enjoy ourselves, explore Oahu and not worry about a thing. We have an appointment to meet with Mr. Murphy the second Monday in January. The driver who brought us here is available to us night and day; we only need request his services from the front desk.

Katherine sat stunned. Neither spoke for several minutes, but their thoughts ran along the same lines. *Could there have been a mistake?* They were just two twenty-two year old kids from middle-class families. They'd done nothing to earn or deserve this wonderful gift. It all seemed like a dream, one neither of them wanted to wake up from.

Suddenly Tom slapped his knees and said, "It's probably too good to be true, so let's enjoy it while we can, and deal with it when we have to. So Mrs. Tyne, how about a moonlight swim?"

Paradise Inherited

"Oh yes. I'm sure the pool would be quite refreshing, Mr. Tyne," Katherine replied with a smile that made her face shine.

"Pool?" Tom replied, amazement in his voice. "Have you forgotten we are in Hawaii? You know, Waikiki, beach, ocean waves?"

Katherine laughed and Tom gave her a squeeze.

The couple reclined on towels looking up at the stars in the sky after their moonlight swim. Tom was just drifting off to sleep when Katherine remembered the package the Captain had given them and the letter from her father.

She gently tapped Tom's shoulder to awaken him, then reminded him of the package.

For just a moment Tom looked into her eyes, then reached out and took her into his arms rolling her over onto the warm sand. Checking to make sure no one was near the secluded place they had found on their walk along the beach, Tom slowly began to remove the strap of Katherine's bathing suit down her shoulder as he kissed her, at first tenderly and then with more urgency. All thoughts of the package and letter left Katherine's mind for the time being.

Many minutes later they strolled slowly arm-in-arm back to the hotel and their room, and enjoyed a warm shower together

Wrapped in a big fluffy towel, Katherine once again remembered the package given to them before leaving the ship. Retrieving it from the drawer where she'd placed it while unpacking, she held it toward him as he exited the bathroom.

"Shall we open this now?

Tom took the package from her hands and set it on a nearby table. Pulling her toward him, he seemed more interested in opening the package wrapped in the towel. With a slap to his hands, and a giggle, she told him to get serious.

"I am serious," Tom playfully pouted, as he stopped his search and seizure maneuver, but left his hands firmly gripping her towel.

Smiling at him and shaking her head Katherine again picked up the package and proceeded to open it. They were delighted to discover it contained a photo album of pictures taken on board ship.

There were pictures of the two of them learning to hula, decorating cookies, playing shuffleboard, and even one with their table mates, Stafford and Ellen. They also found several wonderful pictures of their wedding, with extra copies of in a separate envelope.

"Perfect." "I can mail these pictures to mother and father," Katherine stated, as she reached for her father's letter.

She gasped when she opened the envelope and pulled out a check for $10,000.

Tom's eyes popped open when he saw it.

Letting out a low whistle, Tom asked, "What's this for?"

Katherine didn't respond to his question, as she was intently reading the letter to herself. When finished she handed it to Tom, as tears rolled down her cheeks.

"My Dearest Daughter," He read aloud.

"I believe with all my heart that this marriage is a direct result of God's planning for your life. Be happy my dear. The check enclosed is a combination of the amount Mother and I have saved to give you as a wedding gift and pay for your wedding and of course the money left to you in your grandmother's will that was to be given to you on your wedding day. When Susanne eventually marries she will receive the same. I know you to be an intelligent young woman and, I'm convinced, quite capable of making good financial decisions, as you've handled the bookkeeping and ordering at the store for the last five years. However, I strongly suggest you consult with Tom, as the new head of your home, so that you both may use this money wisely. Enjoy all that life has to offer on this, the 'Great Adventure' you and Tom have plotted and planned since childhood. The road may not always be easy, but if you keep to the straight and narrow, it is a road that never ends when God is your guide.

Much love,
Father."

Tom took his wife into his arms and held her. Years of being Katherine's friend had taught him when to talk and when to be quiet. They would discuss the money later.

Over the next couple of days the newlyweds splashed in the warm ocean water, played volleyball with other guests staying at the hotel and strolled hand-in-hand down the streets of Honolulu. The love each of them had for years quietly harbored for the other blossomed into something richer and deeper than either of them expected.

A few days in to their honeymoon, while they sat on the beach, Tom noticed his wife's skin was turning a deep shade of pink. "Wow. You're getting burnt. We'd better go in," he told her.

Katherine agreed and gathered their towels and beach bag. Just a few steps from the hotel a couple of little boys approached them. Each boy carried two wilted flower leis.

"Wanna buy a lei, Mister?" one of the boys asked.

"How much?"

"Twenty-five cents apiece," the child responded.

Tom looked at Katherine and winked, "Well, guys, that seems like a great deal. Let's see-you have four. I'll take them all."

The boys handed over the leis as Tom reached into the beach bag Katherine was holding and pulled out his wallet. He then handed the boys four dollars and said, "Keep the change guys."

With a whoop of excitement, the boys took off running and jumping. One of them finally remembered the manners his mother had taught him, turned back toward the couple and hollered, "Mahalo Mister!"

"Mahalo to you too!" Tom hollered back.

Katherine leaned toward Tom and said, "What does mahalo mean?"

Tom shrugged his shoulders and said with a laugh, "Darned if I know. But I don't think it's anything bad, unless the kid just called me a sucker or something."

This brought a smile and a chuckle from each of them as they entered the hotel lobby swinging four wilted flower leis.

A few days later, while visiting a museum, a tour guide leading the group of tourists explained that mahalo meant 'thank you.' Everyone laughed when one of the tourists in the group commented that he thought it meant 'garbage can,' because it was stenciled on the side of the cans he'd seen all over town.

While talking to a lifeguard one morning, Tom learned that Waikiki Beach was man-made. He hurried back to where Katherine was sitting to tell her what he'd learned.

"This entire area was once wetlands. It wasn't good for anything but growing mosquitoes," he teased.

Katherine rolled her eyes and smiled.

"Anyway, in order to make the land usable, the Ali Wai Canal was dug to drain the wetlands. And get this!" Tom exclaimed, "The sand for this beach was brought here from Manhattan Beach, California."

Kate's eyes widened with surprise. She looked down at the sand beneath her and started to laugh. "And here we've been comparing this sand to the sand back home, saying how much softer it is, and now you tell me it's the same sand! Oh, brother! How did it get here?"

"Very carefully," Tom joked. He loved to make Katherine laugh.

Getting the response he had desired he continued, "It was transported by ships and barges to Waikiki."

Letting some sand slide through his fingers, he told Katherine that the sand she sat on was probably not the same sand, because at times replenishment was needed.

"One sand replenishment project turned disastrous when man-made sand was used."

"What happened?" Katherine asked.

"The surf turned it into a concrete-like surface. I wonder if it had been left like that we would now be sitting on Waikiki Dam?" he teased again.

The honeymooners took full advantage of the available car and its driver, who introduced himself as Kimo, and turned out to be an excellent tour guide. They spent several days just riding around the island, stopping at various sites of interest. They passed fields of pineapples, and would stop at a roadside stand to sample fresh cut pieces of the fruit.

While visiting the North Shore, they were amazed to see waves taller than most buildings. Tom had considered surfing, but upon seeing those waves, he decided they were way out of his league-much to Katherine's relief.

At Waimea Falls Tom got a gleam in his eye as he watched divers leap off the top of the forty-nine-foot-high falls.

Seeing the look in his eyes, Katherine grabbed hold of his arm and firmly exclaimed, "Oh no you won't Tom Tyne!"

Tom laughed and replied, "Aw ma, you never let me have any fun."

Realizing she'd just performed her first nagging-wife moment, Katherine blushed.

Tom laughed again, took her hand that still held his arm, and kissed it tenderly.

Tom found the avenue for his adventurous spirit at Waimea Beach, as he joined several other young people in climbing the rocks and leaping, with a Tarzan yell, into the ocean. The rocks weren't nearly as high, and Katherine hadn't objected to this jump.

Maybe this will get it out of his system, she thought, and laughed as she watched him jump and heard his yell.

One afternoon Kimo took them up into the crater of Diamond Head. They hiked up the rim to look down on Waikiki and gazed with wonder at the beauty of the sight before them.

"The ocean looks bluer from here," Katherine mentioned.

Another day they took a drive up to the Nuuanu Pali lookout. From here they marveled at the 985 foot-tall cliffs of the Koolau mountain range.

"The wind here can be very extreme," Kimo told them. "There are days when it blows through here so hard you can lean into the wind and the gusts will hold you up."

"Right now, you are standing in the place where the most important battle in Hawaiian history took place."

"In 1795, Kamehameha I wanted to rule the entire chain of islands. So he and his army invaded Oahu, arriving in a fleet of war canoes. They marched to Nuuanu Valley to face the troops of Kalanikupele, the 'alii nui,' or chief, of Oahu."

A small crowd began to grow as other tourists who had stopped at the lookout stood by and listened along with Tom and Katherine.

"The battle was fierce, bloody, and unrelenting. Kamehameha's men gained an advantage, which led to Kalanikupule's men being pursued and driven over the steep cliffs to their deaths."

"Oh my!" Several women responded.

He continued, "In 1897 an engineering firm hired to build the Pali Road, a winding road that is used to carry traffic across the mountains, discovered an estimated eight hundred human skulls and other human bones at the foot of the cliff.

Several women in the crowd gasped, including Katherine. However, the men looked around as if envisioning the great battle scene that must have taken place, and wanted to hear more.

On Sunday, Kimo suggested they attend services at the Kawaiahao church to worship. "There are two services," he explained. "The first service is in Hawaiian, and the second one is in English."

As they entered the building, Katherine had the feeling that she had been here before, but also knew that was impossible. After giving this some thought she whispered to Tom, "This place reminds me of pictures I've seen of Westminister Abbey. It must be the English style of architecture that would have come from the first missionaries."

Reading the back page of the church bulletin they had been handed upon entering, they learned that the first sermon was preached on the island by the Reverend Hiriam Bingham on April 23, 1820, just three days after the first group of Christian missionaries arrived on Oahu.

After the morning services, while eating lunch, Tom read to Katherine from the tourist brochure he had picked up before leaving the church.

"It says here, the first sermon Reverend Bingham shared was from Luke 2:10, 'Fear not, for behold, I bring you good tidings of great joy, which shall be to all people.' The initial houses of worship consisted of four huts made of pili grass."

"Wow!" Tom exclaimed. "Pili grass grows to 90 centimeters in length and was pulled out in clumps and hung upside-down to thatch roofs and walls, and twined to make rope. It repelled water and had a pleasant smell. King Kamehameha III had called a meeting of chiefs in 1836 to develop plans for a new stone church, with Reverend Bingham contributing to the design. The church can seat four thousand five hundred people."

"Can you imagine!" Tom exclaimed. He thought for a few moments before reading from the brochure again.

"Hey, get this! It took five years and more than a thousand men to build this church. They collected wood from their own lands and hand-quarried fourteen thousand coral slabs from reefs ten to fifteen feet under water. I won't even begin to guess how much they weighed, but I'll bet it was extremely hard, heavy work!"

After lunch the couple took a tour of the compound where the Mission Houses of the Reverend Bingham were located. The tour guide told the group of tourists that the structures had been built between 1821 and 1841, making them the oldest surviving western-style buildings in Hawaii. They learned that the White Frame House, as it was called, was the residence of several prominent missionaries over the years. The Chamberlain House, as another building was named, had been used as a storehouse and separate home, and in the Coral House the first printing press of the Pacific had been established. The first printed sheet in Hawaii was produced on January 7, 1922, with Oahu Chief Keeaumoku having had the privilege of pulling the lever.

At the end of the tour, Katherine told Tom that it was obvious that the missionaries made significant contributions to the Island. But after listening to the guide's presentation she had come to the conclusion that they had also caused irreparable harm.

"I find it appalling," she stated, "that for years, the Hawaiian people were not allowed to speak their own language. The beautiful Hula was forbidden. And so much of the land was taken away from the people!"

The last few days of their honeymoon found them swimming in the ocean and sightseeing. A visit to the statue of King Kamehameha, located in downtown Honolulu, was next on their agenda. This time Katherine read the brochure to Tom.

"The original figure was modeled in Rome in 1879 by American sculptor Thomas R. Gould. A year later, it was cast in bronze in Paris and shipped from Germany. During its voyage to the islands, however, the ship caught fire and sank off the coast of the Falkland Islands. A second statue was cast from the original mold and sent to Honolulu, where King Kalakaua dedicated it in 1883."

"It's huge," Tom commented, as Katherine continued to read aloud from the brochure.

"It stands eight and a half feet tall and depicts Kamehameha in his royal clothes, including a helmet of rare feathers and a gilded cloak. The spear in his left hand serves to symbolize the Hawaiian's willingness and ability to defend themselves from hostile nations. His right hand, however, is extended in a welcoming gesture of 'Aloha'."

A lady walking by stopped and shared with the couple that every June 11 the statue is adorned with fresh flower leis of all types. "It's a state holiday, Kamehameha Day," she told them.

From there they went to the National Memorial Cemetery. It had opened to the public just ten years earlier with services honoring five war dead, including an unknown serviceman, two Marines, an Army lieutenant and one civilian. The civilian was famed war correspondent Ernie Pyle, who had been killed by a Japanese sniper. Katherine remembered hearing that bit of history in a conversation that she had overhead once as her father and grandfather had talked.

Finally, they visited the USS Arizona Memorial on "Battleship Row." A new memorial was under construction- a picture of the proposed memorial hung on an entry wall of the ticket booth. The plans call for a 184-foot-long gleaming white structure consisting of three sections: the entry and assembly room; a central area designed for ceremonies and general observation; and the shrine room, where the names of 2,390 people who died on December 7, 1941 during Japan's infamous attack on Pearl Harbor, would be engraved on a marble wall.

Kate shuddered as she learned that 1,177 heroes were still entombed in the Arizona.

***

New Year's Eve 1960 came in with fireworks and an evening of good food, dancing, and moonlight strolls. They were able to catch up with Ellen and Stafford and enjoy the friendship that had begun aboard ship. Best of all, Tom and Katherine found themselves more in love each day, and both felt more alive and happier than they could, ever remember. For them, life was just beginning.

They spent the last day of their honeymoon trip at Hanauma Bay, another popular tourist location for swimming and picnicking. Tom invited Kimo and his family to join them. At first the driver was hesitant, but at Katherine's insistence he had dropped them off and returned later with his lovely wife, Lani, and their three children. He introduced them as his 'wahine' and the three 'keike."

Everyone played games, rested and then swam and played some more. At the lunch break, Tom prayed over the simple meal of 'musubi', a spam and rice block wrapped in dried seaweed and apples.

Then Kimo responded with a prayer in the Hawaiian language that he had been taught by his grandmother, or 'Tutu', as he called her. Tom and Katherine thought the words sounded beautiful, even though they couldn't understand them.

Kimo finished the prayer by saying "Aloha Ke Akua," which he said meant, 'God is Love.'

The couples shared the small talk of people just getting to know each other, but when they each realized they shared salvation in Jesus Christ, all the barriers came down.

"Kimo, what's the Hawaiian word for family?" Tom asked.

"Ohana," he supplied.

"Well then," Tom smiled. "Since we are all God's 'keiki', that makes us 'Ohana'."

It was also during this rest period that Lani more fully explained the meaning of Aloha to Tom and Katherine.

"It's a word we use to express love, affection, compassion, mercy, sympathy, pity, kindness, sentiment, grace, charity, greeting, salutation, regards, sweetheart, lover, loved one; it also signifies to be loved, be fond of, to show kindness. But it's more than just a word. It's a feeling, an action, a piece of your soul, your being, your breath. It's 'Aloha'. It's a way to show the light of Jesus to the world," she finished with a smile.

Katherine responded with a hug, and Lani laughed and said, "This too is Aloha."

Chapter Five

The Monday morning they had been waiting for finally arrived. Tom and Katherine were up early, each taking time for their morning devotional. Katherine liked to sit on the lanai with her coffee, read her Bible, make notes in her journal and stop from time to time to pray and just be quiet before the Lord. Tom would park himself at the table inside, where he could also enjoy his coffee, read his Bible, pray, and take secret glances at his wife. It still amazed him how things had worked out so perfectly. But then he believed God was in control, and though a man makes plans, God directs his path. Once again this morning he gave thanks for the path that God had put him on that included Katherine.

When Tom had finished his prayer he stepped out onto the lanai and stretched as he marveled at the beautiful morning. "It's about time we head for the lobby Kate. Kimo will be here soon."

"Yes, I'm ready, just let me put these books away," she said, entering the coolness of their room.

Before she could get by him, Tom caught her arm and pulled her back to him. As he wrapped his arms around her, Kate sighed as she experienced once again the contentment of being held by her husband. They stayed locked in each other's arms for just a moment and kissed, starting again the passion which was new and exciting for each of them.

"Didn't you say something about leaving soon?" Katherine whispered as Tom continued to kiss her neck.

He groaned and released her.

"I'll remind you where you left off when we get back," Kate teased.

Tom groaned again, and with a husky sound in his voice replied, "I don't think I'll forget."

Kate hugged him again and then quickly stepped away, laughing as she did so.

Ten minutes later they sat in the backseat of the black Rolls that had been their means of transportation for the past two weeks. Kimo was back in his chauffeur uniform, but the high professionalism of their first meeting was replaced with a warm greeting of friendship and a bag of cookies that Lani had sent along.

They talked and laughed as they recalled their day at the beach. Kimo maneuvered through the morning traffic and had them downtown in no time.

"Second floor, third door on the left. Every door has a name plate on it," Kimo directed, after opening the limo door for them. He patted Tom on the back. "Hang loose cousin," he encouraged with a laugh before climbing back into the driver's seat. "I'll be waiting."

It didn't occur to the couple to wonder why Kimo knew the location of the office they were looking for. It also didn't occur to Kimo to explain that he worked for Jonathan Murphy.

Instead, Katherine gave Tom a playful slug and smiled at the two men, saying, "That's good advice. Hang loose cousin."

Kimo had explained that on the island you were a visitor for five minutes, then everyone becomes family. Even if not blood-related, they were deemed, a cousin, and as an indication of respect, every adult was referred to as Aunty or Uncle by those younger than them.

Tom, having no extended family of his own, thought this was a great idea. Katherine enjoyed it as well, but it made her realize she hadn't heard from her parents since they had waved from the peer. It was also a bit puzzling not to have heard from Susanne. She and her sister had never gone more than two days without being in contact in their entire life.

So why haven't I heard from her or mother or father? I suppose they are allowing us our privacy during our honeymoon, she thought, and then firmly decided to write a long letter to each of them when she returned to the hotel.

She wanted to send the wedding pictures and tell them about all the things they were seeing in Hawaii. *I must remember to tell mother how friendly the natives are.*

Finding Jonathan Murphy's office turned out to be as easy as Kimo had said. Standing in front of the office door, Tom reached for the knob, then stopped.

"What's wrong?" Katherine asked, as she reached for his hand.

"Nothing really." "It's just....oh, I don't know, I'm just nervous, I guess."

Katherine squeezed his hand. "Whatever this appointment brings we'll face it together. But more importantly, remember that God has promised to never leave us or forsake us, and where we go He will always go with us. One day at a time, remember?" she said, as she looked into his eyes and smiled.

"Right! Thanks, I needed that. See, I'd never had made it without you Kate," Tom said, smiling back at her.

"And don't you forget it," she said, squeezing his hand again. "Now let's go in before we get arrested for loitering. That elevator operator is giving us funny looks."

Kate smiled at the operator, who was indeed watching them, and gave Tom a gentle push.

As the door to the reception area of Jonathan Murphy's office closed behind them, the private entrance to Jonathan's office opened down the hall. An elderly man, silver haired, and sharply dressed, smiled to himself as he passed Jonathan's office door.

"Glorious day, Ralph," Thomas Kalama said to the elevator operator as the doors slowly closed.

Paradise Inherited

In the office, the receptionist greeted the Tynes warmly, then ushered them immediately into the lawyer's office.

Jonathan Murphy was about fifty years old, with red hair, just starting to gray at the temples. He stood when the couple entered the office and greeted them with a strong handshake and an 'Aloha', spoken with an Irish brogue. His secretary then offered coffee, tea or passion fruit punch as everyone made themselves comfortable.

"Before I get started," the attorney said, "Do you have any questions?"

Tom and Katherine looked at each other and then returned their attention to Mr. Murphy.

"Oh, one or two I guess," Tom answered.

This caused everyone to laugh and created the perfect ice breaker.

"But I'd really like to hear what you have to say first, Mr. Murphy."

"Okay, I'll start, and you can jump in anytime," the older man began.

"First, please call me Jonathan. I'm not too formal unless I'm in the courtroom."

As he sat down, the attorney said, "Your uncle was actually a client of my former partner. When my partner retired your uncle asked that I continue handling his affairs."

"Were you aware that I didn't even know he existed until I received your letter?" Tom asked. "Actually, I don't even know his name."

Jonathan nodded his head.

"What was he like?"

"Ah, a very good question," replied Jonathan. "Your uncle was a very private person-so private in fact that in the ten years I'd handled his affairs I only met him face to face in this office once. He traveled a lot."

After a moment the lawyer said, "From what I know, he was a hard worker, and lived a very simple life. Most of the money he earned he saved and invested- wisely, I might add."

Kate noticed that her husband had repositioned himself to sit on the edge of his chair

"He did have a financial partner, although I never met the partner either," Jonathan stated. "Tom, you should know you have been left with a considerable fortune. It is to be divided into five parts of money and property-One part of each will be given to you at the end of each year that you remain in the islands.

Katherine sat quietly through this initial briefing, trying to take in as much as she could about this mysterious uncle, his partner, and the five-year directive.

"Should you decide to leave the islands before the five years is up, the remaining inheritance will be transferred to and divided among some predetermined charities, since there are no other living relatives. Your uncle and his partner were quite specific in those terms."

"I see," Tom laughed nervously. "Can you tell me why it was necessary for me to have a wife?

Katherine clinched her jaw at this question. Some of the insecurity she'd felt when they left California jumped into her thoughts. *Is he sorry he married me?*

"And why must we live here for five years?" Tom continued.

"Well if we have to live someplace, this is definitely the place to be," Katherine inserted timidly, still feeling the effects of her insecurity.

"Some people can't handle living on an island, totally surrounded by water, with no place to go but around and around. It gets to some people," Jonathan replied.

"These are excellent questions, but unfortunately I can't answer them right now.

I promise you however, that at this time next year, should you still be here, I will be able to answer more of your questions."

No one spoke for a moment as they absorbed that information. Katherine gazed at the view from the window, wondering how anyone could not want to live in such a beautiful place. But, she reminded herself, this is Tom's inheritance. The decisions about it are his to make.

Abruptly, Katherine noticed that she could see the Iolani Palace from where she sat. Her thoughts turned to the day they visited the palace and learned it had been build in 1882 by King David Kalakaua and his wife Queen Kapiolani.

Kimo, acting as their personal tour guide, had shared his wealth of knowledge regarding historic sites of his island home.

"The palace had electricity and telephones even before the White House. When Hawaii gained statehood, the Iolani Palace became the only royal palace in the United States," he'd said proudly.

Katherine had read on the ship about the last reigning Queen, Liliuokalani. She had also paid close attention to Kimo's dialog when she realized it was in that very palace that the queen had been imprisoned during the overthrow of her government.

He had finished his story by telling them, "Some people claim you can still hear the Queen pacing back-and-forth in the room where she was held captive."

Breaking away from that memory Katherine thought, *We've passed here several times over the last two weeks and didn't know we were anywhere near this office. I wonder how many times we have passed Tom's uncle's farm?*

With that thought in mind, Katherine spoke up. "Where on the island is the farm located?"

"Oh yes-the farm. Actually, the farm is not on this island. There are actually several pieces of property," Jonathan said, with an expression on his face and a tone in his voice that gave the impression he was letting the couple in on part of the secrets.

Tom and Katherine sat up a little straighter, with their mouths open, yet seemingly speechless.

Jonathan laughed at their expressions. "The family home is located on the island of Kauai. Several generations of your family have lived on and around this place. Tomorrow you will be flown to Kauai and taken to your new home."

Tom's mind was still running over the words, several *generations of your family.* Except for his Aunt

Beth, he had never experienced 'family.' On hearing those words, Tom realized that a big part of his past that had been missing was being re-discovered.

He suddenly remembered that the attorney had not answered his earlier question. "What is...or rather was my uncle's name? I know it seems silly but nothing has been said about his name. All I know is "Uncle."

Jonathan gave him an understanding smile. "Unfortunately right now, per his directive, I am not at liberty to tell you his name or the name of his partner."

Jonathan could see that Tom was exasperated with this answer, so he leaned forward, patting Tom's hand where it rested on the desk in front of him. "I can tell you this much, in business and formal matters, he went by his initials, 'T.K.', but everyone else just called him 'Uncle'.

"An initial," Tom whooped. "The last name starts with a 'K', Tom stated sarcastically.

Again Jonathan smiled. "I can tell you that your uncle was your mother's older brother. Older by about sixteen years. He never married, so his Will was designed to leave everything to her, or, her children should she not be living."

"How long has he known about me?" Tom asked.

"My understanding is that he had regular written contact with your mother, up until her death. You were too young to remember, only about fifteen months, I'm told, when your mother and father brought you here for a brief visit before the three of you continued on to China."

"Wait," Tom held up his hand. "Let me get this straight, I was with my parents on the mission field?"

"Oh yes," Jonathan replied. "Your Uncle told me it was a miracle you survived the train wreck that killed so many. After receiving news about his sister's death, it was your uncle who went to China to get you. After much thought about his lifestyle as a bachelor, it was decided that your Aunt in California should raise you."

Seeing how this information had affected the couple, the attorney called for a brief break in their meeting, and asked his secretary to refresh their drinks and bring in a light snack.

When their business resumed Jonathan explained how their finances would be handled. He handed them a checkbook and ledger and he explained that every month an allowance would be deposited into their checking account.

"How much?" Tom asked.

"At this point, your income will be drawn from the interest on the existing investments, so there could be some slight variations from month to month. However, if you budget wisely, I have no doubt there will always be enough to see you through from one month to the next."

He took a piece of paper from his desk drawer and showed them what their projected income for the next three months was expected to be.

"That's not bad," Tom spoke his thoughts aloud. "A job to cover extras and insurance, and we shouldn't have any trouble at all. At least it would be enough in California. I'm not sure about here."

Half listening to Tom and Jonathan talk, Katherine's father's words returned to her. "Trust in God first, He will provide, and then trust in Tom for wise counsel regarding your finances."

She gave Tom a quick look out of the side of her eye, and silently whispered a prayer. *Father, guide and direct Tom. I trust you, Father, and I'll trust my husband as you would require me to. In Jesus name I commit this to you. Amen.*

The meeting ended with Jonathan telling them they were in good hands. "I'll be in touch throughout the year," he assured them.

As promised, Kimo was waiting with the car. "Man, you two look like you've been knocked over by a North Shore wave! You ok?" Kimo asked, with genuine concern.

Tom nodded and said, "Kimo, do you know a nice, quiet place where we can have lunch and talk about this?"

Kimo smiled and said, "Sure, I know just the place, maybe not so quiet, but the food is good.

Moments later, as they pulled into the driveway of a residential home, Katherine spotted Lani out in the yard hanging clothes on a line to dry.

"Oh, Kimo, you've brought us to your house!" she exclaimed.

"Yep. Best place to relax and get good food is always at home."

Katherine was out of the car almost before it had stopped rolling. The two women ran to each other and hugged tightly, like they'd been best friends forever and hadn't seen each other in years, when in fact it had only been one day. Tom and Kimo watched with amused expressions on their faces.

Just as they started to enter the house, three tiny bodies, with squealing, happy laughter came running from the back yard.

"Aunty," "Uncle." they cried. The youngest leaped into Tom's arms and the other two wrapped themselves around Katherine's legs.

"This makes it official. You are definitely now part of the family," Lani said.

"Yeah, like, when can you babysit?" Kimo asked.

Everyone laughed and the tension of the earlier meeting vanished.

After lunch the children were put down for their afternoon naps and the adults found lawn chairs and sat in the shade of the trees. Tom relayed the story that he and Katherine had heard that morning. When he was finished no one spoke for several minutes.

"I knew it was something big by the V.I.P. treatment you have received, but I had no idea it was anything like this," said Kimo.

"Hey, you never told me you been hanging out with V.I.P.'s!" Lani swatted at his arm, which he ducked as if this was a well practiced move.

"So you are 'Uncle's heir'?" Lani asked, with a new tone of respect in her voice.

With raised eyebrows and a surprised expression on his face Tom said, "You know or knew my Uncle?"

"Well..." Lani glanced uncertainly at Kimo. "Sort of," then added quickly, "But everyone has heard about Uncle."

"Aren't you exaggerating just a little?" Kimo asked his wife.

"Okay, so not everyone. But I've heard stories from my mother's, sister's, brother-in-law's, third cousin-she lives outside of Kona you see-and 'Uncle' was well known in her town." Lani said with emphasis.

"Sounds like a reliable source," Kimo teased, and then ducked when Lani's arm swung around.

Tom and Katherine exchanged a quick glance and then broke into laughter.

"Maybe we should tell Lani about House Rule #1," Tom said, and they laughed again.

When the laughter subsided, Katherine asked where Kona was located on Kauai.

"No, no, not Kauai, Kona is on the Big Island of Hawaii.

"Oh," Katherine said, with a confused look on her face. "We are flying to Kauai tomorrow, not the Big Island. I guess the 'Uncle' you've heard about is a different one."

"Yes maybe," Lani replied, again flashing a quick glance Kimo's way.

Everyone was quiet for several minutes after that. Finally, Tom stood up and reached for Katherine's hand.

Paradise Inherited

"Kimo, I suppose we should get back to the hotel, we have some packing to do and a bit of shopping to take care of before leaving." To Lani he said, "Thank you for a wonderfully relaxing afternoon and lunch. We do appreciate your hospitality, especially since you had no notice of our comings."

Lani smiled and shrugged slightly. "No problem, you two are welcome anytime. No reservations needed," she teased.

Tom and Katherine smiled back and then Tom said, "I'm not sure when we'll be back in Honolulu, but we'll keep in touch."

Lani and Katherine hugged again and promised to write.

"We'll be praying for you," said Kimo. "In fact, let's do that right now."

The two couples stood in the middle of the front yard of Kimo's home, joined hands, bowed their heads and prayed for each other.

Back at the hotel Tom and Katherine packed their trunks in silence. The information given, or the lack of information they'd been given, was heavy on their minds.

Suddenly Tom slammed the lid of his trunk. "It doesn't make sense! Why all the secrets? Why can't I be told anything? This is crazy!" He said, running his hands through his hair.

"How am I supposed to take care of you? Where will we live? Am I supposed to just sit around and wait for the years to pass?" With a heavy sigh he sat down on the edge of the bed and hung his head and said, "Ah Kate, what I have gotten you in to?"

Katherine slowly walked over to him and put her arms around his head and cradled him against her stomach. "I can't answer those questions. But don't worry. Remember what the Bible says in Matthew 6:34, 'So do not worry about tomorrow for tomorrow will care for itself. Each day has enough trouble of its own'."

I only pray I'm strong enough to walk the talk, Katherine thought to herself, and then spoke aloud. "As I recall, I volunteered for this adventure. You didn't get me into anything I wasn't willing to go through with you."

Neither spoke for several minutes. Tom stood up and took Katherine in his arms. "You continue to amaze me," he said softly into her ear. "Just promise me if whatever comes gets to be too much, you'll tell me. I promise I'll take you home immediately."

"I promise," she whispered back. "Now where were we earlier when we were so rudely interrupted?" She spoke with the huskiness of desire filling her throat.

Later the couple went for one last stroll through Waikiki, stopping at several tourist shops. Katherine purchased her first muumuu and some pretty hawaiian floral print letter writing paper. Tom picked up a nifty straw hat and ukelele.

"What are you going to do with that?" Katherine asked, pointing to the ukelele.

Plopping his new hat on his head Tom replied, "Why ma'am I'm going to learn to play this here ukelele and give Don Ho a run for his money."

Katherine laughed at Tom's silliness, but also hoped he was serious. In just two weeks she had fallen in love with Hawaiian music, and even more in love with Tom. *Or Don Ho?* She laughed at her thought.

Chapter Six

After early morning pillow talk and time spent in prayer about their concerns, the couple was once again filled with the excitement of the adventure before them as they boarded the plane for the short flight to Lihue, Kauai.

The last two weeks had been filled with delightful fun and surprises. They both had more questions than when they had first left California. Each had individually decided to be patient and see what came next. That was easier said than done as they realized that their outside calm hid an inside shaking, despite their efforts to dispel their concerns.

Upon exiting the plane, Katherine's nose was filled with a glorious variety of tropical aroma-Gardenia, Tuberose, and Plumeria. The warm morning breeze wrapped its arms around her and made her feel welcome. The ground was wet, indicating the morning rain had only recently stopped. As the couple walked hand in hand toward the terminal the sun began to peek through the clouds as if to smile its welcome on the newlyweds.

Standing just outside the gate was a young woman holding a card that had TYNE printed on it. Tom spotted it first, then smiled and waved at the girl.

Seeing Tom, she, too smiled and returned his wave.

"Aloha! Welcome to Kauai! I'm Alice," she said, as she reached out her hand for a handshake with each. "We are neighbors. Mr. Murphy asked me to pick you up and take you to your house."

"Thank you," Tom and Katherine replied in unison.

"Can we pay you for your gas?" Tom asked.

Alice laughed, "Well you can if you want to, but it's your Jeep and your gas."

This was said just as Alice stopped in front of an army green Jeep that had seen better days.

"My Jeep? Wow this is great," Tom said, as he walked all around the Jeep examining it from top to bottom.

"Um, Tom, you can look it all over when we get to the house, but I think we should get going before the rain starts again," Katherine said.

"Oh right. Sorry, it's just that I've wanted one of these for years," he said with a stupid grin on his face.

Katherine muttered something about boys and their toys, which Tom missed, but Alice heard quite clearly and nodded in agreement. The two girls laughed, and a friendship had begun.

"It's beautiful here!" Katherine exclaimed as they drove along. She knew there would be some settling in to do at the new house, but couldn't help being excited about the sightseeing that was ahead of them.

The first thing they noticed was that Kauai was not as built up as Oahu. There were a few hotels, but for the most part, the land was still untouched.

"It looks like it must be just as God created it," Katherine spoke out loud to no one in particular.

The narrow two lane road was cut through a sugar cane field. On both sides the cane grew so tall and thick there was no way to see the ocean that was just beyond them or much of the mountain range on the other.

"Look at the color of the ground!" Tom exclaimed. "It's rusty red."

"Oh, roosters!" Katherine excitedly put in. "They are strutting along just everywhere you look. In the parking lot, alongside the road, just everywhere," she laughed. "I've never seen roosters up close."

"Dinner!" Tom hooted, using his thumb and index finger as a gun.

"Nah, those birds are too tough. Nobody eats them, they just run free," Alice explained.

"They are beautiful birds," Katherine interjected.

"Beautiful, yes, but also a royal pain in the neck. They crow at all times of the day and night. You wait. You'll see," Alice laughed.

"Where do they come from? And why are they everywhere?" Katherine asked.

"The wind blew them in," Alice laughed.

The dumbfounded expression on Tom and Katherine's faces was enough to cause Alice to laugh again.

"Actually they were brought here in the 1800's, originally, to provide food for the coconut and sugarcane workers. But mostly they were brought here to be used for 'cock fights'. Plantations would have several hundred of the birds. When the plantations began to die out, the owners sold off parcels of property to the workers, basically the lot their small house was on. The parcels were too small to maintain all the birds, so they were left to run free. Of course you're also likely to hear stories about the birds being scattered across the island by a hurricane."

They hadn't journeyed long when Alice turned off the main road and headed in the general direction of the beach. A small community came into view. Katherine spotted a general store, post office, bank, one gas station, and a couple of hotels a little farther down the road they had just turned off.

Some locals had set up some stands along the side of the road, and were selling fresh fruit, flower leis and other Hawaiian trinkets that the tourists liked to buy. Alice stopped at the general store and invited the couple to look around.

"Need to pick up a couple of things for Mama," she explained. "And, since I have the use of your Jeep...well." She shrugged her shoulders and grinned.

Tom smiled in return and said, "Sure go ahead," then he turned to Katherine and added, "We might want to pick up a few things as well. I'm not sure what we'll find when we get to the house"

Katherine agreed and walked into the cool air inside the general store. Although it was still relatively early in the morning, the Hawaiian sun was already heating up the air outside.

Alice introduced the Tynes to Mrs. Wong, who stood behind the counter.

"If you don't see what you need you ask, ok? Mrs. Wong said, and smiled sweetly at Katherine.

Katherine nodded and began her first tour of the store. Not actually knowing what they would find when they reached the house made it difficult to make any decisions, so Katherine settled for a loaf of Sweet Bread and Guava jelly. Tom picked up a couple of sodas and a bag of chips.

"Some first meal," they laughed, when they compared their purchases at the counter.

Walking back out into the sunshine felt good. Alice had already finished her shopping and was stretched out in the jeep, head back, eyes closed, enjoying the warmth.

"Sorry to keep you waiting," Katherine said.

"Oh, no problem. We aren't far now," Alice replied as she sat up and stretched.

That statement turned out to be more than true, for approximately one hundred and fifty feet down the road Alice turned into a driveway. A moment later she stopped the Jeep, leaped out and threw her arms open wide. "This is it."

Tom and Katherine sat in the jeep with their mouths hanging open, unable to speak.

To their right was a beautiful blue lagoon with gentle waves rolling up the sands, and to their left was the most run down, weather beaten shack they had ever seen.

The house obviously had not been lived in for quite some time. It stood off the ground on stilts. The metal roof was a rusted brownish red that appeared to need a couple of sections replaced. Bamboo window shutters in various stages of usability hung from windows, most of which had no glass in them, and the screens were torn or missing altogether. An open-air porch appeared to wrap all the way around the house. Several pieces of railing lay on the ground at various spots.

After a moment of silence, Tom finally spoke. "This is a joke right?" Fighting anger and the urge to burst out laughing he looked first at Katherine then at Alice.

"Oh my," Katherine whispered, tears threatening to spill down her cheeks.

Katherine recovered a bit sooner than Tom. She climbed out of the Jeep, put her hands on her hips, and said, "Well, Tyne, it looks like we've got a little work to do before supper!" then headed up the front porch steps toward the front door that hung on only one hinge.

Tom still sat in the Jeep, staring, shaking his head, and running one hand through his hair. For a moment he wasn't sure if he would laugh, cry, or holler for Katherine to get back in the Jeep and race back to the airport. Finally laughter won out, great gulping laughter that brought tears to his eyes and caused his stomach to hurt.

Through his laughter and with a bit of anger still in his voice, Tom announced, "Kate, the next time I see Murphy I may have to kill the man."

"Hey are you coming?" Katherine asked, as she looked back at Tom, who still sat in the Jeep.

He jumped from the Jeep, then he ran up the stairs two at a time and caught Katherine just before she entered the house.

"Hold it, we have to do this right," he said.

Across the road a silver-haired old man was sitting on his porch, observing this first glimpse. He smiled and nodded his head.

"He'll do," the old man said to no one in particular, then continued to rock in his chair and stroke the cat that slept peacefully in his lap.

Katherine laughed as Tom scooped her up into his arms and carried her across the threshold of their new home. Once inside he gently set her down and then whispered in her ear, "Welcome home, Kate."

She turned and wrapped her arms around his waist and lay her head on his chest, not speaking, just looking around, as Tom was doing.

Katherine was the first to speak. "It's going to take some work, but if you look past the mess, it was once a really beautiful place to call home. And I believe with some love and attention it can be again."

Tom gave a slight shrug and let out a deep sigh. "Kate, you never fail to amaze me. I was practically ready to turn tail and run, and you are already imagining curtains!"

He laughed and she joined him. She was rewarded with a gentle kiss and a look in Tom's eyes that promised more later.

Alice came in carrying Katherine's trunk.

"Here, let me get that," Tom said, as he reached to take the case from her.

"So, what do you think?" she asked when she stood next to Katherine.

"To be honest, I'm a bit overwhelmed, but we'll just take one day at a time and pray a lot," Kate replied.

"A whole lot," Tom interjected as he headed out to the Jeep to retrieve the other trunk and their small bag of groceries.

Meanwhile Katherine and Alice began removing dust covers from the furniture that was still in the house. Dust flew everywhere, causing both girls to sneeze and laugh. When all the dust covers had been removed they discovered several incredible pieces of hand carved Koa wood furniture. They uncovered a beautiful long side table, several chest-of-drawers, and a dining room table. The chairs would need to be rebuilt or thrown into the fire pit if it was determined they were unsafe to sit in. There was also an exquisite hand-carved headboard uncovered in the master bedroom, but no mattress or bed springs.

"If I didn't love these pieces so much, this furniture would be the start of a great antique store," Kate commented to Alice

Alice agreed, and then the two sat quietly for a few minutes and just looked around them.

"We'd better let the dust settle before we do anything else," Katherine stated. Alice nodded in agreement as she sneezed again.

Tom returned with his trunk and grocery bag in time to see the dust storm in the house.

"Wow, Kate! I can't leave you alone for a minute without you already getting into trouble," he said, and then ducked when Katherine pitched the dust cover she was holding at his head.

"Stick with me kid. You haven't seen anything yet!" she replied, joining in his laughter.

"This old house ain't heard so much laughter in a good long time," came a voice from the doorway.

"Daddy!" Alice said. "Come meet Tom and Kate Tyne."

She had only heard Tom refer to Katherine as Kate, and didn't realize she had any other name.

"Aloha, nice to meet you Tom, Mrs. Kate," Alice's father replied, as he shook hands and smiled warmly. "Call me Joe."

"Nice to meet you, Joe," Tom and Katherine replied at the same time.

While the two men talked, Katherine thought of the greeting she had just received. *Mrs. Kate. I like it.*

Joe took the Tyne's on a tour of the house and outside to check out the property. "It's a mess now, but oh, you should have seen it when Aunty and Uncle were alive. Always full of music, laughter, and clean as a whistle. I had a crush on their daughter, Mele, but she went off and married that Haole," he said with a slightly disgusted tone in his voice.

Paradise Inherited

"Now, Daddy, you said he was a pretty nice guy," Alice popped in after a quick side glance at Tom.

Seeing his daughter's glance, Joe quickly added with a nervous laugh, "Oh, yeah, he was alright for a white guy."

Alice, who knew every inch of the property, having grown up in the next house down the road, excused herself from the tour and went over to visit the old gent across the road and invite him to share lunch with them. Leaning in, she whispered in his ear, "I like them. They are very nice."

He nodded and thanked her kindly for the luncheon invitation. "Not just yet Alice. Perhaps another time. For now I prefer to just sit on this porch, in my rocking chair, and pet this old cat."

"Alright Uncle, but Mama expects you for Sunday dinner," she said giving him a quick hug.

When Alice came back she pointed him out to Katherine, who looked over to the house across the road and waved. He waved back.

I'll have to make it a point to meet our neighbor soon, Katherine said to herself.

After Alice and Joe had gone home, Tom and Katherine sat on the floor and leaned against the wall to relax and reflect on what the day had provided- new friends and a home badly in need of repair and cleaning.

"Blown up and rebuilt might work better," Tom had teased half seriously, then added, "And the first day almost gone of the one thousand eight hundred twenty four days left to go."

Katherine laughed. "But who's counting?"

"We have no electricity, no running water inside the house, no bathroom inside the house, and no bed, bedding, or pillows. Oh-And because there is no electricity we have no stove or refrigerator, no washing machine, and no television or radio. What do you suggest our first priority should be?" she asked with a smirk on her face.

"Gee, you make it sound so bleak," Tom said, and laughed along with her.

Tom suggested their first priority be to get a room at one of the hotels they had passed, but his wife would not hear of it.

"Not tonight," she protested. "It's our first night in our first home. We have a roof over our heads in case it rains, and the doors and window shutters can be closed. What else do we need?" she said as she gave her husband a seductive smile.

Tom put his arms around her and pulled her close. "What do you suggest we use for pillows and covers?" he asked, not quite convinced.

Katherine jumped up, went to her trunk and brought out two of the wedding gifts they had received from friends they had made on board ship. Holding them up for Tom's review were two deflated air mattresses from the pool, and the quilt she had taken from her bed at home.

"I almost didn't bring this," she said through a big grin. "Susanne convinced me to take something to remind me of home."

"Looks like we are set for tonight anyway." Tom replied. He then got down to the business of blowing up the air mattresses while Katherine went on a hunt

Paradise Inherited

for matches to light the candles she had found in a cupboard while cleaning the kitchen.

"Alright, let's get serious," she continued. "I think we'd better make a list of the items we need to make this place a home."

Tom agreed, suggesting things should be put in order of priority. "Starting with this," he said as he pulled her closer and began unbuttoning her blouse.

"Tom, I'm serious," Katherine giggled.

"Oh I'm serious, dead serious," he said as he covered her lips with his.

Sometime later in the glow of the candle light, Katherine picked up her notepad, gave Tom a loving glance and said, "Well, let's see, where were we?"

Tom moved her hair from her neck and started kissing her gently sending chill bumps down her arms. "I think we were here," he teased.

"Tom, we'll never get this done," she purred.

"Exactly," Tom said, as he blew out the candle on the floor next to them.

Before settling in for the night, and much to her dismay, Katherine eventually had to make a trip to the outhouse. It was quite dark so she made Tom go with her.

Upon exiting the smelly building she stated, "That was the most disgusting experience I've ever had and one I do not wish to repeat for any longer than is absolutely necessary. I vote we list indoor plumbing and a bathroom in the house as top priority."

Tom laughed, and Katherine gave him a disgusted look.

"Yes ma'am he replied, "I'll get right on that first thing tomorrow."

"Ugh," Katherine replied. "Good help is so hard to find. If you start now surely you could have it done by morning." She laughed and ran back into the house, with Tom in hot pursuit.

Finally, the couple settled down for their first night in Kauai. A gentle rain had begun to fall, and even though Katherine had been concerned about the noise of the metal roof, she found it actually provided a relaxing beat, added to the sound of the waves from the beach and the winds that blew gently through the trees.

Tom on the other hand heard the drip, drip, drip, in various places around the small house and knew tomorrow he'd be repairing the roof as top priority.

As they lay on their air mattresses, each was lost in thought, but basically thinking the same thing. There was still no real indication as to what they were here for or what they should do for five years, but one day was done and they had agreed once again to trust God to lead and give them direction, and to take life one day at a time.

"He's brought us here for a reason Tom," Katherine spoke into the darkness. "Our job is to be alert, and to watch for His leading."

Tom agreed, and then kissed her. "I love you Kate, I'm a lucky man."

She smiled and rolled over into his waiting arms. And *I love being called Kate*, she thought to herself. *It's so quiet and peaceful here. I hope it will stay this way for a long long time.* Kate though, as she drifted off to sleep.

Kate awoke early the next morning and rolled over and watched her husband who lay beside her, sleeping peacefully. Quietly, she stood up and walked to the front door. Opening it she discovered the view of the little cove provided a wonderful frame for the rising sun. She stood there for a few moments and offered up a prayer of thanks for the beauty before her. She stepped out onto the front porch and then decided to walk down to the beach. After a quick check to make sure Tom was still sleeping, she hurried down to the beach.

The sand was cool to the touch and still damp where the tide had come in and gone out again.

"It is so peaceful here," she said to herself.

"Watch out for the little crabs," said a soft voice.

Kate jumped at the sound and spun around. Behind her stood the old man who lived across the street.

"Oh, good morning," she said.

"Sorry, I didn't mean to startle you," the man replied.

Kate chuckled, "I didn't realize anyone else was here. You said crabs. What crabs?"

"Just watch the sand around your feet, you'll see them." The old man pointed towards Kate's feet.

Looking down she noticed little ripples of sand moving all over the beach. Suddenly out of one of the ripples popped a tiny crab. She was fascinated and stooped down to see them more clearly. They didn't bother her, just popped in and out of tiny holes all over.

"Do they come out like this all the time?" Kate asked.

"Yep, every morning," he said with a gentle smile on his sun leathered face.

Standing up she walked toward him and introduced herself. The old man said his name was Tom, at which Kate laughed and said, "Well that should be easy to remember, that is my husband's name." Old Tom smiled again and nodded his head.

"Have you lived here long?" she asked.

"Oh, on and off for a long time." he responded.

They chatted a few minutes then Kate excused herself mentioning that her Tom would probably be awake and wondering where she had gone off to.

"I'm glad to have met you, Tom. Come over later and meet my Tom," she said as she turned and headed back to the house.

Old Tom watched her walk away, then turned back toward the beach and let go with a contented sigh.

"She'll do too," he said to no one except maybe the sand crabs.

Tom was sitting up on the air mattress when she entered the front door. "Thought you fell in," he said, with one of the goofy looks he gave her when teasing.

"Ha Ha, very funny," Kate laughed. "No, actually I was down at the beach getting a lesson in crabology from our neighbor across the street."

Tom gave her another goofy look. "Crabology, what's that?"

Kate laughed. "It's my new word for the day. Seriously though, Tom, you should see it. Little tiny crabs burrowing all over the beach. It was fascinating."

Tom loved it when Kate got excited about something. When she couldn't think of the correct word for what she needed, she just made one up to suit her purposes. It was something she'd done as long as he'd known her.

"Oh-and our neighbor and you have something in common."

"Really, such as?" he asked.

"His name is Tom also."

"Tom Also. Interesting name. Do you think 'Also' is a Hawaiian name?" he asked, then ran out the back door. Kate laughed and ran after him.

"Beat you to the throne room," Tom cried over his shoulder.

At that, Kate stopped dead in her tracks.

"Oh no, you go right ahead, your highness, the throne room is all yours."

They both grinned and Kate hoped she could wait to relieve herself at the restaurant down the road when they went for breakfast.

After breakfast the couple took care of some business before heading back to the house. At the bank, Tom introduced himself to the manager, as Jonathan Murphy had instructed. They opened a savings account and deposited the check Kate's father had given them. Tom had advised her that earning

Paradise Inherited

interest was a wise decision until they decided what to do with the money.

Next stop was the Post Office where they established a PO box to receive any mail that might eventually come to them. At noon they found themselves back at the General Store. Mrs. Wong once again greeted them warmly and loaned them a Montgomery Ward and the new Spiegel and Sears catalogs to browse through so they could better determine what they needed for the house.

It became very clear quite quickly that almost everything had to be ordered and shipped in, something neither of them had considered before.

"We'll need to pick carefully and prioritize," Tom remarked. Depending on how we use the money, it could be a very long, hard year, or a very peaceful one."

Kate nodded her head in agreement while flipping through the catalog pages.

When they arrived back at the house Kate started a list from the catalogs of items she thought were needed. Tom went outside to explore the shed, the one area Joe had not shown him the day before. Suddenly Kate heard Tom give a whoop and call her name.

"Kate, come look at what I've found," he yelled.

She quickly ran out to find Tom standing at the shed door, a grin spread across his face. He stepped away from the entrance, so she could look inside. She too let out a hearty whoop of excitement.

Before her was a claw-foot bathtub, a toilet, and a sink.

Tom took her hand and ran toward the back of the house. Moving some high grass and weeds, he exposed some water pipes sticking out of the ground.

"Looks like at sometime, rather recently, someone had started the process of getting indoor plumbing," he explained.

Kate was overjoyed. "Do you know how to finish this?"

"No, but we'll ask Joe if he knows someone who can help"

Joe was delighted to be of assistance to his new neighbors. "I ran the plumbing into our house a couple years ago," he stated. "Much better than the outhouse," he laughed.

When the work was done Tom wanted to pay for Joe's services, but Joe wouldn't take it.

After the plumbing project was completed Kate purposely walked out to the outhouse. Tom followed close behind and laughed when he saw what his wife was doing. With hammer and nail in hand she placed a sign on the outhouse door. 'OUT OF ORDER, PERMANENTLY' it read. They both laughed as she stood back to admire her work.

As they walked back into their little home, Tom mentally checked off the first priority item and Kate prepared herself for a nice long soak in the tub. Of course Tom would have to start up the barbecue and heat water, as there was no water heater. By mutual agreement it was decided the next priority would be getting electricity.

Days turned into weeks and the little house began to look more like a home than a deserted shack. Walls were painted inside and out, flower beds had been cleaned and replanted, the electricity was connected and a new refrigerator hummed in the kitchen. Pieces of furniture began to fill the tiny home.

Kate continued to visit the beach before Tom got up each morning. Often she would meet Old Tom there, always urging him to come meet her Tom. In the end it took a gift of a couple of dozen homemade cookies to lure the older man into a visit.

He strolled over one afternoon as Tom worked up a sweat preparing the garden for planting.

"Need some help there Bud?" he asked.

Tom had not heard the old man approach and spun around. After the initial shock of discovering he was not alone, Tom smiled and said, "Sure, I'll take all the help I can get.

As the two men shook hands, Tom said, "My wife tells me your name is Tom."

Old Tom nodded and replied, "Just call me 'Uncle'."

With a flash of a smile and a twinkle in his eye the old man took up one of the garden tools lying on the ground next to his feet. The men worked long and hard all afternoon indulging in small talk now and then to get acquainted. By dinnertime the garden was ready for planting. As they walked toward the house Old Tom patted the young man on the back.

"You've done well. A man not afraid of hard work and getting dirty-I appreciate that in a man," Uncle said.

Tom beamed. He had rarely had a compliment from another male, and once again realized how much he had missed not having a father as he grew up, a male to teach and encourage him.

"Thank you sir, I really appreciate the help."

Old Tom nodded and smiled.

Learning to live with the roaches and gecko's everywhere and the early morning wake-up call from the neighborhood roosters crowing had been one of Kate's challenges the first few weeks on the island. That and sleeping on the floor was getting old.

I hope a mattress for the bed reaches the top of the priority list soon, she thought one morning as she stretched to get the kinks out.

One thing or another had gotten moved to priority above the roof repair. When the day finally came, this project turned out to be a bit more painful and not at all what anyone expected.

"Looks like you broke this arm in two places and the leg too," stated the emergency room doctor as he reviewed the x-rays. "So how did you manage this?" he asked casually.

"Needed to do some roof repair. I climbed the tree next to the house to gain access to the roof. Before I was completely settled up there the limb I was on broke and the rest is history," Tom said as he grimaced at the pain of his arm being set.

When asked why he'd climbed the tree, Tom replied, "I didn't have a ladder."

After the accident several members of the local church came by along with Joe and old Tom and finished the yard cleanup and house repairs.

On their six-month anniversary of being island residents, Tom and Kate celebrated by going to dinner at the CoCo Palms Resort Palace Restaurant. As they waited for their meal to arrive, Tom sat smiling, his eyes sparkling.

"You look like the cat who swallowed the canary," she teased.

"I've got news," he laughed. "I got a job today."

"Where?" Kate leaned forward in her chair.

"Here," he laughed. "I've been hired for the grounds crew."

"Oh Tom, that's wonderful!"

Over dinner he told her about his job responsibilities, and ended by saying, "We've done alright on our monthly allowance, but the extra money will come in handy."

"More than you know," Kate laughed as she handed Tom a small square gift-wrapped box, tied with a ribbon.

"What's this for?" Tom asked surprised.

"You'll see. Just open it."

Tom lifted the lid and his expression grew even more puzzled for a moment.

He looked at Kate, and seeing the huge smile on her face, it suddenly registered with him what he had seen. He lifted the one pink and one blue bootie, and yelled with excitement as he jumped up from his chair. "We're having a baby? When?"

"Around Valentine's Day," Kate stated as tears of joy streamed down her face.

Next thing she knew she was wrapped in Tom's arms and the entire restaurant was filled with the sounds of clapping, laughter and shouts of congratulations.

Chapter Seven

Kate was miserable during the early stages of her pregnancy and almost beside herself that after seven months in the islands she still had not heard from her family.

On his way home from work each day, Tom stopped at the Post Office to check the mail. A smile spread across his face when he opened the box and discovered they had finally been rewarded with three letters. One was for himself, from Jonathan, the attorney in Honolulu. The other two were the long-awaited letters from Kate's parents and from Susanne. *Kate will be so excited*, Tom thought as he hurried to the Jeep to get the letters home. "And I hope it improves her general attitude," he spoke out loud.

The first weeks of pregnancy had not made Kate the most exciting person to be around. If she wasn't in the bathroom struggling with morning sickness, "that lasts for twenty-four hours," she'd complain, she was moody and hard to satisfy, no matter how hard Tom tried to comfort her.

They had come to shouting matches a couple of times over very trivial things. These usually ended with Kate crying and slamming the bedroom door and falling asleep, or Tom storming out of the house and spending the afternoon or evening in the shed puttering around with whatever project he was working on at that time.

After one such hard day, Kate had cross-stitched a sampler that now hung in their bedroom.

> Be angry, yet do not sin;
> Do not let the sun go down on your anger.
> Eph 4:26

"Some days it's easier said than done," she had laughed, and Tom agreed the afternoon he hung it on the bedroom wall.

Kate was almost her old self, laughing and jumping for joy as soon as Tom handed her the letters from home. She opened first the letter from her parents as she settled onto the couch. Her heart leapt with joy just to see her mother's handwriting.

Dear Katherine,

Your father and I were delighted to receive your letter and wedding pictures. You were indeed the beautiful bride I thought you'd be when Susanne and I purchased the dress for you. I'm so glad you were pleased with our surprise. It gave me great pleasure knowing you wore the locket on your wedding day.

Something borrowed and all that. But of course I want you to keep the locket.

I'm sorry we haven't written sooner. You father and I have had quite a time since the evening you and Tom left for Hawaii. It has taken me several weeks to adjust to both my girls being gone.

Surprised and confused, Kate stopped and reread the last line again.

"Where did Susanne go?" she questioned aloud.

She quickly read the rest of the letter.

Sometime during the night after you left, Susanne slipped out of the house and eloped with Mason. You remember him, the new bank president's son. They ran away to Reno and were married in a cheap wedding chapel. No wedding dress, nothing. We were crazy with worry, but a telegram arrived the next day telling us that she was happily married, and that they would be home the end of the week. Oh, she also apologized, asked our forgiveness, assured us that she and Mason were fine and asked us not to worry. Not worry, she says. She's only known that boy for, what, a month? And we knew nothing about this! After all, she was engaged to and about to marry Tom just the day before.

Anyway, not long after the telegram arrived our doorbell rang and Mason's parents stood there just as upset and angry as your father and I.

The long and the short of it is that it is now July and they still have not returned from Reno. Susanne does write from time to time. Apparently Mason took a job there, although I'm not clear what type of job and they have decided to make their home in Reno. Of all places! Yes, well, I have forwarded your address to your sister and enclosed hers for you. Hopefully you will hear from her soon.

The rest of the letter contained news about neighbors, church activities, and father's hardware store updates, but Kate couldn't concentrate on it, as her thoughts were miles away with her twin.

She and her sister had always possessed a knowing sense about things that concerned each other and Kate now knew, without a doubt, that something wasn't right about Susanne's situation.

Remembering she also held an envelope from Susanne, Kate then gave her full attention to that letter.

Dear Kat,

I'm sure you've heard by now that I beat you to the altar. You have no idea how relieved I was when a door opened for me to get out of the wedding with Tom and marry Mason Anderson instead.

From the moment he moved into town I knew he was the man I wanted to marry.

We have decided to make our home in Reno, where Mason has been offered a wonderful opportunity that simply can't be passed up. We are well and happy. Write soon and tell me all about your 'little grass shack'.

Seriously, my dear, I hope you are doing alright. I do worry about how you must be surviving. Glad it is you and not me. Ha.

Love Sus

Short and sweet, Kate thought. She certainly said a little bit of nothing.

Sighing deeply, she got off the couch. Her feelings about the content of both letters had become almost overwhelming.

It was sometime later while rereading her mother's letter that it dawned on Kate that her mother had not made one mention about her pregnancy.

"I'd give anything to have a telephone right now."

***

On the other side of the ocean, across the desert, Susanne sat listening to classical music with Mrs. Lawson, the dear older lady who had so graciously opened her home to Susanne after Mason abandoned her.

As Mrs. Lawson slept peacefully in the rocker beside her, Susanne wondered with a sense of longing what her sister and parents were doing. She'd accepted that she would have to go on wondering for awhile longer.

"Maybe forever," she whispered as a tear trickled down her cheek.

Mason why did you do this to me? Susanne silently cried, as she rubbed her rounded belly and then picked up her needlepoint and tried to concentrate on it instead of the road outside.

***

After discussing the family letters with Tom, Kate asked, "What did Jonathan have to say?"

"He's coming for a visit next week. Apparently he has another client on the island he needs to see. After that business is done, he will make a point to stop by to see how we are managing," Tom informed her.

"Checking up on us is he?" Kate joked. "I suppose he must continue to look after your Uncle's interests. Does he say what day he's coming?"

Scanning the letter again quickly to make sure he hadn't missed anything, Tom said, "No specific day mentioned, just next week."

"Oh great, a surprise attack," Kate replied.

"Sometimes surprise attacks are the best action to take," Tom laughed, as he jumped out of his chair and attacked Kate from behind with several quick kisses on her neck

Kate squealed in surprise when Tom picked her up and started toward their bedroom. She weakly responded with something about needing to finish the dinner dishes before he was kissing her lips.

"That can wait," Tom said, as he gently lowered her onto their bed.

The next morning Tom found Kate standing at and gazing out the living room window, gently rubbing the tiny bulge that was beginning to grow and make her jeans fits snugly.

"You can unbutton the top button you know," he told her as he came up behind her and slipped his arms around her expanding waist.

"Are you saying I'm getting fat?" she asked as she turned to face him and snuggled against his chest.

"Nope, just beautifully having my baby," he replied.

"Nice save," she laughed.

"Seriously, are you still worried about your sister?"

"Something is wrong, Tom. I don't know what, but I feel it inside."

Tom didn't know how to respond other than to hold his wife tighter. After a moment he spoke softly into Kate's ear, "God knows, Kate, whatever is going on with Susanne, He's still in control and will provide for her. Trust Him. It's really all we can do, besides pray."

Kate nodded as Tom pulled a handkerchief from his pocket and gently wiped away the tears that threatened to slide down her cheeks.

Making an effort to calm herself for his sake, she sent him off to shave while she finished getting breakfast.

"Tom's right, prayer is all I can do for my sister right now," she said to the eggs in the skillet. It also dawned on her that she felt hungry for breakfast for the first time in weeks.

Young as she was, Kate had also learned that God uses his people in ways they would never dream of and sometimes he uses unpleasant or unexpected circumstances to get their attention to guide and teach them.

"I have a feeling the lessons here aren't just for Susanne," she admitted to herself.

The rest of the week flew by for the couple, and while Kate thought of her sister often, she didn't dwell on her concerns. When Saturday morning arrived, Tom, Kate and Uncle, climbed into the jeep loaded with a picnic basket and a cake for the church auction. A family down the road had lost everything to a fire and the church family, of which Tom and Kate were now members, were gathering for a fundraiser auction to help the family meet some of their needs.

Along with a freshly-baked cake, their offering also included a baby blanket Kate had crocheted. The old man contributed some books from his collection of first editions. Tom's contribution had been to design and pay for the advertising of the auction. It was hoped that people and tourists from all over the island would come to support this worthy cause.

The trio in the Jeep joined the line of cars, bicycles and foot traffic making its way into the churchyard. Many carried items to put up for sale, but most were there to participate in the auction. The prevailing mood was festive, but there was no lack of genuine care and concern for the victims.

Several people had come with guitars, drums, and ukuleles, and music filled the air. As they pulled into the churchyard Kate noticed several people swaying to the music, many times women and children would begin to dance.

As Kate watched the dancers she leaned over toward Tom and whispered, "Hula is so graceful and peaceful to watch. I wish I could be that graceful."

Alice had offered to continue teaching her the Hula lessons she'd started on the ship. Kate felt quite awkward when she danced normally, and the baby bump wasn't helping her to feel any more coordinated.

"It takes time. Stay with it, you'll learn," Alice encouraged at each lesson. "The dancers you'll see performing have danced in most cases since they were babies.

It's so cute to watch. Babies who haven't taken their first solo steps will stand hanging on to tables, or whatever is in their reach and sway those little fannies."

Before the auction officially began, Kate and Tom walked around the tables checking out the items up for bid. There were handmade grass skirts, monkey pod dishes that were hand-carved, and bolts of Hawaiian print material. Tom made note to come back and bid on the dinner cruise, while Kate kept an eye on a beautiful handmade koa-wood cradle. At the end of the day both were delighted to discover they had won the items they had bid on.

At the end of the day the family that had been burned-out was presented with a check from the sale that included a matching amount from an anonymous donor. Keys to a house, rent free, for one year came with the check. The family was overwhelmed with this outpouring of love.

The following Monday morning, as Tom was leaving for work, he noticed Old Tom preparing to enter a taxi.

The old man saw Tom, waved and hollered, "I have some business to take care of on the mainland. I'll be back in a couple weeks," then climbed in to the taxi and drove away.

"I wonder what that's all about?" Tom asked, watching the tail lights of the departing taxi.

"He never said a thing about leaving," Kate remarked, as she handed Tom the lunch bag he'd left in the kitchen.

Looking across the street Kate spotted a note tacked to the front door of Uncle's house. While Tom climbed into the jeep to prepare to leave, Kate calmly walked across the road to see what the note said.

I'll be back. Feed the lazy old cat. Thanks, Uncle.

"Not long on good-byes or words, is he." Tom chuckled.

Kate shook her head in response and said, "You'd better get moving, too. Don't want those coconuts falling on the guest's heads."

Tom puffed out his chest and replied, "Yeah, they can't get along without me."

Kate laughed and slugged his arm. "Ok Wonder Worker, get moving."

Rubbing his arm, he gave her a stern, yet comical facial expression and said, "Hey, do we need to go over the house rules again?" He then slugged her back.

"Yes maybe we do," Kate laughed, rubbing her arm.

With the warm sun on her skin and the light breeze in her hair Kate decided to sit on the lanai and enjoy a few moments of the morning before getting ready for the cooking class Alice's Tutu was giving her.

As much as she hated to admit it, Kate knew she was a pretty good baker, but didn't know much about cooking meals. Tom had been a big help, since he was a good cook, but now that he was working he didn't have time to help her. One meal at Alice's Tutu's house had convinced Kate to ask her for lessons. At first they had worked on the basics. Today she was learning how to make true Hawaiian dishes.

"When we pau you be one very good cook," Tutu praised Kate's efforts one day.

"Pau?" Kate mouthed at Alice with a quizzical look on her face.

Alice laughed and silently mouthed the words "all done."

Kate has blushed slightly and thanked Alice's grandmother with a warm hug.

"I can only hope to be half as good a cook as you, Tutu.

***

The flight to Honolulu was short. Uncle reached his destination in record time. "Kimo, you still drive like a crazy man." The old man grinned into the rearview mirror.

"Sure, I know, but I never get my passengers to their destination late," Kimo replied.

Laughing, Uncle gave Kimo a healthy tip as he exited the vehicle and said, "You make sure to get Lani and those beautiful keiki of yours something special today."

Kimo smiled and gave the old man a hug. "Yes sir," he replied, as he touched his cap and winked at his mentor.

As the old man walked toward the elevator that would wisk him up to his attorney's office, he reflected on when he had first met Kimo.

He had been living and working for a church in Honolulu as a youth pastor, which involved leading a youth bible study group. He remembered the night a tall, skinny, eighteen year old young man entered the room. Kimo had been invited by a young girl named Lani. Lani was a friend to anyone and everyone, and had convinced the homeless young man to come for the dinner to be served that night at the church.

During the course of the evening he noticed that Lani stayed by Kimo's side and introduced him to everyone in attendance. It was during the sharing time that he learned that Kimo was a high school dropout and probably headed for trouble.

He's had a rough time of it, Tom had thought, as Kimo told the group something about himself.

At first a bit shy, Kimo's normal friendly personality eventually broke through and he talked and laughed as each person took a turn sharing. He had been amazed that a group of young people could get together and have so much fun without a trace of alcohol anywhere. Not that he drank much, but he'd been smashed a few times.

At the end of the evening he stayed after the others had departed and talked to Pastor Tom for a couple of hours. The result was that before Kimo left that night he had become a born again child of God, acquired a job, as well as a place to live.

Tears gathering in his own eyes, Tom had watched as the young man had cried with joy and relief when he took it to heart that God loved him just the way he was. He hadn't done anything to get his act together, only acknowledged that he was a sinner, and asked Jesus to forgive him and come into his life. Tom had hugged the boy and told him he was a new creation in Christ. From that day forward Kimo diligently sought the will of God for his life. He read his Bible daily and became a mighty prayer warrior.

"Finding God was the best thing that ever happened to me," he always told everyone. "The next best thing was meeting Lani." He'd also tell anyone who would listen, "I'll always remember, with much Aloha, the man who took the time to talk to a half starved, cocky Hawaiian boy and save his life.

Pastor Tom would always smile and remind him that, "God saved your life, Kimo, I was only a willing instrument."

Reaching the office he needed, Tom entered and was greeted by the receptionist with a warm Aloha then ushered immediately into the office where Jonathan stood to greet him.

"Pastor Tom! Wow! This is a record, two times meeting in my office! It's great to see you. How's it going?" Jonathan asked.

Uncle grinned and chuckled, "Jon, my boy, I haven't been your pastor for years, but I thank you for the compliment of respect. To answer your question, it's going great. Better than I'd hoped, actually."

Jonathan smiled broadly.

Uncle smiled back and asked, "So what did you think of my nephew?" Without waiting for an answer he continued. "Those two are quite a pair. They work hard and love easy. Kate has had quite a time with the various bugs here, and lack of television, but she's adjusting, and I think this will work out just fine."

Jonathan paused before speaking to make sure his client was finished. When the old man didn't continue he spoke up. "The short time I had them in the office, I sensed they would be a great couple. Are you sure you don't want to tell them, sir?"

The old man sighed, "No it's better this way. How could I ever explain why I allowed things to turn out the way they did? Not that his aunt did a bad job raising him, mind you, but I should have taken a more active interest. He is my only sister's only child."

Jonathan said nothing, just slightly nodded his head in agreement.

"Besides, that old doctor only gave me five years, maybe six if I'm lucky. I don't want to waste the time explaining and run the risk of Tom becoming angry and leaving. This way I can enjoy him, teach him a few things about his heritage and then go out quietly, you know, without a lot of fuss."

Jonathan wasn't sure he agreed with the plan, but it wasn't his decision to make, so he remained quiet. They got down to the other business Uncle had come to discuss before he boarded a plane for the mainland and the team of doctors in California who monitored his heart condition.

Chapter Eight

Jonathan arrived from Honolulu without announcement early Wednesday evening while Tom and Kate were at the church actively involved with the mid-week youth group. Not knowing for sure when the attorney would arrive, Kate had left a note on the door every time they left the house, giving the information of their expected return time.

While he waited, Jonathan took a stroll around the yard, noticing the Tynes had definitely worked hard to repair and landscape the old home of the Kalama family. It had certainly changed since the meeting here, almost a year ago, when his client, Tom Kalama, had asked Jonathan to join him in Kauai and instructed the attorney with what Kalama had called 'the plan'.

"I want to see what my nephew is made of," the old man had stated. "The boy was raised by his prissy Aunt. Who knows what kind of influence she had on him? I need to know how he handles life's challenges."

"Looks like he's doing quite well," Jonathan replied out loud to his own thoughts.

Settling into a rocking chair on the lanai, Jonathan watched a couple of roosters strut across the yard. By their movements and chatter it was obvious that one was the dominant bird and the other a new guy on the block trying to take possession.

"You guys are sure pretty to look at, but I'm guessing not so pleasant to hear early in the morning," he said out loud to the passing birds.

The peaceful setting and faint lulling sound of the ocean was so relaxing that Jonathan unintentionally drifted into a light sleep. The sound of tires crunching the gravel on the driveway brought him quickly awake. Seeing Tom and Katherine in the approaching vehicle, he raised his arm to wave.

"Surprise," Kate said just under her breath, doing her best to give an honest smile as she returned the wave and thought, *I knew he was coming, but I'm tired and really not in the mood to entertain or make small talk.*

"Tom, Katherine, it's good to see you again," Jonathan said, as he walked toward the Jeep.

Tom shook Jonathan's outstretched hand.

"Call me Kate," Katherine said, as she too shook his hand. "Everyone does now."

Kate served glasses of iced tea and jumped right in with her own questions before Jonathan had a chance to swallow his first sip.

"Mr. Murphy, I was under the impression Tom has inherited a rather large fortune. If this is true why has our monthly income jumped up and down, *really* down to be quite clear?" We barely got this wreck of a house put back together with the income, leaving next to nothing to live on."

Tom reached over and gently put his hand on Kate's shoulder. He could tell by the rising tone of her voice that she was on a roll.

Kate gave him a quick side glance, brushed away his hand and continued, her voice beginning to tremble.

"Do you have any idea how expensive it is to live here? We don't have a television or telephone because we can't afford one. There are no decent shops and..."before she could finish and without giving the attorney a chance to speak she began to cry, jumped up and ran from the room.

From her bedroom Kate could only hear the muffled voices of Tom and the attorney. She washed her face after a few moments and rejoined the men in the front room. All three acted as if nothing out of the ordinary had occurred.

This time Kate sat quietly and let Tom do the talking. She realized she'd made a spectacle of herself and hoped Tom wasn't angry with her. She also hoped Murphy wouldn't stay long, but much to her dismay Tom, insisted that Jonathan stay at the house during his visit to Kauai.

"Kate's done a crackerjack job of decorating the guest room," Tom stated with pride.

"That's very kind of you," Jonathan said, then gave Kate a hopeful look as he added, "I'd love to stay, if it's not too much trouble."

"Of course it's no trouble," Kate assured with slightly forced graciousness. Then, feeling a little ashamed of herself she added, "Providing you don't mind putting up with the moods and lack of energy of a pregnant hostess."

"Congratulations!" Jonathan said, with genuine surprise and pleasure showing plainly on his face.

As Kate had been wearing a full length muumuu since he arrived, he hadn't noticed the small bulge of her belly. But now that the news was out he joked about being a dumb and blind bachelor and not noticing these things.

I wonder if Kalama knows, He thought while shaking Tom's hand.

As he settled into the guestroom Jonathan was pleased his gamble had paid off. He had hoped for just such an invitation, which is why he hadn't booked a hotel room before arriving. He wanted a chance to get to know the couple a little better. If the invitation hadn't been extended, he wasn't concerned; there was always the suite Kalama kept at the CoCo Palms Resort.

After a good night's sleep Kate awoke in a better frame of mind. She rarely suffered with morning sickness now and when she was rested she was almost her old loveable self.

After breakfast Tom had to rush off to work, but returned at lunchtime so that Kate didn't have to entertain their visitor alone. To his surprise, Jonathan was not at the house when he got home.

"He left shortly after you did this morning. I guess he really does have other business here," she said, feeling a bit ashamed of her earlier attitude toward the man.

The next two days Jonathan left early and returned long after the dinner hour. The first night Kate had set aside a plate for him.

"That was very kind of you, Kate," he told her. "I'm sorry, I should have told you I had several meetings scheduled with clients on the island and those meetings tend to run late."

He spent the weekend with Kalama's family. It encouraged him and also strengthened the old man's case that 'the plan' was working out better than either could have expected. The accountant in charge of distributing the Tyne's finances and recording the financial statement Tom furnished each month indicated that the couple was spending and saving wisely. Kate's outburst about having so little money when he first arrived had confused him at first, but later she had explained that she was really missing having a television and telephone and even though Tom had promised they'd get one, it hadn't yet happened and she had assumed it was from lack of money.

"My emotions have been all over the place recently and I even momentarily forgot about the money my father gave us," she'd explained. Looking at Tom, she gave him a weak smile. "We agreed to save that for an emergency, and neither of those fit that category.'

From other conversations with Tom and Kate, Jonathan also determined that the Tyne's were adjusting to island life quite well in spite of the lack of those household items. He was pleased to see they were making friends, as several people had come over Saturday night for a barbecue held in his honor.

As the ribs cooked and music played Kate introduced Jonathan to all their friends. After Alice welcomed him, she mentioned to Kate, "Too bad Old Tom is away, he loves a party."

Playing his part, the attorney fanned ignorance, and asked, "Who is Old Tom."

"He is a dear old man who lives across the street," Kate said as she pointed to the old man's house. We've gotten to know him quite well. He's practically like family."

On Monday morning Jonathan boarded a plane headed back to Honolulu. While he sat waiting for his flight to be called he passed the time by opening his briefcase and started a letter to Tom Kalama.

'Tom Tyne is turning out to be a dependable, hard worker,' the attorney wrote. 'He's careful with his money and has managed well during those months when we purposely reduced his monthly allowance, and has saved wisely when we raised his income. Being rushed into an unplanned marriage has turned out well, as it is obvious he picked the right woman.'

After boarding and when the plane was in the air, Jonathan accepted a cup of coffee from the stewardess then continued his report.

'It appears very likely that the couple will be here at the New Year and I recommend the first segment of the inheritance be given to the Tyne's.'

Jonathan smiled as he sealed the envelope that contained his report and slipped it back into his briefcase.

***

Uncle returned after a two-week absence. He didn't say where he'd been or what he'd done, so Tom and Kate didn't ask. They were curious and a bit concerned, as he seemed to have trouble breathing from time to time, but decided they didn't feel comfortable asking questions that he obviously didn't feel the need to answer. Each day that passed they had grown to care more about the old fellow, yet some boundaries still felt too awkward to cross.

On his first day back on Kauai, Uncle picked up his mail at the Post Office and was pleased to see a letter from his attorney in his box. He read the letter with a sense of satisfaction.

Now that he was getting to know his nephew, the old man began to once again experience the feelings of regret about the way he had spent so many years traveling the world and not being an active part of the young man's life.

Later that evening while sitting in his rocking chair watching the stars come out, Uncle let his mind wander back to the time when he'd returned to the islands nearly thirty years ago and had purchased the old coffee farm, sight unseen, on the island of Hawaii.

It was on the farm that he came back into a right relationship with the Lord. Auntie Lou, his mother's youngest sister and a long-time resident in one of the farm cottages would come by every morning to prepare his breakfast and clean up after the bachelor. While she cooked and cleaned she could be heard softly singing songs of praise to her Lord.

One morning while he was eating she sang a song that broke through the hardness of his heart. *Just As I Am* hit his heart and broke the chains of bondage. Jesus loved him just as he was that moment. Warts and all. He didn't have to clean up his act first to be good enough for God. Kalama thought of himself as a pretty good guy. "I've never killed anyone," he'd told missionaries who had witnessed to him in the past. "I go to church on Christmas and Easter. My parents took me to church as a kid. I'm a Christian," he'd proudly proclaim.

'Oh you go in the garage too, that don't make you a car," Auntie Lou had gently scolded. "You a sinner boy. Just like me. Like da Bible say, 'For all have sinned and fall short of the glory of God'."

He knew he was a sinner and yet God loved him so much he'd sent His son, Jesus, to die for those sins. He had sat there, a grown man, with tears streaming down his cheeks. Auntie Lou stopped what she was doing and wrapped her arms around the grieving man, who for the moment was a child again reaching out, seeking forgiveness after years of denial, admitting his need for a Savior, Jesus Christ, to be Lord of his life.

Several changes took place after that day. He began reading his Bible daily, regularly attended church and memorized scripture. Eventually he went to the mainland to attend Bible school

He met Anthony Tyne while in school. Anthony was almost twenty years younger than himself, but their friendship grew as the two men studied together.

Along with his parents, Tom Kalama hoped his sister Meleana, called Mele, would settle down with a nice Hawaiian boy. But after meeting and getting to know Anthony, Tom had decided that if she were to marry a haole, a Caucasian, or non Hawaiian, Anthony was just the type of fellow he'd pick for her. He'd pray on it, he decided, leaving the details up to God.

As it turned out Mele also went to the mainland to do her nursing studies, which happened to be in the same town where Anthony was working as a youth pastor at his home church. Delighted with this outcome, Tom had advised Mele to attend services there and had asked Anthony to watch out for his little sister.

One look at the pretty Hawaiian girl was all Anthony needed. He watched very carefully and by the end of her two-year nursing course the two were engaged.

They were married shortly after Mele's graduation. Only Tom had been able to attend, as their parents were sickly and unable to stand the journey. He was delighted that Anthony had become part of his family and even more delighted when a year and a half later his sister placed his nephew, his namesake, into his arms.

Mele and Anthony had stopped for a short visit to Hawaii on their journey to China, where they were going to serve as Missionaries for three years. Mele wanted her Mama and Papa to be able to hold their grandson and to have him dedicated to the Lord at the little church she had grown up in. Little did anyone know on that glorious Sunday morning as they smiled for pictures, that it would be the last time anyone from home would see Mele alive.

Word of the train wreck had reached Tom first, since he was listed as the emergency contact for Meleana. Anthony had lain in a coma for several days before passing on, but Mele had died at the scene. Amazingly little Tom had survived without a scratch.

Tom had sent word to Anthony's older sister, Beth, letting her know he was headed for China to get the baby and that he would be in touch as soon as possible.

Beth took the news of her brother's death hard. She had been estranged from Anthony because of her dislike of his marrying a "foreigner," and because she didn't want him going to China, but after receiving word of the accident she had sent a cable to Hawaii to let Tom know that she would be willing to raise the boy.

It had been hard to give little Tom to Beth, the old man remembered. He had considered raising the child himself, but came to realize that because of his lifestyle as a bachelor, the little boy would be better off with his aunt and her husband.

It was several years later, in one of their rare conversations that Beth told Tom Kalama that her husband had died of a sudden heart attack several weeks after little Tom arrived.

Old Tom sighed heavily and shook his head over the old memories, and how one always led to another. He'd rarely allowed himself to think about Mele since her death, but now he could not stop the memories and didn't want too. She had been the flower of his life. Mele had been born when he was 16-years old. His parents had been as surprised as he was by this little addition to their family. At first he had been embarrassed by the fact that his mother was pregnant, but when Mele was born, it was love at first sight.

He'd rush home from school, change her diaper and take off with her to whatever activity filled his afternoon. As she grew, she delighted everyone with her sweet songs and graceful Hula. Before she could walk Mele would hold onto whatever was close and sway as Papa had played his ukulele, he remembered. Seeing his nephew after all these years brought memories of Mele to his mind until it seemed she was all he could think about. It also didn't help that young Tom was the spitting image of himself at the same age.

Now that he was back on Kauai, he planned to make every moment count with Tom and Kate. He was having less trouble with chest pains and his breathing difficulty seemed to be improving. The doctor had been pleased, but still was doubtful that he would live beyond five years. He only hoped the doctor was wrong. He desperately wanted more time, a chance to make the most of every precious moment.

He and Kate continued to meet each morning at the cove. He had grown to love his new niece and was pleased at his nephew's choice of a bride. She shared story after story of the adventures she and Tom had experienced throughout their growing up years. The stories sometimes made him laugh and sometimes nearly brought him to tears as he realized anew how much he'd missed.

Each evening the old man would watch for Tom to return from work. He'd wait a few minutes and then mosey over. At first Kate had to insist he stay for dinner. Now it was just expected. His contribution to the meal usually consisted of fresh fruit or a dessert he had prepared himself.

The three were becoming a family. It was a very satisfying experience for all of them. After dinner, while Kate cleaned up, the men would settle on the front porch discussing the events of the day, whether it be local or world news.

Six weeks after Uncle returned from his mysterious trip Kate was surprised and thrilled to see him placing the third of three new varnished Koa wood rocking chairs on her front porch. After sitting and rocking for a few minutes, enjoying the comfort of the chair, she also noticed the workmanship had a remarkable similarity to the furniture found in the house when they'd first arrived. Tom and Uncle were talking about the garden and she didn't want to interrupt so she didn't say anything at that time. She mentioned it to Tom after Uncle had gone home for the night, but he'd been preoccupied with a project he was working on and hadn't given her words much if any consideration.

Many times over the next few months as the old man watched his nephew and niece work in their garden, or chase each other with the hose, or just walk hand-in-hand on the beach, a deep sense of satisfaction filled him as he had not experienced since his parents had been alive. Watching Kate's body blossom with her advancing pregnancy made the old man smile even wider.

"I have family once again," he'd spoke aloud one afternoon as he watched the couple as they stood at the ocean's edge and let the gentle waves wash over their feet. He was almost tempted to tell them the truth of his identity, but something held him back.

Letting his mind wander as he worked in the shared vegetable garden one morning he began to reflect on the day he had decided to locate his nephew. It was the same day the doctor had told him of his heart condition and that he had five to six years to live.

After the detective had been hired, Thomas decided to update his will and while talking with his attorney had come up with the idea of telling his nephew that he had died and left him all his fortune, which in part was true. At first Jonathan had argued this plan, believing the truth would be better. Thomas however, was convinced this idea was the best way to get to know his nephew, and see what the boy, now a man, was made of.

How could he explain to the attorney that it really wasn't about the money, he could donate that to charity in a flash. *I want to see if the boy is capable of building a relationship with me and not just for the jingle in his pocket*, he'd thought.

But now as he watched the couple splash and heard their laughter, he admitted to himself, I'm old and I want my *Ohana,* my own family.

When Thomas had received word from the train station master that Tom and Katherine were en route he had sighed with relief because it meant they were actually coming. The captain of the ship had also wired about their arrival onboard the ship and Tom's request for a wedding before reaching Honolulu. The old man had gotten a kick out of that. The boy had spunk, and the young woman obviously cared very much about him to head off into the unknown with him.

After their arrival on Kauai Old Tom had been delighted to learn that both his nephew and young Tom's new wife were born again Christians and assumed they were seeking the Lord's guidance every step of the way.

***

The first Saturday after Uncle's return Tom and Kate invited him to go siteseeing around the island with them. They had ventured out on their own several times, but didn't know where they were or what the history of the place might be.

"Where is Kimo when you need him?" Tom laughed.

"We'd love to have your company," Kate said to the man they now lovingly called "Uncle."

"And we'd love to have a free tour guide, if you know any of the history around here," Tom joked.

"Well, I might know one or two little details," Uncle smiled teasingly. "Does some of Kate's fried chicken come with the deal?" he threw in.

The young couple quickly discovered that Uncle seemed to know something about everywhere they went. There were so many of them that the trio's 'Saturday Siteseeing' outing became a weekly event.

On their first venture out they visited the town of Hanapepe on the south shore.

"The town was started by Chinese rice farmers in the late 1800's," Uncle began his tour guide narrative. "It was the only town that was not associated with a plantation. It gained a reputation as a wild spot with numerous bars and brawls."

Kate spotted the swinging foot-bridge over the river that ran through the town, but decided with her baby-belly throwing her off balance anyway, she'd stay on firm ground. Tom and Uncle however, acted like kids racing back and forth, purposely causing the bridge to swing wildly. This continued until a policeman stopped their fun.

"I'll keep them in line officer," she promised the policeman as he walked away, then turned to her pair of Toms and teased, "Can't take you two anywhere.".

It was then off to see the Russian Fort, which was merely the stone foundation of its former impressiveness. Once again Uncle began a narrative of the historic site.

"This fort was built by George Scheffer in 1816 with the assistance of the Kauai King Kaumuali'i. Officially Kauai had pledged allegiance to King Kamehameha. However, Kaumuali'i thought he could reclaim his kingdom with the help of Russia. When the Russiana heard of Scheffer's promises and plans, they sent a ship to bring him back home. He fled from the Russians to Oahu and finally to Brazil. Needless to say, Kaumuali'i didn't reclaim his kingdom,"

"What promises and plans?" Kate asked.

"Got me," Uncle teased. "I wasn't around then. Didn't know the guy."

"Oh brother," Kate laughed as she put her arm though Uncle's arm and the two walked back to the Jeep with Tom bringing up the rear.

Another weekend adventure brought the threesome to Spouting Horn. Kate thought the site was fascinating and listened carefully to Uncle's explanation.

"This natural wonder occurs when water rushes under a lava shelf and bursts through a small opening at the surface. Every wave produces another spray. Spouting Horn frequently spurts salt water 50 feet into the air. We must come one evening at sunset. It is especially exciting when the spray becomes irridescent with the colors of the rainbow." he told them.

"This particular blowhole is different from others found throughout the state, as another hole nearby only blows air, making a loud groaning sound.

Legend states that this coast was guarded by a large mo'o (lizard) that ate everyone who tried to fish or swim here. One day, a man named Liko entered the water. When the mo'o went to attack him, he swam under the lava shelf and escaped through the hole. The mo'o became stuck and was never able to get out. The groaning is the cry of hunger and pain from the lizard still trapped under the rocks. There used to be a much larger blowhole called Kukuiula Seaplume adjacent to Spouting Horn. It shot water 200 feet into the air. However, as the salt spray damaged a nearby field of sugar cane, the hole was blasted away in the 1920's."

Waimea Canyon was Kate's favorite.

"People call this place the Grand Canyon of the Pacific," Uncle told them.

Kate looked over the edge into the deep canyon. "It's so peaceful here. The red of the ground, the various greens of the forest, and the waterfalls off in the distance. It's breath-taking." And, by simply turning around and crossing the road, the mighty Pacific Ocean could be seen off in the distance twinkling in the sunlight. "I love it here," she'd told her men.

They had barely gotten out of the Jeep at the lookout rest stop when Kate spotted several roosters heading their way.

"Goodness! They are everywhere!" She laughed

Reaching back into the Jeep, she took a sandwich out of the picnic basket and fed the birds. In no time birds were coming at her from all directions. She quickly climbed back into the jeep then hollered for help and decided quite fast that feeding the birds had been a bad idea.

On another outing Kate suddenly realized as she watched the scenery pass that the mountain range to their left looked like a large face. Actually it looked like an entire body in a reclined position.

"You've lived here nearly a year and you've just noticed that," Tom teased.

Kate prepared to slug his arm, but she couldn't move quickly enough around her belly to hit the intended mark. The couple laughed.

Uncle smiled at their antics and then explained. "That is the Nounou Mountain Ridge which bears a striking resemblance to a sleeping giant, which is why it's called 'Sleeping Giant'," he laughed. "Legend states that this giant once roamed the land and was much loved by the Hawaiians. They planted taro fields in his footsteps. One day the village chief wanted a new heiau, a sacred temple, to be built. The villagers were much too busy farming, so the giant volunteered. It took him two weeks to complete the project, and when he was done, the village had a luau for him. It is said that after eating so much at the party, the giant laid down and has not awakened yet.

"You will also hear stories which claim that in ancient times, the people of Kauai planned to discourage any invaders to their island by lighting fires behind the mountain. This would illuminate the figure of the giant and thus scare off any invasion forces."

Their next stop on the tour that day would be at Holoholoku Heiau, and later the Hikinaakala Heiau. Once there he explained that a Heiau was comprised of a stone platform with various structures built upon it. The structures on the platform were used to house priests, sacred ceremonial drums, sacred items, and images that represented a god associated with that particular temple. There were also altars used for plant, animal, and human sacrifices. The heiau were sacred places; only the Kahuna, priests, and certain sacred ali'i, or high chiefs, were allowed to enter.

With the coming of Christianity the heiau practices were eventually abandoned. Most were destroyed over the years. Often they were broken up and plowed under to make way for fields of sugar cane.

"Uncle, how do you know so much about this island?" Kate asked. She noticed that he hesitated.

"I was born here," he replied simply and changed the subject.

Later that evening, while Tom and Kate sat alone on their lanai enjoying the cool breeze, Kate asked, "I wonder why he never married."

"He told me that life just got away from him and that I met you first," Tom said as he smiled at Kate, lowered the ukulele he'd been playing and leaned over to gently kissed her on the nose.

Uncle also sat on his lanai at his house across the road from the Tynes. Gently rocking and petting the cat that always curled on his lap whenever he sat down, he also smiled when Tom stopped plucking on the ukulele and saw his nephew kiss Kate. Looking back up at the stars of heaven he continued the silent prayer he'd been saying for the couple.... "And Lord, remind me that I've got to teach that boy how to play that thing before somebody gets hurt."

Chapter Nine

In late September Kate received a letter from Mrs. Bertha Lawson, the woman Susanne had briefly mentioned in her last letter.

Dear Mrs. Tyne,

Your sister was delivered of a beautiful baby girl on September eighth. Susanne has named her Polly Katherine. Both are doing well. I am writing to you because I am concerned about Susanne. I will be leaving Reno come December and I fear Susanne and baby Polly will have nowhere to go. The man Susanne married last December, has not been seen or heard from since five days after their wedding.

"WHAT!" Kate cried out loud. Her mind flashed back to the few letters she'd received from Susanne. She never mentioned anything about a baby, only glowing reports about her husband and marriage.

Tom looked up from his paper and started to ask what was wrong when he saw tears running down

Kate's cheeks. He dropped the paper and rushed to her side. Kate was too upset to continue reading, so she handed the letter to him.

Reading quickly, a deep frown formed on his face.

Susanne has refused to notify her family about the situation in which she has found herself. As a friend, and Christian, I could not bring myself to leave her without notifying someone. Susanne speaks so lovingly of you that I decided to contact you instead of your parents. I hope I've done the right thing. I'm sure Susanne will be furious with me for doing this, but she needs help with her finances and her baby. The money she received from your father after her marriage is gone. The small allowance I give her for being my companion will also be gone after my departure.

If there is anything you can do I pray you will find it in your heart to do so. Susanne had told me you are expecting a child as well, and that you live on a poor farm in the Islands, but perhaps you can contact your parents, as Susanne will not.

"I knew something was wrong. I just knew it," she said through her tears.

Taking Katherine's hand, Tom immediately prayed with her for Susanne, and baby Polly. Thanking God for Polly's safe arrival, he then asked for guidance and wisdom on what, if anything, they should do for Susanne. When he was done, he kissed Kate's tear-stained cheeks.

"Let's continue to pray on this for a few days and wait on the Lord for an answer," he suggested.

"Alright," Kate agreed. "But something must be done soon."

"True, but let's not get ahead of what God has already planned for Susanne," he advised gently.

In the end, Kate decided to wait awhile longer to see if her sister would tell the truth herself.

"I'll play along for a little while, but if she doesn't 'fess up by Christmas, I'm going to notify father," she emphatically told Tom one evening as they walked home from church.

After a couple of weeks Kate wrote a long letter to Susanne, being careful not to mention baby Polly or what she'd learned about Mason's abandonment. She filled her letters with descriptions of the house, the beach cove, the flowers and even tried to explain that the property was located on an old sugar cane plantation that was no longer in use. She closed the letter with an open invitation to come visit anytime and a statement that had made her laugh.

Sus, you'd love it here. You won't even have to use the outhouse.

***

Reno, Nevada

Susanne re-read her sister's letter over and over. She had cried at Katherine's kind offer to come and visit anytime. At first she had decided she couldn't go there after the spectacle she'd made the night Tom had made the announcement to go to Hawaii. She'd written back thanking Katherine for the kind invitation, but insisted her social schedule was too full right now, with the holidays coming up.

But as the holidays grew closer Susanne realized that all she could think about was the situation she would be in when Bertha left town.

"And we can't go home," she'd whispered to Polly as she nursed her daughter late one night.

The week before Mrs. Lawson was to leave, Susanne finally came to a decision. "Don't worry about us, Bertha," she said through a forced smile. "I've called my parents and we are going back to California."

"That's wonderful," Mrs. Lawson said as she reached to pull Susanne into an embrace. "When do you leave?"

"Tomorrow morning. I've called the airport and I have just enough money for plane fare. Now, if you'll keep an eye on Polly, I need to get packed," Susanne said as she gently withdrew from the older woman's hug.

"I'm finally getting out of this blasted desert," she whispered as tears filled her eyes and threatened to spill down her cheeks. *"Whatever possessed me to believe this was a romantic place I'll never know.* With a forced laugh she added, *"And why I decided to run off with Mason and make a total fool of myself is the real question."*

After closing the latch on her truck, Susanne stood staring out the window into the Nevada night. Spinning the tiny gold wedding band she wore so people wouldn't know she wasn't married, she sighed and said to herself, *Mason, if I ever see you again,*

*I'll I'll...*but couldn't continue the thought. She knew in her heart that half of the situation she found herself in was her own fault.

Pounding her fist on the top of her truck she hissed, "Someday you will have to face me, Mason Anderson, but I won't sit here waiting another day!"

"Good girl," Mrs. Lawson said, having brought Polly to her mother just in time to hear Susanne's vow.

Startled, Susanne spun around and smiled when she saw her daughter.

"I'll miss you, Bertha," Susanne said as she bent down to place a kiss on the woman's cheek. "Truly, I don't know what I would have done without you."

Bertha Lawson smiled back at her. "I've been happy to have the company, and our Miss Polly has been the icing on the cake," she said as she reached over and tickled Polly's tiny toes.

***

Kauai, Hawaii

In October a harvest festival was celebrated at the church with a carnival for the children of the community. Tom was the festival scarecrow.

Time passed quickly and in November, Thanksgiving was shared with Uncle, Alice and her family, and Pastor John and his family.

As each group of guests arrived, Kate greeted them with a warm Aloha and a orchid flower lei she had made herself. Each family contributed a favorite family dish to add to the meal. There was the usual turkey, dressing, and cranberry sauce, but also lomi salmon, fried banana lumpia, and of huge bowl of poi.

When Pastor John arrived he handed Uncle a sealed envelope. "I found these while cleaning the attic at the church. I thought you'd enjoy having these pictures."

Setting the envelope on a side table by the door, Uncle thanked him but did not open the envelope right then because Kate had called from the kitchen that she needed help with the turkey.

Just as everyone got seated and Pastor John started to pray for the meal, a car drove up the driveway.

"Now who could that be," Tom asked looking at Kate.

From her chair at the dining room table, Kate looked out the front window and let out a shocked squeal.

"Susanne!" she cried, as she struggled to get up from the table.

"Susanne?" Tom responded with a tone of disbelief in his voice. "Where?"

Before Kate reached the door tears began to stream down her face. Susanne took a deep breath as she walked up the three steps to the porch. Tom held open the screen door and gave Susanne a brief brotherly hug before she entered the house. Upon seeing her sister, Susanne too began to cry. Seconds later the two young women held each other tightly laughing and crying at the same time. Through it all, Baby Polly slept peacefully in her mother's arms.

The dinner conversation was all about Susanne's surprise arrival, talk about Polly and Nevada. Kate had more personal questions to ask her sister, but determined that those questions would wait until after all the other guests had gone home. Susanne was grateful her sister hadn't pressed her. The last two days in airports and on airplanes had left her exhausted.

She wasn't looking forward to the conversations that would take place between them. The effort of keeping up the lie to Bertha about going to her parents' home had completely worn her out.

I'm tired of lying; she thought as she curled her legs and feet under her on the couch and watched her sister cuddle Polly. *But I'm just not up to the truth yet*, she sighed.

After dinner, while everyone sat and talked, Uncle remembered the pictures Pastor John had said were in the envelope he'd set aside. Retrieving it, he opened the envelope then went pale when he saw the images on the photos. At that same moment Susanne looked over at Uncle and noticed immediately that something was upsetting him. Just as she started to ask if he was all right, he quickly turned and walked out the front door.

Everyone in the room stopped talking when the screen door slammed and looked from the door to Kate, who shrugged, not knowing what to say.

***

The remaining guests didn't stay long after Uncle had left the house. Susanne helped Kate clean up and then emptied her travel trunk and made Polly a bed in it, being careful to adjust the lid so it wouldn't close on top of her baby. Gently putting her down until her next feeding, Susanne kissed her daughter softy and sighed.

"She's beautiful," Kate whispered to her sister. "She looks just like you."

"No, she looks just like Mason," Susanne replied, trying hard to hide the anger behind her words.

Kate chewed her lip and waited quietly to see if Susanne would tell her the real story regarding Mason Anderson. But as minutes passed, she realized this was not going to happen. She also wasn't sure she should tell Susanne about Mrs. Lawson's letter. After all, she had decided to wait until Susanne wrote with the news. But she never had and it was becoming obvious that Susanne wasn't going to mention anything about her marriage either. Maybe she's just too tired to talk right now, Kate said to herself.

Kate said goodnight to her sister then quietly closed the bedroom door to Susanne and Polly's room. As she walked slowly toward her own room, Kate's thoughts turned to her parents. *I wonder if they know Susanne is here, or about baby Polly.*

***

Two weeks before Christmas, Kate received a telegram from her father announcing that he and her mother would be arriving to spend the holidays with them on Kauai.

The Hampton's still did not know about Polly or that Susanne and the baby were living with Kate. Susanne had begged her sister not to tell them. Kate had reluctantly agreed, but only because Susanne seemed so depressed and Kate didn't want to upset her sister anymore than she already was.

Susanne had been with them a little over three weeks, and except for taking Polly for walks along the beach each evening, she rarely left the house. The story from Susanne remained the same-Mason was away on business.

When Uncle heard the news of the upcoming visit he insisted on taking the family to Honolulu and spending Christmas and the New Year at the Royal Hawaiian Hotel. "Notify your family that we'll meet them at the dock and not to worry about hotel accommodations."

Susanne had whined and tried to convince everyone to let her and Polly stay in Kauai.

"It really won't be Christmas without Mason," she told Kate.

When that didn't work she'd next tried to convince her sister that as Polly was only three months old she shouldn't travel.

Kate was just about ready to call her sister on her lies when Uncle, who had been sitting on the lanai rocking the baby, stood up and walked over to Susanne. Softly he spoke to the two women standing before him as he gently laid the baby in her mother's arms. "Susie-Q, don't waste precious moments on foolish pride. The truth is much better than lies, trust me on that one."

Susanne started to argue, but recognizing a look on Kate's face as one she'd seen once too often in her life from her sister she sighed. This was the look that said Susanne was not being honest and Kate was on to her. Susanne took a deep breath as her shoulders slumped.

Looking from Kate to Uncle she weakly asked, "How much do you know?"

"I'm sure not everything, but I know about Mason leaving you and Polly," Kate replied.

Uncle nodded indicating that he knew as well. "We've been praying for you, Susie-Q, for awhile now," he said putting his arm around her shoulder.

At first Susanne looked confused, and then comprehension cleared her thinking.

"Bertha?" she asked, already knowing that would be the answer. At that moment she was thankful even Bertha didn't know the whole story. *I'm just not ready to face that*, she thought, as she tried hard to keep her emotions from showing on her face.

"Yes," Kate answered softly.

"I should have known I couldn't trust her, bless her sweet, wonderful heart." Susanne spoke just above a whisper.

***

Honolulu, Oahu
December, 1960

Much to Kate and Tom's delight, they were given the same room they had spent their honeymoon in the year before. Connecting suites were reserved for Kate's parents, and one for Susanne and Polly. Uncle's suite was just across the hall.

Tom was concerned about Uncle spending so much money. When he offered to help pay for the lodging using money from the savings account, Uncle chuckled then leaned over and whispered in Tom's ear. "You can't pay for what you already own."

Tom's head popped up like a jack-in-the-box, his eyes the size of quarters.

Uncle laughed at Tom's expression. "Not the entire hotel, but a sizeable stock holding, that comes with the authority and ability to reserve these suites at any time for as long as desired. The only time they are not available is when the President takes a vacation." He laughed again.

Kate walked in just as Tom's knees gave out from under him and he missed the chair and landed on the floor. She went from concerned to totally confused when she spotted Uncle doubling over with laughter. Kate was equally surprised when Tom explained, but he made sure she was safely seated before he told her what he had just learned.

"You mean the President slept here?" she asked in awe.

Paradise Inherited

Both men laughed at her, causing her neck and cheeks to turn bright red.

"I love it when she blushes," Tom commented as he planted a kiss on the top of her head.

Finally the very special 'Boat Day' arrived. As on the day of their arrival, Kimo and the shiny black limo waited outside the hotel to transport them to the pier. Tom had been surprised when he realized Uncle and Kimo knew each other.

"Small world, isn't it?" Uncle questioned with a chuckle.

"Getting smaller every day," Kimo laughed and gave one of his face lighting grins. "Lani always wants to hear about my days. She's gonna love this story."

Kate, Tom, Uncle and a very nervous Susanne arrived just in time to see the big ship slowly making its way to the dock. The Royal Hawaiian Band was playing festive greeting music. Dancers swayed and young men dove off the dock to retrieve coins that passengers tossed into the water.

With all the noise of the band, other greeters and the ship's horn, Sarah Hampton was sure that her daughter and son-in-law would never hear her greeting, but she yelled and waved frantically anyway.

It was all Tom could do to keep Kate from jumping up and down as she spotted her parents. Tom smiled and waved back, and his smile became even bigger when he noticed that their sweet friend, Martha stood right beside his in-laws. Susanne also

Paradise Inherited

spotted her parents and tried hard not to look too conspicuous as she tried to hide behind Uncle.

Kate had brought leis for her parents that she and Susanne had made. They had even made a tiny lei for Polly, who was quite interested in trying to eat it.

When the Hamptons made their way off the boat and through the crowd, there were tears and exclamations of joy over Kate's rounded tummy.

"About six more weeks," Kate told her mother.

Susanne stood slightly away from her sister and Tom, again feeling unsure of how she should respond to her parents who had not seen her yet. Tom noticed and stepped over to her.

"It's an answer to prayer that you are here with us. Everything will be fine," he assured her as he gave her a brotherly hug.

Samuel noticed Tom's movement from the corner of his eye and as he turned his head he saw Susanne for the first time. Reaching over he gently touched his wife's arm.

The touch of her husband's hand drew Sarah's attention, but as she turned toward him she noticed another familiar face in the crowd. Shocking surprise kept her from accepting the sight of her other daughter for a moment or two, so it took even longer for her to realize that Susanne held a baby in her arms.

"Oh, my dear precious girl," she whispered as tears began to stream down her cheeks and she closed the distance between herself and her daughter. Samuel followed close behind. Tom stepped aside and Kate, who was also crying walked into his waiting arms.

Standing to one side, Uncle smiled at the group.

Thank you Heavenly Father, he offered a silent prayer. *This is going to be a wonderful Christmas, a blessed reunion, and a coming together of family. Disappointments and hurts of the past can now be replaced with a new sense of wonder at what the future holds.*

***

On Christmas morning Kate woke early and quietly made her way to the lanai off of the bedroom for her morning devotions.

She had just finished praying when she spotted Susanne and baby Polly sitting on the beach. Setting her Bible and notebook aside, Kate grabbed her camera and quietly slipped out of the room taking care not to wake Tom since the men had stayed up late Christmas Eve talking and enjoying each other's company.

Approaching quietly from behind the pair, Kate paused briefly to watch her sister and niece and thought how sweet they looked together. At that moment Susanne looked totally relaxed and at peace. It was so unlike her body language, whenever their parents were around. Moving up beside her sister and niece she lifted her camera and softly said, "Say cheese."

She snapped the picture as Susanne smiled and Polly, leaning against her mother, continued to squeeze her tiny toes in the soft sand.

After taking the picture Kate sat down beside her sister and quietly said, "I'm really glad you are here. I missed you, Sus,"

Maybe now Susanne would open up, Kate thought to herself.

"Me too, you," replied Susanne.

Both women sat watching the waves roll in and out. After several minutes of silence, Kate heard a sob. She looked over at her sister and watched as tears spilled down Susanne's face.

"Talk to me, Sus, what's wrong?" Kate pleaded.

For several minutes Susanne just sat and cried. Kate put her arm around her sister and hugged her. Susanne began talking hesitantly at first, and as the dam within her cracked, the whole story poured out along with her tears.

When Susanne finished she sighed deeply and looked through swollen eyes at her sister. "Oh Kat, I've made such a mess of things."

Kate said nothing for several minutes absorbing the story then she said, "First let's take this to God. Then we'll go talk to mother and father."

Susanne hadn't prayed in ages. At times she wasn't even sure she believed in God anymore. What kind of God would allow this kind of thing to happen to her? She knew she didn't share the same degree of faith that her sister seemed to have. At that moment she was too emotionally exhausted to argue religion so she just lowered her head and closed her eyes, holding tightly to Kate's hand as her sister prayed.

A short time later a humbled and weary young woman sat between her parents to tell of the deception of the last year, her hands nervously twisting a tissue.

"I thought I was in love with Mason. I thought he loved me. He said he loved me. He begged me for weeks to run away with him. I knew I wasn't in love with Tom, but I didn't know how to get out of the wedding that mother had spent hours putting together. When Tom found out about his inheritance, well, it was just too perfect. As soon as Kate and Tom left, I phoned Mason. He seemed so excited about it. 'Now we can get married', he told me."

Susanne looked at her parents through tear filled eyes and silently cried. *How do I tell them?*

She took a deep breath and let it out slowly, trying to calm herself.

"When we arrived in Reno, Mason told me it was too late to get married that night. And like an idiot I believed him. Reno is a 24-hour town, but I didn't realize that at the time," she spoke softly. "But it wasn't too late to go out to party and gamble. The party lasted for four days and nights. I have little memory of most of it."

Susanne began to tremble and turn red around her neck, something she'd always done when she knew she was in trouble.

"We'd been there almost a week when Mason told me he had everything arranged for our wedding. I was so excited. He told me to take a shower and put on my nicest dress. He said he had a last-minute errand to run and he'd be back in ten minutes. I never saw him again," she whispered.

"He what?" Samuel Hampton thundered.

"Oh Susanne, why didn't you tell us? Katherine, did you know about this?" their mother asked with a sob in her voice.

Kate shook her head. "I just found out about most of this myself. I have known that Mason left and about Polly since September."

"And why, may I ask, did you not tell us?" her father growled.

"Because you taught us not to tattle on each other, remember. The story was Susanne's to tell when she was ready."

"I'm so sorry," Susanne cried. "It was embarrassing enough that I ran away from home, was foolish enough to let Mason. . ." She bit her bottom lip and looked at her father, then continued. When I discovered I was pregnant I just couldn't tell you. I was so ashamed."

Susanne dropped her head into her hands and sobbed. Her mother stood up and knelt in front of her daughter.

Gently stroking her hair, Sarah crooned softly, "It will be all right. It will be all right."

Tears spilled down Kate's cheeks, one fell off her chin landing on the sleeping baby in her arms. At that moment she was fighting extreme anger at the man who had used her sister so cold-heartedly and amazed that for the first time in memory, her mother had not fainted at the mention of a crisis.

Kate's anger, however, paled compared to the degree of fury that appeared to be raging through her father. She had never seen him so rigid. His fists were clenched and his eyes had a cold and threatening look. He hadn't said a word since Susanne's confession. Kate could only guess at what his thoughts were toward her sister, but she was pretty sure Mason would have been a dead man if he walked into the room at that moment.

Kate put Polly in the crib then quietly walked out of the room. Susanne needed some time alone with their parents and she needed to tell Tom what had just been revealed.

Chapter Ten

1961

The family rang in the New Year on Oahu, by attending a luau hosted by Kimo and Lani's family on a private beach. Kate's parents quickly learned that a real luau was much more than just a whole roasted pig and a lot of food. It was a celebration complete with games, dancing and native ceremonies.

Before dinner the men challenged each other at trying their hand at some old Hawaiian games. Uncle won the *'O'o ihe'*, Spear tossing.

"'O'o ihe," Kimo explained, "once trained young warriors in hand-to-hand spear fighting and helped develop skills for food gathering. A target, was set up, sometimes the stalk of a banana plant, and contestants would stand 15 feet away and attempt to stick a lightweight wooden spear in it."

Next, Tom tried his hand and won the game called, '*Ulu maika,*' or '*olohu,*' meaning 'rolling stone disks'. This game was one of the most popular sports in early Hawai'i. It consisted of rolling carefully-crafted playing stones, somewhat resembling modern hockey pucks, on specially prepared courses. The idea was to roll the stones between stakes to test a player's skills or down long courses to show strength.

"There are only a few 'ulu maika courses left. The best one is located on the island of Moloka'i. It's about five hundred feet long, and a real challenge." Uncle told them, as Tom rolled the disks.

The young man hosting the games demonstrated the next game called *'Moa pahe'e'*. He showed them how a player slides a *moa*, or wooden dart, between two stakes for long distances, much like the competition in 'ulu maika. The moa slides though, rather than rolling like an *'ulu*, and is much more unpredictable in its course.

Not to be outdone, Kate's father took a shot at it and proudly won the dart sliding game.

Much to the amusement and eventual annoyance of the ladies, each man bragged about their personal success off and on for hours.

The ladies weren't left out of the fun activities. Kate held Polly and they watched Susanna and her mother learn to make Leis and weave palms into headbands.

The sound of the conch shell being blown called everyone at the luau to participate in the Hukilau ceremony.

Once again Uncle's vast knowledge of his culture was put to use as he explained to the family that a Hukilau is a way of fishing that was used by the ancient Hawaiians.

"The word comes from Huki, meaning pull, and lau, meaning leaves. A large number of people, usually family and friends would work together in casting the net from shore and then pulling it back. The net was lined with ki leaves, which would help scare the fish into the center of the net. Anybody who helped could share in the catch."

Sarah held her granddaughter while the rest of the family participated in the Hukilau ceremony. Everyone laughed and tugged as the nets were pulled from the ocean to the rhythms of a conch shell and Hawaiian chants.

They also enjoyed watching a young man climb a coconut tree, barefooted. To their surprise, once he reached the top he showered the onlookers with flower petals from a pouch he wore on his hip.

Another blast of the conch shell called family and friends to watch the procession of those chosen to represent the King and Queen presiding over the Imu ceremony in which a roasted pig was removed from a pit that had been dug earlier that day. Uncle explained that the pit is approximately six feet, by four feet, by three feet. Extremely hot rocks are placed in the pit and then a salted pig is placed inside and covered with banana leaves to preserve the flavor and the heat. Then it is covered with burlap and soil, and left to steam all day. Once removed from the imu, the meat is ready to be served.

The sight of the head still attached with an apple stuffed in its mouth caused Kate's mother to gag, then squeal in disgust, and finally frown as her daughter's laughed at her. Tom put an arm around his mother-in-law's shoulder and gently squeezed as he spoke into her ear.

"Don't let the looks of it now discourage you. You must taste it. Kalua Pig is the best."

"Well," she replied tentatively, "I'll admit it does smell good."

"Oh mother, you really have to try the poi," Kate added as the family walked back to the tables where their meal would be served. "It's wonderful."

"That stuff is nasty," Tom shot back. "It looks and tastes like wallpaper paste."

"And just how often have you eaten wallpaper paste, may I ask?" Uncle asked which cause everyone within hearing distance to laugh.

As they sat down on the ground next to the low tables, Kate dipped her finger into a bowl containing a purple-gray pudding. She then gently stuck the goo covered digit into Baby Polly's mouth, much to the Susanne's alarm.

"What are you doing? What is that stuff?" Susanne cried out in alarm.

Laughing at the reaction of her sister, Kate stated, "This stuff is called Poi, and I think she likes it and wants more."

"Don't worry Susanne, babies have been fed poi for generations. It's good for them," Uncle reassured the nervous mother. "It contains plenty of vitamins, and you may even find she'll sleep better."

Susanne considered this for a moment then quickly turned to Kate and said, "In that case, give her more. I could use some extra sleep!"

Each table was provided a dish containing ten small white squares of coconut pudding called Haupia.

"Go easy on the Haupia," Tom warned the newcomers. "It can have some interesting effects on people," he laughed, without elaborating.

"He knows from personal experience," Kate laughed, as Tom began to blush.

Susanne and her mother followed Kate's example by taking only one of the Haupia squares, but Samuel offered to eat any that nobody wanted from the tables surrounding theirs.

"These are very tasty," he said, picking up his tenth square.

Kate sat biting her bottom lip as she slowly shook her head from side to side and waited. She knew it was only a matter of time before her father would realize he should have heeded Tom's warning.

After the meal beautiful young men and women dressed in island costumes performed traditional Polynesian dances. A man twirled a fire baton, and before the evening ended the singers sang a Hawaiian wedding song. Newlyweds and those celebrating anniversaries were asked to come up and dance. Kate didn't want to go because of her big baby belly, but she finally agreed after much insistence from Tom and her family.

The grand finale of the evening occurred when several guests, including Kate's father, suddenly stood up and raced as fast as they could go to the bathrooms as the Haupia took effect. Roars of laughter filled the night air.

"Can't say I didn't warn him," Tom said through his laughter. Facing his mother-in-law, Tom explained, "Too much Haupia works as a great laxative."

"Kamehameha's revenge!" Uncle added with a burst of laughter.

Back at the hotel the family joined other guests out by the pool and sipped delicious fruity tropical drinks. Some danced to music coming from a club just a short distance up the beach. As the clock struck midnight everyone stopped what they were doing and watched as fireworks filled the sky. People cheered and whistled as 1961 began.

Taking Kate's hand, Tom helped her out of the deck chair she was sitting on and pulled her behind a palm tree, then kissed her with the same tenderness as their first kiss.

"You are the most beautiful woman here tonight," he said softly.

"I'm as big as a house. How can you say I'm beautiful? Were you watching the stage tonight?" she asked as a tear began to roll down her cheek.

Tom smiled. "Yes, I was watching. Those women are professional dancers. It's their job to be beautiful, Kate. Your beauty starts in your heart and radiates throughout your body and mind. As for being as big as a house, well, maybe you are growing a football player in there."

Kate looked down at her bulging belly, gave it a pat and smiled. "Or a sumo wrestler."

She kissed him once more before they walked back to their room.

***

Neither of them noticed Susanne, who sat in the darkness a few feet away. No one heard the sob that erupted from her throat or saw the large tears flow down her cheeks. The old flames of jealousy and envy of her sister's relationship with Tom had begun to steal back into her heart over the weeks she'd been with them. But she also knew she loved her sister and was happy to see Kate so happy and in love. Wiping her tears away, Susanne stood up, straightened her shoulders, determined within her mind to stop feeling sorry for herself and do something about her situation.

"I just don't know what yet," she spoke softly into the warm night air.

The next morning, while Polly and her grandmother slept peacefully, the others gathered again out by the pool for coffee and danish. The men discussed the events of the past year, with each expressing opinions and concern about the U-2 spy plane that had been shot down by Russia. They shared a fascination regarding the first nuclear-powered aircraft carrier, the Enterprise, which had been launched from Virginia, and had varied opinions about Kennedy's election to the presidency by a narrow margin. Some for and some against, since Uncle and Tom were diehard Republicans and Samuel Hampton a firm

Democrat. After one heated discussion, the men agreed to disagree, thus keeping peace in the family.

Kate and Susanne talked about movies and movie stars. Kate hadn't seen a movie in a year and wanted to know all the latest.

"We have movie theaters here. We just haven't taken the time to go. There is so much beauty to discover outside, that Tom and I just preferred to be tourists."

Susanne gave a scene-by-scene description of her favorite parts of *Gone With the Wind*, which she had seen twice while in Las Vegas. Eventually they talked about Susanne's pregnancy and other baby-related topics.

Two days later everyone gathered again at the pier to send off the Hamptons. Susanne still had a few misgivings about staying with Kate and Tom. Nonetheless, she was determined to make the best of the situation so that Kate would not be alone as she had been when Polly was born. Of course she realized Tom was there, but Susanne remembered how she had wished for her mother and her sister when her time had come.

I'll decide what to do about my life after Kate has delivered and is on her feet again, Susanne thought as she waved goodbye to her parents on the departing ship.

Later that same day Tom, Kate, Susanne and Polly boarded a plane for the short flight back to Kauai. Uncle was headed to the Big Island. He'd told Tom he needed to take care of some business and would be sure to be back on Kauai before the baby was born.

As pre-arranged, Alice met the travelers at the airport in Lihue. She talked non-stop all the way back to the house, which allowed Susanne the opportunity to once more take in the beauty surrounding her. The swaying palm trees and gently rolling waves off the crystal blue water that sparkled in the sunlight reminded her of the travel posters she had seen before coming here.

I thought those tourist pictures were too good to be true, but it's all real, she thought, as she smiled and then took in a deep breath of the air around her. Aromas from moist earth in the morning rains, a combination of tropical flowers and salt air filled her senses. She loved it.

Their first night back from the holiday in Honolulu, after Polly had been fed and was fast asleep, Susanne lay upon her bed looking out the window at the moon and thought about all that Kate had told her over the past several weeks.

Why do all the good things happen to Katherine? My life is such a mess.

For the ten months she had lived in Vegas, every morning she awoke certain that this would be the day he would walk up the road and beg her forgiveness. She never actually considered how he might find her since she had moved in with Mrs. Lawson shortly after he disappeared. But by bedtime, after no sign of Mason she would again start to cry and sink a little deeper into the depression that had overtaken her.

Now that she was in Hawaii, the same thoughts and feelings were beginning to fill her nights.

As had happened many nights before she went to sleep, Susanne rehashed the night she had made the decision to run off with Mason. She would relive in her mind those exciting days before he disappeared and on occasion would find herself hoping one day he would come back to her.

Just as she started to drift off to sleep another thought struck, her causing her to sit straight up in bed, do I want him back? After the way he deserted me, penniless and pregnant, why would I want him back?

***

Life went back to normal after the holidays. Tom went back to work and the girls took time to sew little sleepers and diapers for Kate's baby and to play with Polly. Every evening Kate and Susanne took long walks along the beach. For the most part, Susanne talked and Kate listened. She described her year in Reno and filled Kate in on Mrs. Lawson. Only once did Susanne mention Mason.

Kate had decided not to push on this subject. She knew her sister well and could tell this was a very embarrassing and painful topic. Susanne would talk when she was ready.

Some days Kate prayed that Mason would somehow learn of Susanne's location, and come to take care of her and his daughter. Other days she

Paradise Inherited

wished and hoped he'd fall off the face of the planet and never bother her sister again.

Uncle returned as promised the first week in February. He seemed to walk taller and smiled more frequently. He filled his days with improvements to the little house across the street.

Every evening after dinner Uncle told the others stories of the islands. One of Kate's favorite stories was about the 'Menehune', a mythical race of small people who were supposed to live deep in the forests of Kauai.

"They have been called pixies or trolls, even pygmies," Uncle said. "There are those who have claimed to see them, but for the most part only their superb craftsmanship has been seen. The Menehune work only at night. As if by magic, roads, temples, a canal and the Alekelo Fishpond appeared literally overnight. Generations of Hawaiians have avoided the woods fearing that they held evil spirits. Of course today, the Menehune are jokingly blamed for anything that goes wrong."

Kate loved this part and jumped into the story telling. "If you lost your wallet, the Menehune took it. If your car won't start, Menehune have been tinkering with it."

Susanne laughed and said, "Well there you go, that explains the burnt toast this morning. The Menehune were cooking, not me.

The kitchen where everyone was gathered filled with laughter. It was the first real smile that reached her eyes that anyone had seen on Susanne's face since her arrival.

Susanne kept a watchful eye on her sister as Kate's delivery date approached. Kate was uncomfortable no matter if she was sitting, standing, or lying in bed. Around 3a.m., Valentine's Day, Susanne thought she heard someone moving about the house. It was too early for anyone to be up, but hearing a noise again, she got up to check. She found Kate pacing between the living room and the kitchen. She spoke softly so as not to startle her sister.

"Is everything alright, Kat?"

"I'm not sure. I have this weird feeling in my back, and I'm trickling water. The baby must be sitting on my bladder," Kate replied.

A smile slowly began to cross Susanne's face.

"What are you smiling at?" Kate snapped. Then it hit her. "Oh my, is this labor?"

Susanne nodded her head and started to tell her the trickle of water was probably her waters breaking. However, before she could get the words completely out, Kate gave a squeak as water gushed from between her legs.

"Yep, that's it," Susanne laughed, as she ran to get a towel.

Tom woke at the sound of Kate's loud squeak and Susanne's giggle. He got out of bed and stumbled into the living room to see what was going on. For a minute his brain was too sleep-fogged to make sense of the reason for this middle of the night gathering. But seeing the puddle of water beneath Kate's feet, his head cleared instantly and sharply.

Even though they had practiced for this moment many times, everything they had prepared for went right out the window

"Get dressed," Tom ordered Kate. "No! Don't get dressed. I'll get dressed."

He raced to the bedroom then instantly returned, while trying to pull his pants on over his pajamas. "My keys!" he shouted. "Where are the keys? And my shoes?"

"On the table by the door," Kate said, trying not to laugh.

"What are my shoes doing on the table?" Tom spun around and caught sight of Susanna. "Why aren't you dressed? You can't go to the hospital in your pajamas. They won't know which one of you is having the baby. Where are my keys?"

"Tom! Calm down!" Susanna ordered.

Tom stopped running in circles long enough to stare at her as if she had suddenly grown an extra head.

"This isn't the time to be calm! It's the time to hurry! But we're stranded because I can't find my keys. Or shoes. Wait. What's the date? Good grief! I don't even know when my child's birthday is!"

He ran across the room to look at the calendar. "The thirteenth. Our baby's birthday is the thirteenth."

"Sweetheart, today is the fourteenth," Kate said gently.

"Are you sure?" Tom turned back to the calendar. "Oh! Okay, right. The fourteenth. February fourteenth. Our baby's birthday is February…" Tom went still for a moment then turned to face Kate. He planted his hands on his hips and demanded, "Do you have to do this now? It's a holiday!"

Both Kate and Susanne burst into fits of laughter at the sight.

"Tom!" Susanne finally got his attention, "Go take a shower. There is plenty of time."

"Are you sure?" he asked, concern and excitement in his voice.

"Oh yes. First babies take a long time to be born," Susanne replied.

While waiting for Tom, Kate made him a lunch to take to the hospital. It gave her something to do between contractions, and she knew Tom would never leave the waiting room except for a call of nature.

With that task completed, she decided to walk the short distance to Uncle's house, as the plan had included him staying with Polly, if needed in the middle of the night.

Kate knocked softly on Uncle's door. She was surprised when it opened just seconds later. Seeing Uncle fully dressed, she giggled as she realized he'd been sleeping in his recliner chair that sat next to the front door.

Blinking his eyes several times Uncle tried to focus on Kate's face. He rubbed his hands over his eyes, cleared his throat and finally spoke. "Is it time?"

Kate giggled again and nodded. "Do you always sleep in your clothes?"

Uncle looked down at his rumpled clothing. "Only when on baby alert," he responded, with a grin spreading across his face.

Fifteen hours and thirty-five minutes later Meleana Susanne Tyne arrived with a cry that announced well formed lungs.

Standing outside the nursery, Tom beamed with pride as he looked through the viewing window at his tiny daughter. Susanne glowed with pleasure at the sight of her niece, and Uncle, who had arrived after his replacement had come to watch Polly, cried softly and whispered, "She looks exactly like Mele."

"She has Kate's nose," Tom said beaming with pride.

After checking on Kate, Tom went right out to send the wire to Kate's parents announcing the birth of their second granddaughter.

***

The telegram was delivered an hour later to the Hampton's door. They were delighted with this news about the new addition to their family.

Later that afternoon, as Samuel Hampton left the bank after making the day's deposits and spreading the news about his new grandbaby, he got a less pleasant surprise. There at a taxi stand only a few feet away, was Mason, the man who had ruined his daughter. The two men stared at each other briefly before Mason escaped in a cab.

"Are you absolutely sure it was him?" Sarah asked when her husband told her the news.

"Yes, I'm sure. He looked right at me then made a quick exit in a waiting taxi," he stated firmly.

They waited all day for Mason's parents to come over with news of their son, but no one came.

Later that afternoon Samuel announced, "I'm going over to talk to them right after dinner."

Kate's mother nodded, but said nothing.

Samuel Hampton returned an hour later in a fury.

"That boy had the nerve to tell his parents that Susanne was in Reno awaiting his return from his business trip. He never mentioned Polly. He obviously knew nothing about her pregnancy. And he told his parents he'd only made a quick stop in town to close his savings account, since he and Susanne had opened accounts in Reno."

Quite calmly, Sarah asked, "Do you think the Anderson's even know about Polly?"

"They didn't mention her, either. I don't know what they know!" he yelled.

"Calm down, Samuel, there must be a reason," his wife tried to soothe him. "We shouldn't think the worst until we know more."

"That hoodlum is not going to get away with abandoning and neglecting my daughter and granddaughter!" Samuel said before going to his study and slamming the door behind him.

Chapter Eleven

Mason sighed deeply as the taxi headed to the airport. The meeting with his father and stepmother had gone well, considering he had lied almost nonstop during the time he had spent with them.

A twinge of guilt had surfaced when he saw Susanne's father, but it was only a twinge. He realized then that he hadn't even thought about Susanne until he had come home to get a few things he left behind. When his father had asked if his wife had come with him, Mason had to think fast and struggled to keep his facial expression calm.

Was she still in Reno? He wondered. Apparently she had even gone so far as to make up wild stories about his whereabouts. *Why is she covering for me?* It didn't make sense to him.

Mason had planned to stay a few days. He could use a few home-cooked meals, and cooking was about the only thing his stepmother did well. However, with the questions about his job and Susanne, he had decided to cut and run as fast as possible before his parents figured out his stories and Susanne's weren't lining up.

On the plane Mason's mind turned back in time.

The Andersons had moved to California just before Halloween of 1959. At twenty-two years of age, he was still living with his parents. Not because he wanted to, necessarily, but because he was too lazy to get a job. He'd made it a point not to be in the house much, preferring to stay out late, hanging out at the local bar drinking and playing pool until the wee-hours of the morning.

He spoke to his father only when a direct question was asked, and avoided his stepmother as much as possible. In fact, he avoided most people outside of his local hangouts, and even then generally preferred to keep to himself.

On a few occasions, when the alcohol had control of his thoughts he, would get to feeling sorry for himself, and would remember that he hadn't always been a loner. As a child he had been loving and happy, making friends easily. That had all changed when his mother died suddenly and his father remarried just two weeks later. At first his stepmother had been nice to him, but as time went on he saw a drastic change. She was still pleasant in his father's presence, but when he was alone with her she became cruel and threatening. Confusion and anger quickly took hold of him, and he began to close himself off from his friends.

His stepmother had requested that he call her 'Mom,' which he had objected to, but his father had insisted. She expected him to clean the house and take care of the yard. His father beamed at his new bride, giving her the credit for taking care of their home so well. She never told him that Mason did the work. Within a few months of the marriage, while his father would be working, Mason had watched a stream of men come and go. When he tried to tell his father, his step-mother had cried and called Mason a liar. It hurt him deeply when his father believed her and became even more distant from his son.

By the time he was fourteen years old, he had a few new friends. They were the type of boys that were every mother's nightmare. The group, including Mason, had been picked up by the police several times for one law violation after another. The last time his father had picked him up at the police station they did not go home. His father had driven him several hundred miles and enrolled him in a military school specially designed for wayward boys.

Looking out the plane window, as he flew toward Mexico, he remembered the fear and bitterness he felt toward his step-mother. His father had simply handed him his packed suitcase at the school and then walked away. Even after all these years he still blamed her for the division between himself and his father.

The years had passed quickly for Mason. He'd graduated only to discover that he had no place to go but back to his father's home. Jobs were hard to come by, and for weeks he had done nothing but lay around the house, much to the dismay and annoyance of his step-mother. When his father had accepted the job in California and moved, he had just packed up and moved along with them.

He clearly remembered the bright fall afternoon when he had first noticed Susanne Hampton with her hourglass figure and long, blond ponytail, that swayed with the movement of her hips. He had casually asked around to find out about the girl, and learned that she was the daughter of the owner of the thriving hardware store. Thinking that her family probably had money, he instantly decided that he'd be more than happy to help her spend it. And that body wasn't a bad thing either. A wicked smile crossed his face as he also recalled how as she passed him, she would swung her blonde mane and flash him a flirtatious smile and wink at him, laughing as she did so.

Immediately plans to meet his personal needs began to consume his thoughts. Something about her actions had kicked off memories of his step-mother's actions years earlier. He knew one way or another he woud get that sweet young thing to bed and teach her a thing or two about life and men. Even then he knew when he was done with her or the money ran out, whichever came first, he would dump her before she could do to him what his step-mother had done to his father.

He had learned that she was to be married at Christmas, just over a month away. That didn't set well with his plans, so he had made it a point to be wherever she was, laying on the flattery hot and heavy.

Despite being engaged, Susanne had eaten up the attention he gave her, like a starved dog. It caused him to seethe inside at the thought that she could profess to be in love with someone else and at the same time be so flirtatious with him when the groom-to-be was not around. On more than one occasion he had tried to convince her to leave Tom, 'the loser', and be his girl.

He was surprised when, while at his favorite bar the night before Susanne's wedding, he had received a phone call from her. She was excited and talking so fast he'd had to work hard to calm her down so he could understand what she was saying. Once the message became clear, it had been easy to convince her to run away with him. It never dawned on him that the girl might actually be interested in him, or that she had actually taken all his false flattery as truth.

He knew as they drove off into the night that he had no plans to marry her, but she had been insistent that there would be no sleeping together unless they were married. A few nicely planned lies and several drinks later, Mason got what he wanted and Susanne, convinced that he loved her, had given herself to him freely. He also kept her just drunk enough for the rest of the week that she believed anything and everything he told her.

For a day or two they had had fun, drinking, dancing, gambling, and having sex. By the end of the week, however, he was bored with Susanne and they had spent all of the money she had brought with her- a pitiful piggy-bank allowance and some stolen cash from daddy's desk drawers.

He recalled how disappointing it had been that there hadn't been as much money as he had envisioned, and on top of that, after the first few days, all Susanne had done was complain when she wasn't flat on her back.

She complained that the hotel was too cheap, and it didn't have room service. She wanted a flashy diamond engagement ring, and a big fancy house to live in.

The topper for him had been all the crying about not having the big wedding she had always dreamed of, and "couldn't they go home and plan a big wedding so all their friends could attend?"

Mason wasn't sure if it was the going home part, or the big wedding part, or just being trapped with this whining woman that bothered him the most, but when he awoke early their fifth morning in Reno, he knew he had to get out and fast. As he lay watching her sleep he planned his last lie. And later that day, as he closed the hotel room door, he muttered "Stupid broad."

A passing stewardess interrupted his thoughts when she stopped and asked if he would like a drink. After giving his order he looked out the plane window. There was nothing to see but desert, and so his mind returned to his earlier thoughts.

I would have bet money she'd have run home to Daddy just as fast as her sweet legs would carry her.

For just a moment he considered going back to Reno to check on her, but just as quickly he decided that would have too many unnecessary consequences.

Paradise Inherited

Besides, Mexico was his planned destination now, and he saw no reason to change his plans.

Let her stay and wait-it would serve her right. She had played a fast game and lost, that was her problem. He didn't need her, he didn't need anybody. There were plenty more dumb females out there for the taking, and next time he'd be smarter and find one with tons of money.

I'll bet that's why she hasn't gone back, he decided. *She can't face her father after stealing his money, not to mention running off with me.* A wicked laugh erupted from his mouth, causing the man sitting next to him to glance his way.

***

One afternoon while Uncle rocked Polly, then six months old with strawberry blond curls and dimples in her cheeks, Susanna overheard him tell the baby that her dimples were placed there when angels had kissed her the moment she was born. While Susanne was grateful for the attention Uncle paid to her baby, she couldn't help but think, *it should be your daddy holding you*.

Thinking about Mason was something she tried not to do, but it was becoming harder not to think of him, as Polly's appearance changed daily and she began to look more and more like him.

Your daddy doesn't know what he's missing, she silently told her daughter.

Sometimes it was a struggle not to let the frustration and anger at Mason's abandonment spill over into the sweet relationship that was developing between her and her daughter. There were days when she wanted to run away from the responsibilities of motherhood that exhausted her both physically and emotionally.

Susanne knew that what frustrated her most was that she had every right to be furious with Mason, but when she tried to express that anger she would begin to feel guilty and would end up blaming herself for the situation she was in. Single and raising a baby by herself. No job. No money. Not even a home she could call her own. She was grateful for Tom and Kate's help, but that didn't stop the depression that continued to build.

It was Uncle who first noticed Susanne withdrawing into herself. She rarely talked and almost never laughed. Polly's smiles and giggles were about the only thing that brought a smile to her face, but even that would disappear as fast as it came.

One evening after dinner Uncle watched as Susanne picked up her daughter and quietly walked out the front door. He continued to watch as she slowly made her way to the beach. He had grown fond of the young woman in the weeks she'd been living with Kate and Tom. He wanted to help, but first he'd have to find out what she needed.

Taking note that Tom and Kate were occupied with their own daughter, he, too quietly left the house and walked to where Susanne and Polly were sitting playing in the sand. When he reached them he softly asked, "Mind if I join you?"

"Sure." Susanne shrugged, patting the ground next to her, inviting him to sit down.

At first Uncle gave his attention to Polly, making her squeal with delight when he poured soft sand on her tiny toes. Then, while continuing to play with the baby, he started to talk to Susanne.

"Life can sure get complicated sometimes," he said.

Susanne just nodded her head.

"Look Susie Q, I know you can talk to your sister anytime. But if you ever need another ear, I'm a pretty good listener."

Several seconds passed with no response from Susanne, who aimlessly drew circles in the sand, making Uncle wonder if perhaps she hadn't heard him. Suddenly she forcefully smashed the small mound of sand she had made earlier for Polly.

Tears began rolling down her cheeks as she told him about the feelings and questions that had been growing inside her since Mason disappeared. Then, to her own surprise, she went on to tell him things that she'd kept locked inside herself for years

She told him of her years of jealousy and comparing herself to her younger sister and always feeling inadequate. This lead to her admitting to the trap she'd placed Tom in, knowing all the while that Katherine loved him. She also confessed that she'd originally been attracted to Mason because she thought he had money and because the things he said to her made her feel good.

Uncle just nodded without making any comments or asking any questions.

In the flash of an instant Susanne realized she'd just bared her soul to a man she hardly knew. She also realized she saw no trace of disgust in his eyes. Only understanding. Seeing that acceptance seemed to loosen something in her chest. Relief at no longer carrying such a heavy burden all alone flooded through her. She knew that the consequences of her actions were still her own, but they no longer felt so overwhelming.

They sat there for several minutes not speaking. Finally Uncle took her hand in his and simply said, "Thank you."

Surprised by his words and actions, Susanne's mouth popped open for a brief second, and then closed as she chewed on her bottom lip.

"What for?" she asked quietly.

"For trusting me enough to tell me your story. That was quite a leap of faith you just took. I assure you our conversation will be just between you and me," Uncle said, as he wiped the tears that again slipped down her cheeks.

Susanne sighed deeply and gave him the first smile he'd seen on her face in days, then leaned, resting her head on his shoulder.

"What am I going to do, Uncle?" she asked hesitantly.

"Well, for starters, let's head back to the house before Kate and Tom begin to worry. We've been AWOL for awhile now and managed to get out of helping with the dinner, too," Uncle said with a laugh.

"You really don't know my sister well, do you?" She laughed. "When it's my turn to do the dishes, the dishes wait for me."

This time he gave her a big grin as he stood up and reached to help her stand up.

"It's good to hear you laugh," he said. "As for your question, let me give it some thought. Between the two of us I'm sure we can come up with some ideas for you and Miss Polly."

Walking back to the house, Susanne knew nothing had really changed, but she felt better just having told somebody how she was feeling. She hadn't wanted to burden her sister. It was enough that she and Polly were living under her sister's roof, being fed and clothed through Kate and Tom's generosity.

As she prepared for bed that night, she recalled that Kate was always telling her to have faith and trust God. Even Uncle had mentioned faith during their talk at the beach.

"What is faith?" she asked herself. She wasn't sure at all about trusting a God who would allow her life to fall apart so fast.

"I'm a good person. I've never abandoned anyone. Never killed anybody. I even go to church on Easter and Christmas. I deserve good things in return. Don't I?" she questioned the stars that shone brightly outside in the night sky.

After walking Susanne back to Tom and Kate's house, Uncle had returned to his little house across the street and sat in the rocker on his front porch, gently rocking back and forth, while petting the cat that was curled up on his lap. Knowing his time on earth was running out, he slept less and enjoyed the moments more. He especially liked those moments in the night just after the last car of the night passed by on the highway, when all the children had been put to bed and the dogs had stopped barking. It was a peaceful time. A quiet time to talk to God.

He also loved to look up at the stars that filled the sky. On rainy nights, which happened more often than not, the sound of rain tapping the leaves and ground, and the winds gently blowing seemed to steady his heart that was having trouble finding its beat. He talked to God about that, too. Mostly he just tried to listen, waiting to hear what his God had to tell him.

Over the years there had been many times he had regretted not getting married and having a family. But not for one moment did he ever regret his surrender to God's calling, receiving the free gift of eternal salvation and the relationship he had shared all these years with Jesus, his Lord and best friend.

That particular night the prayers he sent up to heaven weren't for himself. He didn't ask for healing this time. Rather he stood in the gap between earth and heaven and prayed for Susanne, baby Polly, and finally for Mason. Uncle didn't know how God would work things out for them. He wouldn't even try to guess. Instead, he just prayed for God's best and perfect will to be done in the lives of these two young people and their precious daughter.

Chapter Twelve

Kate leaned against the bedroom door and watched Tom as he snuggled on their bed next to their one-month-old daughter who Tom had nicknamed Mele. If Mele was napping when he came in the house this is where Kate would find him. If she was awake he would pick her up and hold her for hours.

"She's amazing," he'd say, at least nine times a day.

A smile of perfect contentment appeared on Kate's face and sparkled through her eyes, as it always did when she saw Tom with their daughter.

I had no idea you would be such a sweet and attentive father, she thought.

Kate loved sharing a part of those moments with her parents through letters.

Meleana is a tiny little girl, with delicate features and her hair is curly and black just like her daddy's, she wrote in her latest letter.

Of course there were parts she didn't share, such as the fact that generally Tom stroked the baby's head while she was nursing, and that he would lean down and tenderly kiss Kate's forehead at the same time.

Marriage had certainly added new dimensions to the couple's relationship. Sometimes it was surprising to both of them that after all the years of knowing each other there was more to learn. Little habits one would not know about unless you lived in the same house. Some of them annoying.

Kate discovered that Tom was a middle-of-the-toothpaste-tube squeezer, and always left the toilet seat up, which drove her crazy. If he got home while she was out Kate could tell exactly what he'd been doing or eating and where he'd been in the house by the trail of discarded socks, newspaper sections or dirty dishes from his snack.

For his part, Tom had learned that Kate had a real problem with the milk bottle being left on the table while he ate his breakfast. It had been the only thing they'd argued about during the first year of their marriage.

"I want the milk handy in case I want a second or third bowl of cereal," he had stated firmly.

Kate was just as firm in her wants and opinions. "I want my milk cold! Just because I don't eat... Lukewarm milk is disgusting!" she'd announced with a dark frown wrinkling her brow.

The other thing Tom learned about Kate was that she was a collector of "stuff."

Whenever time allowed, Kate and Susanne would take the Jeep and travel the island looking for yard sales. When they returned from these outings, Tom was often enlisted to help unload boxes of fabric, tea cups, wooden carvings and bowls of all shapes and sizes.

He always asked the same question, "What are you going to do with all this stuff?"

Sometimes Kate just laughed at him. Other times she became exasperated, putting her hands on her hips and repeating again what was becoming her mantra!

"It may be stuff, but its good stuff and you never know, we might need it one day!"

Tom would sigh and head for the shed muttering to himself. Somehow he always managed to make more room for storage. Generally, he tried to ignore what was inside the boxes, but occasionally he spotted items he liked. He never said a word, but Kate always smiled to herself when she discovered one of her garage sale treasures strategically placed inside the house, knowing full well who had placed it there.

***

Uncle knew that Kate and Tom both had become great supporters of the idea of building a permanent memorial for the USS Arizona after their honeymoon harbor cruise that had taken them past the sunken ship.

"I still get chills when I remember seeing parts of that ship sticking out of the water and realizing a thousand men are entombed inside of it," Kate would state whenever the topic of Pearl Harbor came up.

Word was spreading across the island that Elvis was doing a concert to raise money to assist in the building of a memorial and both Kate and Susanne had expressed the wish that they could go to Oahu.

When Uncle came to supper that evening, he made a show of looking Kate and Susanne over and shaking his head slowly. "You girls are looking a little drawn. I think you need a break."

He smiled broadly as he handed them tickets to the Elvis Presley concert to be held in Pearl City on the island of Oahu. Seconds later his smile turned in to a wince as the young women started squealing loudly while jumping up and down, which caused the babies to squeal and start to cry.

He picked up both little girls to distract them but still had to wait a good three minutes for their mothers to quiet enough to hear him say, "I'm perfectly capable of taking care of these two little angels while the rest of you have a night out."

As Uncle's words registered, the women abruptly stopped their celebration and stared at each other as if suddenly remembering their responsibilities.

"Oh, Uncle, that's so sweet but Mele is so young..." Kate began, at the same time Susanne said, "I don't want to impose. I really don't think..."

Uncle mocked a sulky frown. "Are you too trying to say that you don't think I can take care of your children?"

"Of course not!" Kate said, quickly.

"Not at all!" Susanne jumped in. "You've always done wonderfully with Polly."

Thinking he really was hurt, Kate took his hand in hers. "There is no one we trust more with the kids, but two babies to feed, bath and put to bed is such a handful. We'd feel guilty about leaving you with all that work, and wouldn't be able to enjoy the show."

Uncle couldn't hold back his grin. "Okay, I confess. I've already talked to Lani. She's willing and eager to come to the hotel and assist in this babysitting adventure."

Kate turned to Tom with an expression that was as excited and hopeful as a child's on the night before Christmas.

Tom was tempted to tease both her and Uncle a little by pretending to show reservation but he wasn't sure that wouldn't cause a mutiny, so he just smiled and nodded, which earned him another ear piercing squeal from his wife, followed by a big kiss.

The girls talked nonstop late into the night discussing what needed to be done before the family could board the plane for Honolulu in three days, including washing, ironing and giving the house a good cleaning.

"You know, we don't really have to do all that before we leave," Susanne suggested.

Knowing her sister's long habit of avoiding as much housework as possible, Kate mimicked perfectly their mother's often said phrase and southern belle tone, "One should always have a clean haven to return to after a time of being away."

She giggled when Susanne rolled her eyes and sighed the same way she had always done when their mother said such things.

Now with a home of her own, Kate understood what her mother had been teaching, and thought it cute that she was carrying on her mother's tradition.

Susanne still thought it completely unnecessary and had no trouble telling her sister how she felt. Despite her grumbling though, she was always there with a mop and bucket doing her share and doing it well.

I shouldn't complain, Susanne scolded herself silently. *Polly and I have a roof over our heads and food in our bellies, and to top that, we get to have these things for free, in paradise.*

***

Pearl Harbor
Oahu, Hawaii

The stadium was filled to capacity. The noise level reverberated across the place, sounding like the dull rumble of an engine. When Elvis Presley took center stage, that rumble became a roof shaking roar accented by female shrieks.

To Tom's dismay, some of those shrieks belonged to Kate on his right and Susanne on his left. Even with the huge speakers around the arena he still missed random snatches of what the rock and roll star said and sang throughout the night.

"Oh my gosh!" Susanne gushed, as they left after the show. "Did you see? He looked right at me once. Right into my eyes. I thought I was going to faint!"

"No, I didn't notice that," Kate said with a glint in her eye and a wink at her husband, "because it was me he was looking at."

"Oh you wish!" Susanne laughed.

Tom joined the fun by stating, "No, Elvis made eye contact with me, and he gave me the thumbs-up for being in the company of two such beautiful women."

The concert, two days of shopping and a wonderful barbecue at Kimo and Lani's home the day before they left made for a delightful vacation.

"It's been perfect," Kate told Uncle, when thanking him for making it possible.

Tom agreed out loud that the time away had been perfect. But to himself he thought, *Well, almost perfect.*

Tom was nearly positive he had seen Mason in Waikiki.

***

The day before the barbecue, Kate and Susanne had gone shopping while Uncle and Tom kept the babies. The men had decided the little girls needed a bit of fresh air and sunshine and had taken them out for a walk in their new strollers.

They were just a few blocks from the hotel, at the corner of Kuhio and Seaside, when a group of rowdy sailors, a man in a rumpled suit and three giggling women had pushed past them. Tom spotted the man in the group and thought it was Mason. Tom had never been well-acquainted with or even noticed

Mason that much, and the group moved on so quickly that he hadn't gotten a good look at the man, so he immediately decided not to mention it to anyone.

After returning from their walk, the men had settled the babies down for their afternoon naps and then talked quietly as the little girls slept.

"Tom, I wonder if you'd do something for me." Uncle asked hesitantly then finished in a nervous rush. "I need to take care of some business, so I'd like to send the girls back home and have you accompany me."

"Sure," Tom eagerly agreed. "I'd like that a lot."

Thinking about the mysterious business trips his Uncle went on had been driving him to distraction.

"Of course we'd better check with the women to make sure they are comfortable with the idea. And I suppose I should let my boss know I'll be taking a few additional days of vacation." he said as an afterthought.

Although Kate wasn't totally thrilled at being separated from Tom, she, because she knew the trip was important to her husband.

Susanne had stepped up in her "big sister" role, and had assured Tom and Uncle that she and Kate and the girls would be just fine. Except for the needed time spent taking care of their children, Susanne was eager to have some time alone with Kate. Uncle was wonderful and had become a reliable confidant for her, and Tom had been more than generous, considering what she had put him through. But some sister time was what she craved.

A few minutes later she confided to her sister "I never realized how much I enjoyed the talks we used to have in the closet until you and the closet were no longer a part of my life."

After hugs and kisses the family separated at the airport. The girls flight west to Kauai took off just minutes after Tom and Uncle's flight farther west to Kona on the Big Island.

Tom had no idea what he was about to do or see. He was just glad and a little bit nervous to be with Uncle on the trip. His gut told him some of the secrets of Uncle's past were about to be revealed, and for some odd reason he couldn't put his finger on, he wasn't sure he wanted to know.

Uncle was a bit nervous, too, unsure of what Tom's reaction would be to what would soon be revealed. At the same time, he was delighted to spend time alone with his nephew. He loved Kate, Susanne and the babies, but from the beginning his goal had been to be part of his nephew's life and make sure Tom was well-taken care of for the rest of his life.

Besides, it's time to show him more of what he's inheriting, he thought and smiled as he looked over at Tom, who, so like a little kid, had his nose pressed to the window watching the waves below.

***

After the flight to Kauai had boarded and the door closed, Mason stepped out from behind a pillar across from the gate. His heart was racing and his palms were damp. He couldn't believe he'd come within a few feet of Susanne, Katherine and Tom Tyne. What was she doing in Hawaii? But more importantly, whose kid was in Susanne's arms? He shook with a mixture of fear and awe as he realized the child looked amazingly like his own baby pictures. For just a moment he toyed with the possibility that perhaps he was a father. But just as quickly those thoughts vanished and he laughed and complimented himself on getting out when he had.

"Could have been trapped for good," he said to himself.

Mason gave an involuntary shake of his head, took one quick glance to make a mental note of that plane's destination and then hot-footed it to catch up with his buddies, who were being entertained by a couple of young ladies who had provided a weekend of fun for Mason and his friends. Seeing them off as the girls headed back to the mainland was their last bit of entertainment before the sailors headed back to their ship and Mason headed to the nearest bar.

Kona, Hawaii

As Tom exited the airplane, his first reaction was amazement at the difference between the scenery here and that of Kauai. The area around the airport back in Kauai was green and lush with flowers and growing sugarcane and pineapple fields, whereas the Kona airport was smack dab in the middle of an ancient lava flow. Black rock was everywhere as far as he could see.

I wonder if this is what the moon looks like? He thought.

When Uncle joined him at the bottom of the stairs a moment later, he already had another question. "Does the entire island look this barren?"

Uncle laughed. "Not all of it."

The look of disbelief on Tom's face caused Uncle to laugh again.

"Tell you what. Tomorrow we'll take a tour around the island and you'll see for yourself."

The next thing to catch Tom's eye was the open-air terminal. The ticket counter and baggage claim were outside under a covered roof reminding Tom of a picnic area he had seen once during a vacation in Arizona when he was a child. The baggage claim area and ticket booth were far enough back that Tom guessed that only a hard wind would push even a mist of rain into it. The restrooms and a tiny gift shop were the only things inside closed walls.

While the men waited for their luggage Tom noticed a big Hawaiian man approaching them with an even bigger grin on his face. Uncle spotted him at the same moment and started walking toward him.

"Aloha, Uncle," said the large man as he wrapped he massive arms around the old man.

"Aloha, Charlie," Uncle replied, as he smiled into the chest of the giant Hawaiian. When he was released from the embrace, Uncle introduced Tom to Charlie. The two men shook hands.

"Charlie and his family are my neighbors. I've know this fellow since he was a tiny boy," Uncle said.

It was the first time Tom had heard anything about Uncle having neighbors here, which of course meant he must have a home of some kind on this island.

Grabbing his suitcase and following Uncle and Charlie, Tom thought he would wait to ask any of the questions that were coming to mind. Instead he would let the afternoon play out and see where he ended up.

Charlie's old car rattled from a dozen different places as he drove down the two-lane roadway. Tom sat in the backseat enjoying the view of the ocean on one side and the sloping mountain range on the other. He realized it had only been two or three minutes before they were out of the black rock and into an area where palm trees and flowering bushes grew.

Taking a quick detour off the main road, they dropped down into Kailua-Kona, the sleepy little tourist town that had once been the summer playground for Hawaiian Royalty.

"Gotta make a quick stop in town and pick up Ruth. "It just take a couple minutes," Charlie said, as he maneuvered the car through the winding road that ran alongside the ocean

"Ruth is Charlie's wife," Uncle explained.

Tom noticed the gentle waves washing in and out, bringing the scent of the sea into the village. Seeing that gift shops lined both sides of the street, Tom said, "Kate and Susanne would love this place."

It then occurred to Tom that this was the first time he and Kate had been separated for more than a few hours since the day they were married.

We need to have a phone installed, Tom decided. I don't like not being able to hear her voice. What if something happens to Mele?

He shook his head to clear his thinking. He had left their side a little less than an hour ago and he was missing his wife and daughter already.

Before Tom could slide into a full bout of homesickness, a petite, dark-skinned, young woman, with dark chocolate colored eyes and long black hair ran to the curb as the car rolled to a stop.

"Uncle," she squealed in surprise, then bent down to place a kiss on the old man's cheek. "Charlie, you didn't tell me Uncle was coming home."

Charlie beamed proudly over pulling off the surprise.

"Does Auntie Lou know?" Ruth asked, still standing beside the car.

Charlie nodded, and then cocked his head to indicate that she should look in the backseat.

Ruth was momentarily startled to realize that there was someone else in the car. As her eyes focused in on Tom's face, her expression changed from teasing and lighthearted, to shock.

Looking from Tom to Uncle and back to Tom again, Ruth quickly recovered and softly whispered to Uncle. "It's him?"

"It's him," Uncle nodded, looking back at Tom, who once again found himself confused and a little bit unnerved.

Tom reached through the open window to shake Ruth's hand.

"Aloha," she said softly.

Not sure what else to say, Tom responded with the same greeting. "Aloha."

Tom gave Uncle a curious look, but said nothing while Ruth climbed into the car and filled the silence, talking a mile a minute, doing her best to catch Uncle up on the latest island gossip as Charlie steered the car back into the light traffic.

It's going to be a long night, Uncle thought. *That boy has a bucket load of questions, and before much longer he'll have even more.*

After returning to the highway, it was only a few minutes before Charlie turned the car onto a dirt road that led away from the ocean and gently climbed the side of the mountain. With the higher elevation, Tom noticed the air was cooler and a light mist was falling. Looking out of the rear window he could see the ocean, which, from there, appeared to be a magnificent shade of deep royal blue. It took his breath away.

I have to bring Kate here sometime. She'd love it.

Turning forward again, Tom noted that they were approaching a two-story country farm house, surrounded by dozens of varieties of flowers and trees

"Who lives here?" he asked.

"I do." Uncle smiled. "Welcome to my home."

Tom let out a low whistle as he exited the car.

It took a moment for him to realize that he was seeing a copy of his house on Kauai. Only this one was newer, much larger, and had the second floor.

And definitely in better condition than mine was the first time I saw it, Tom said to himself.

As Tom climbed the front porch steps a little old lady appeared at the front door.

"Bout time you show up," she said with a toothless grin as she placed a lei around Uncle's neck and welcomed him home.

"Auntie Lou I'd like you to meet...." but before Uncle could get the words out, Auntie pushed by him and wrapped Tom in a warm embrace.

"I know, I know," she said as tears began to roll down her weathered old cheeks. "This our boy, God sent him home just in time."

Tom stood in stunned amazement, looking first at the tiny woman hugging him fiercely and then to Uncle for an explanation.

"Come in, Tom," Uncle said softly. "We have a few things to talk about."

While Uncle excused himself to get them some cold drinks, Tom used the time to look around what was apparently the living room. Directly in front of him he noticed a beautifully carved wood sideboard table. He recognized the pattern and craftsmanship as being the same as the furniture that had been left in the house on Kauai.

His attention was quickly captured by the framed pictures that covered the top of the table. Walking slowly toward the table he looked from one picture to the next. Seeing the subjects of the photos, he began to tremble a little and gulped in air as carefully picked up a picture of his mother that he had never seen before. She wore the white dress and cap of a nurse.

"That was taken when my sister graduated from nursing school," Uncle's voice softly spoke from behind Tom. "She was so happy."

Setting the picture back on the table, Tom turned to face the man he'd just realized was truly his uncle. "And what about the others? How did you get them?" he asked a mixture of confusion and anger in his voice.

He turned back to the table and quickly looked over the photos of himself, at age five, sitting on a pony. In his Boy Scout uniform at age eleven. Standing proudly beside his first car. Then one of himself and Kate in their caps and gowns taken at their graduation just four years earlier. This one he grabbed and thrust toward his uncle, demanding harshly, "Enough secrets. I want the truth and I want it now."

Uncle sighed deeply. "Let's sit down."

"I think I'll stand." Tom said tightly,

Settling in the chair that Tom had refused Uncle ran his hand though his hair, stalling just for a moment as his mind reached back in time.

"When your mother died I took it very hard," Uncle began. "Even harder for me was giving you to Beth. But as a single man and as broken as I was then I didn't feel I could give you the home you deserved. At Beth's insistence, and for reasons that sounded reasonable at the time, I agreed to stay out of your life. For several years I traveled, trying to run from my emotions. I was angry at God. Angry at your father for taking my sister to China and angry at myself for agreeing to your aunt's conditions.

Tom tried to keep an open mind and heart for his Uncle's excuses but when he heard the role his aunt played in keeping him from knowing about his mother's family he was overwhelmed by feelings of betrayal and a rage that he had never known before.

The pain of it buckled his knees, forcing him to sink to the floor. He braced his elbows on his crossed legs and held his head in his hands as the blood pounded through his temples. The anger of so many lost years and denied memories seemed to weigh so heavily on his mind that his neck could no longer support the burden alone.

"I'm not sure why, but from the time you were five years old, packages started arriving that included a picture and brief updates on your progress. Beth never explained her change of heart, but like clockwork I'd get new pictures, report card results from school, and even stories about your friendship with Kate. To be honest, I began praying that she would be the perfect helpmate for you.

"Appears the Lord answered that prayer," he said with a forced chuckle in an attempt to lighten the mood.

Seeing the tense look on his nephew's face, and how he was clinching his jaw, Uncle sent up a silent prayer for understanding and forgiveness.

"Over time," Uncle continued, "Your Aunt and I developed a type of friendship. Between us we made some financial decisions on your behalf."

Tom raised his head at this statement. Remembering things his Uncle's lawyer had said, and then demanded, "Was Aunt Beth the partner Jonathan spoke of?"

Uncle nodded. "Beth was a very intelligent woman, especially when it came to money. She recommended several investment opportunities, the results of which will be given to you at the end of the five years. That was actually her stipulation. Beth wanted you to be older, more mature, before receiving what has been put in trust for you."

It just conveniently fell within my doctor's diagnostic time-frame as well, Uncle added silently.

"I am not at liberty to tell you all the details right now, Tom, but what I can tell you is that eventually you will be an extremely wealthy man. You have your Aunt Beth to thank for that."

Tom wasn't feeling very thankful. His initial flare of anger had diminished to a burning coal, leaving room for his confusion and hurt to grow. He needed time and distance to think clearly. Feeling battered and torn, he slowly rose to his feet. Without looking at his Uncle, he started walking toward the door. "I'm going for a walk."

Auntie Lou slowly walked into the living room from the kitchen as the door closed behind Tom.

"That go pretty well," she said putting her hand on Uncle's shoulder. "He a good boy, can see it in his eyes. You no worry. He be back. Our boy no leave."

Uncle gently patted the dear old hand on his shoulder. "I wish I had your faith, Auntie."

"Ah you only seventy years old. You young yet. Got plenty time. I have ninety-five years practice and most of that faith go to prayers for your funny face," she laughed. "My sister roll over in her grave if she know the trials you put us through. God bring this boy home. He in control, always in control, you remember that, Tommy," she said as she squeezed the old man's shoulder.

Chapter Thirteen

After returning from Honolulu, Kate, Susanne and the babies quickly settled back into their regular daily routine. With the exception of Kate not preparing Tom's breakfast and packing his lunch before he'd leave for work, the last week had gone by pretty much as usual.

Since joining the church, Kate had been actively involved in various ladies' groups. Bible studies, prayer meetings, quilting classes, hula lessons, and she took a turn in the nursery once a week. Mothers could drop off their children, giving them an hour or two to shop, keep doctor appointments, or just have some quiet time to themselves.

Susanne, on the other hand, preferred to stay home. She was still struggling with depression and was uncomfortable being in public with Polly. She had convinced herself that people were talking about her behind her back. *A young woman with a child and no husband was shameful. At least that was the way she had always thought, so why shouldn't they*, she concluded.

The day after their return from Honolulu, Susanne waved goodbye to her sister as Kate headed off with Mele to whatever gathering she was participating in that day.

Polly had gone down for an early nap, which gave Susanne at least two hours to herself. The house had been cleaned before they left for their mini vacation, and she didn't feel like working on her needle point project. Suddenly an idea came to her. "I'll surprise Uncle and clean his house." she said to herself.

After quickly checking to make sure Polly was still asleep in her nap basket on the lanai, Susanne headed for the kitchen to gather the supplies she thought she would need to do the job.

She was sure she would have no trouble getting in, since according to several of the locals, no one ever locked their doors, in case their neighbors needed to borrow something when the residents weren't home.

The open hospitality had been quite unusual to Kate and Susanne at first. Kate seemed to have adjusted, *probably because she's lived here over a year*, Susanne thought to herself. Susanne was only beginning to get use to it.

To her surprise, Susanne found Uncle's house fairly clean. A bit dusty and cluttered, but overall quite clean, considering he had no woman or cleaning lady to look after him. There were stacks of unopened mail, piles of books, many with markers that indicated he read many at one time and wasn't finished reading. The most fascinating thing to Susanne was the little pieces of paper tacked all around the house with what Susanne recognized as Scripture verses written on them.

Susanne knew Uncle had been a Pastor earlier in his life, but wasn't sure why he had placed the verses in so many places around his home.

"Don't Pastors have the whole book memorized anyway?" she asked herself.

At first she tried to ignore the papers tacked to walls, doors, cabinets and those lying on tables and chairs. But as she found more and more, it quickly became a game to look for the next one while she dusted ….and a little exciting when she found a new one. After a while, she started reading each discovery aloud.

"As for me and my house we will serve the Lord."

"Delight yourself also in the Lord and He will give you the desires and secret petitions of your heart."

For reasons unknown at that moment, reading that one had reminded Susanne of Mason.

Is he a desire of my heart? She questioned.

As time passed, Susanne had come to realize more and more that going after Mason had been wrong. *I thought he had lots of money,* she silently whined to herself.

It had been almost a year and a half since she'd seen him and she was finally beginning to realize that it wasn't actually Mason she was wanting. She just wanted to be loved.

I'm lonely, she thought. *Not for company, I have that with Kate and Tom and Uncle. I'm lonely for what Kate and Tom have in each other.*

Shaking her head to clear the thoughts, she decided to go check on Polly. She found her daughter awake and playing quietly with her toes and singing in her baby sweet voice. Polly's face broke into a wide happy grin upon seeing her mother enter the room.

"There's my sweet face," Susanne cooed to her daughter. Picking her up after changing her diaper, Susanne hugged her little girl, then tickled her belly, bringing giggles from the baby.

"Ok Miss Polly, let's say you and mommy go finish our surprise for Uncle."

Polly didn't talk yet but upon hearing the word 'Uncle.' the little girl clapped her hands and smiled.

Later that afternoon when Kate returned, she found her sister rummaging through the boxes in the storage shed. Seeing that sort of activity from her sister was surprising enough, but Kate was amazed to discover that Susanne was actually whistling as she dug though the boxes.

Polly's squeal of delight alerted Susanna to the fact that they were no longer alone. Turning quickly, Susanne saw her sister standing a few feet away, watching her.

"Oh Hi Kat. Come over here and help me will ya?" Susanne asked.

"What on earth are you doing?" Kate asked, looking around at all the boxes that had been opened and the contents spread haphazardly on the shed floor.

"I'm looking for that material we purchased. You know, the one we said would look great as curtains in a man's study," Susanne replied, then whooped as she spotted her treasure at the bottom of the box she was digging through.

"Oh yeah, I remember," Kate replied. "What do you need it for?"

"I'm going to make new curtains for Uncle's house," Susanne said, matter-of-factly.

Kate became excited as she realized this was the first time, probably ever, that Susanne had thought of someone else's needs before her own.

"That's a great idea. Can I do anything to help? She asked.

Susanne smiled at her sister. "Well, actually, I was thinking after I cut the curtains, you could take the scraps and do your quilting magic to make Uncle a new bedspread.

In happy agreement the girls began their labor of love for Uncle. While Susanne sewed the curtains, Kate cut out scrap squares for the bedspread, adding a few other pieces for contrast.

The little girls played happily in the playpen, Polly played sitting up by herself and reaching for the toys she wanted, and Mele lying on her back kicking at the soft toys strung across the inside of the playpen.

The four girls' contentment made the afternoon fly by.

As nightfall set in, Kate took Mele back to her own home to prepare something for their supper. Susanne took a last look around the small one-bedroom house that was now freshly cleaned and newly-decorated.

When Kate finishes the bedspread it will be perfect, she decided.

Making one last swipe to straighten the freshly-laundered sheets on the bed, Susanne stopped and picked up a Bible that lay open on the night table. She had owned a Bible since she was a small girl and understood that it was an important book, but had never taken the time to read it. She and Kate had attended Sunday school classes and Vacation Bible School as children, so words of Scripture addresses were vaguely familiar, but held no meaning for her.

Flipping through the pages, she noticed that some passages had been underlined in red ink and that some words were marked out, with new words written above them. Her first reaction was one of shock. Mother had always insisted that it was a grave sin to write in one's Bible.

Curiosity got the better of her, so Susanne began to read aloud what was underlined and rewritten. "For God so greatly loved and dearly prized 'Tom' that He gave up His only begotten son (Jesus), so that if 'Tom' believes in, trusts in, clings to, relies on Him, 'Tom' shall not perish or come to destruction or be lost, but have eternal, everlasting life."

Susanne swallowed and took a deep breath. She had of course heard the verse from John 3:16 before, but had never seen it or heard it personalized. Gently setting the book down, she turned and began once again going around the house rereading the verses taped and tacked around the house.

In the bathroom she read, "As it is written, none is righteous, just and truthful and upright and conscientious, no, not one." Susanne noticed the symbol '#' and the number '1' were written on the left hand corner.

I wonder if they are all numbered.

It didn't take long to find number two, as well as the rest of the numbered pieces of paper.

She began to read them in order. "Since all have sinned and are falling short of the honor and glory which God bestows and receives."

"Therefore, as sin came into the world through one man, (Adam), and death as the result of sin, so death spread to all men."

No one being able to stop it or escape its power, Uncle had written in the side margin.

She saw that Uncle has written the word 'Why?" next to the beginning of the next sentence. "Because all men have sinned," she read.

Continuing to hunt, she found the fourth paper: "For the wages which sin pays is death, but the bountiful free gift of God is eternal life through Jesus Christ our Lord."

Susanne wasn't sure she understood everything she was reading, but with each paper message her heart beat a little faster.

If anyone were to see me racing back and forth through this house they'd think I was going crazy. She laughed out loud.

"Maybe I am," she said to the walls, as she reached for paper number five.

"But God shows and clearly proves His own love for us by the fact that while we were still sinners, Christ Jesus died for us."

Number six caused Susanne to sit down as she read and reread the message.

"Because if you acknowledge and confess with your lips that Jesus is Lord and in your heart believe, adhere to, trust in and rely on the truth that God raised Him from the dead, you will be saved."

"For with the heart a person believes, adheres to, trusts in, and relies on Christ and so is justified, declared righteous, acceptable to God, and with the mouth he confesses, declares openly and speaks out freely his faith and confirms his salvation."

"For everyone who calls upon the name of the Lord, invoking Him as Lord, will be saved."

Susanne's heart was now pounding hard inside her chest. It seemed so confusing and yet simple. *Too simple!* She knew she had never killed anyone or stolen great amounts of money-well, except for the few hundred dollars she'd removed from her father's desk the night she had run off with Mason. She also knew she had lied to Tom and her family, and dishonored her parents by running off and sleeping with a man she knew her father would not have approved of.

"How is this possible for me?' she cried out to the darkening room. "I still don't understand how faith works," she said, as she began to cry.

Suddenly, she felt a hand gently touch her shoulder. Looking up from the floor where she sat, Susanne saw the concerned look on the face of her sister. Kate knelt down beside her and put her arms around Susanne, holding her close, rocking her slowly, saying nothing while they both cried.

When Susanne had gained some control of her emotions she gently pulled away from her sister's embrace.

"I want what you, Tom, and Uncle have," she said through sniffles. "I just don't understand how to get it. I've never thought of myself as a sinner. But these papers say that everyone is a sinner in God's eyes. How do I put faith in something I'm not sure of when I don't understand what faith is?"

Kate looked at the papers Susanne held in her hand. Speaking softly to her sister she first explained that the words on the paper were indeed scripture verses from with Bible, with a few clarifying words added by Uncle. Standing up, Kate went to retrieve Uncle's Bible from the bedroom. She'd seen it on the night table while assisting Susanne in changing the sheets on the bed.

Opening the book, she turned to the page she wanted, and handed the Bible to Susanne while pointing to the book of Hebrews, chapter eleven, and verse one.

"Read this verse," Kate directed.

Susanne looked hesitant for a moment then began to read aloud, "Now faith is the assurance, the confirmation of the things we hope for, being the proof of things we do not see and the conviction of their reality."

In the margin Uncle had again written, "Faith does perceive as real fact what is not revealed to the senses."

"Sus, when you sit down in a chair, especially for the first time, how do you know it will hold you up? With the chair, we just automatically believe without even thinking about it, that the chair won't collapse when we sit on it."

Kate suddenly remembered the chairs that had broken under the weight of the workers the day they had moved into their house, but decided to keep these thoughts to herself.

"Can you see the wind?" Kate continued. "Of course not. We can only feel it and see the evidence of it."

"It's the same with God. We can't see Him, but look around-there is definitely evidence of His work everywhere. The Bible also says, 'we walk by faith, not by sight,'" she quoted.

Kate then pointed out several more verses for her sister to read.

"And He died for all, so that all those who live might live no longer to and for themselves, but to and for Him Who died and was raised again for their sake."

Susanne's sobs grew louder as she struggled to read the last two verses Kate pointed out.

"For He says, In the time of favor, of an assured welcome, I have listened to and heeded your call, and I have helped you on the day of deliverance, the day of salvation. Behold now is truly the time for a gracious welcome and acceptance of you from God; behold now is the day of salvation."

"Therefore if any person is engrafted in Christ he is a new creation altogether. The old previous moral and spiritual condition has passed away. Behold the fresh and new has come."

"I think I understand what faith is now," Susanne said, as she gratefully thanked her sister for her help.

"What do I do now? She asked while biting the inside of her cheek.

Kate smiled at her sister. "Are you ready for God's free gift? Are you ready to surrender you life to Jesus and by faith trust in Him from here on out? Would you like to tell God you are trusting Jesus Christ as your Savior?"

Susanne nodded as tears streamed down her cheeks.

Kate hugged her sister and then told her to repeat a prayer after her.

Speaking just above a whisper, Susanne repeated the words Kate spoke.

"Dear God, I know I'm a sinner. I know my sin deserves to be punished. I believe Jesus died for me and rose from the grave. I trust Jesus Christ alone as my Savior. Thank you for the forgiveness and everlasting life I now have. In Jesus' name, Amen."

Both sisters were crying by the time Kate asked," Do you understand what just happened?

Susanne quietly replied, "I think so."

Kate laughed and picked up the Bible again. "Look at this," she said handing the book back to Susanne and pointing out another verse.

"He who hears My word and believes in Him who sent Me has everlasting life, and shall not come into judgment, but has passed from death into life."

Timidly Susanne asked, "So is this what it means to be born again and have eternal life?"

"Yes," Kate replied, a huge smile on her face.

The sisters picked up their daughters and walked arm in arm back to Kate's house. Neither spoke as they walked. Kate couldn't help wondering how those particular verses had come to be written out and displayed all around Uncle's house.

I'll have to ask him about that, she decided.

After putting the babies to bed for the evening, Kate and Susanne sat up talking for several hours. Susanne asked to hear again the last verse Kate had shown her. Kate opened her Bible and turned to the Book of John, chapter five, and verse twenty-four.

She read it to Susanne, and then asked, "Did you 'hear' God's word? Did you 'believe' what God said and trust Jesus as your Savior? Do you understand that 'everlasting life' doesn't mean for this body we now occupy, but for the heavenly body we will be given when we die?"

"I honestly don't understand all of this, but for some reason I can't explain, I do believe it," Susanne responded, as she laughed at her feelings of both confusion and certainty.

"God doesn't expect you to understand everything immediately. I don't think we are actually ever meant to understand everything about salvation or the things of this world," Kate stated. "I believe this is where faith really comes in-Trusting Him no matter what the situation we find ourselves in. Sometimes that can be really difficult, almost impossible."

"So what's next?" Susanne asked, excitement filling her voice and her eyes, making them shine as if lit from within.

"I'd suggest you begin reading your Bible every day," Kate directed. "Start in the book of Philippians. Talk to God, regularly. Tell Him what's on your mind. Even when you are angry. You won't hurt His feelings"

Susanne eyes grew wide at this statement. "It's OK to be angry at God?" she asked in amazement. "What if I don't do it right, this Christian thing? What if I mess up? Won't God leave me like Mason did?" she asked.

"God knows we are human, and He knows we will make mistakes," Kate answered. "The key is that He asks us to turn from our sin and follow Him. He has also promised never to leave us or forsake us."

"Susanne, He also knows our thoughts and feelings anyway, but He wants a relationship with us. Good relationships are based on honesty and continuous communication."

"Relationship? I thought we've been talking about religion," Susanne asked, sounding confused again.

"I won't push you about going to church Sus," Kate said. "But worshiping with God's people is what God wants from His children. It's how we grow in the truth and understanding of His Word. It's a wonderful family to be a part of. It's all about building a relationship with our Heavenly Father and His church."

Susanne nodded, but didn't commit to anything at that moment.

"Any other advice?" she asked Kate.

"Well, you should tell others what Jesus has done and about your life being surrendered to His leading. Oh, and when Uncle and Tom get back you should be baptized," Kate said as excitement began to grow inside her again.

"Baptized?" Susanne said, astonished and again confused. "We were baptized as babies. Why do I need to be baptized again?"

Kate carefully considered her next words. "Mother had our tiny heads sprinkled when we were born. That was a decision she and father made. It was sweet and made them feel like they were doing the right thing. The difference is, now *you* have made the decision to follow Jesus. The Bible teaches that we should follow Jesus' example of being baptized to symbolize our own death and resurrection from our sinful state, which would have separated us from God and Heaven. It doesn't give us salvation, it just shows those watching that by going under the water we have died to our sinful nature, and coming out of the water we are washed clean, resurrected as Christ was when He rose from the grave."

Susanna smiled brightly and said, "I hope the guys get back soon."

Sunday morning Susanne and Polly were up and ready for church before Kate had even gotten out of bed. Kate laughed lovingly at her sister's enthusiasm and hurried, so they would not be late to services.

When Pastor John held the altar call at the close of service, Susanne was the first to go up. She excitedly told the pastor about her salvation and asked to be baptized. He was delighted by the news and agreed to meet with her to plan her baptism ceremony, and suggested she attend the New Believers Class.

He then turned her around to face the congregation and made the public announcement of Susanne's decision for Christ. The entire congregation applauded and then each person rose from their seat and walked down the aisle, hugging and congratulating her. Several of the older ladies who wore flower leis removed them and put them around Susanne's neck, wishing her a warm Aloha.

Tears of joy and happiness streamed down faces all around the church. Several of Kate's friends hugged her and gave each other knowing smiles.

"God is faithful to answer the prayers of His children," one woman whispered in Kate's ear.

Kate smiled and laughed as she said, "I just wish He'd answer them in my time instead of His. I was beginning to think this would never happen. I've been praying for Susanne's salvation since our first Vacation Bible School when we were seven years old."

"It's all in His perfect time dear," another woman stated.

Chapter Fourteen

The first rays of sunlight slowly crossed Mason's face as he woke with a splitting headache. He decided to leave his eyes closed for a little longer but that only drew his attention to how much every muscle in his body hurt. Finally, holding his head, he sat up and became aware of the most awful odors surrounding him. He blinked several times in an effort to focus his eyes and was startled as reality hit him.

"I'm in jail?" he said. "How the... when did I...?"

Confused and suddenly frightened, he stood up quickly, then immediately sat back down on the bed as the room began to spin. Patting his pockets he realized his wallet was missing. Even his expensive Rolex watch was gone.

Mason old boy, what have you gotten yourself into now?

Mason looked around carefully and noticed some of the other 'guests.' It was also becoming quite obvious that the ghastly smell, which he couldn't seem to get away from, was in fact coming from his own clothes, as well as from the other occupants of the jail cell.

Standing, slowly this time, he quietly made his way to the urinal in the corner of the room.

"Certainly no privacy here," he informed a small rat that scurried along the wall.

The smell that rose from the urinal made him gag. Mason had to hold onto the wall to keep from falling down, as much from his hangover as from the fumes of the room.

Making his way back across the crowded cell, he finally made it to the bars that prevented the men from leaving. Leaning his head against the cold bars gave him only a marginal amount of relief from the pain he was experiencing, even though it did sooth him enough to try to recall the last twenty-four hours.

"What twenty-four hours? I can't remember the last two weeks," he said aloud.

A foul, "Shut up!" pierced his ears as several men grumbled.

"Sorry," Mason said softly.

"I said 'shut up'," a sailor shouted from across the room.

Mason ducked as a pillow came flying at him.

Rolling his forehead over to the next cool bar, Mason tried to piece together his thoughts as flashes of memory played through his mind.

I remember boarding a plane in Los Angeles. But where was it headed and when did I get here?

"Hey where are we, anyway?" He asked no one in particular.

An old guy who had obviously seen the bottom of a bottle one too many times sat at Mason's feet. He slowly raised his head off of his knees, and with a toothless, lopsided grin replied, "Sonny you've made it to the first class accommodations of the Honolulu Hilton."

This brought chuckles from some of the occupants and slurred threats from others.

Rubbing his temples, Mason slowly sank to the floor next to the old drunk.

"Come here often?" Mason tried to joke.

The old man turned his head toward Mason, and slowly opened one eye. Unable to focus on the man sitting next to him, having apparently used up his sense of humor, the old man responded by turning his back and immediately started to snore.

Leaning his head back against the bars, Mason once again tried to remember what had happened, and how he'd ended up in Honolulu, not to mention jail. After awhile he gave up. Nothing was coming back to his memory and his head still hurt too much to concentrate.

What might have been a half an hour later, a tall police officer walked down the hall and stopped outside the cell door.

"Good morning gentlemen. I trust you all slept well?" He asked with a smirk on his face.

This was met with the same reception that Mason had received, with a few choice words added. The officer opened the door and told the military personnel to come out, then handed them off to the custody of the military police and marched away. Mason expected the door to be closed again after the last man stepped through. Instead, the officer continued to hold it open and called out "Mason Anderson."

Mason shot his hand into the air at great cost to his head and aching body, and replied, "Here sir," as he struggled to stand up.

"Come with me Pretty Boy, we need to get you cleaned up. You've got a date with the judge," the officer stated, as he took hold of Mason's arm and gave him a slight tug, bringing him to his feet more quickly.

Mason staggered at first, slowly shook his head trying to clear his vision, and then followed the officer down the hall.

Putting his head under the cold water faucet, Mason would have liked to stay right there for several hours. But prompting from the officer at the door caused him to turn off the water. His mouth felt like it was full of cotton.

I need a drink, he told himself.

***

The courtroom wasn't much different from any of the others he had stood in over the last couple of years. The difference this time was that Mason had always known before what it was that brought him into court. Speeding tickets. Overdue parking tickets. Minor stuff. Mason had a feeling, for reasons he couldn't quite put his finger on, that this time it was different.

"Man, I wish I could remember," he spoke softly.

The officer standing next to him turned to look at Mason, then turned back to face the front of the courtroom.

Finally it was Mason's turn. His court-appointed attorney sat next to him, flipping through several pieces of paper. After the swearing-in the judge looked right at Mason and said with a deep sigh, "Mr. Anderson, are you bored with Honolulu or do you just like my courtroom."

Mason blinked. "Excuse me your honor?"

"Well, let's see, according to my records you have been a guest in our facility five times in the last two weeks. You've stood before me four of those five."

Mason was dumbstruck and just stared at the judge. Finally he whispered, "I have?" Mason had absolutely no recollection of what the judge was telling him.

"Son, what were you thinking when you tried to tackle one of Elvis' body guards? Your actions started quite a brawl, I'm afraid. Fortunately for you, Elvis won't be pressing charges."

As the judge continued to talk to Mason, bits of memory began to surface in his fuzzy brain and he noted two things. One, his attorney had not said one word since the judge walked into the room, and two, a flash of recollection from the concert he had attended the previous night with a group of people he also couldn't remember. As if a lightning bolt shot through his brain he suddenly recalled seeing a profile of a young blond woman in line at the concession stand that he had thought was Susanne. He remembered looking away and then quickly looking back again, but she was gone.

Now my drinking is causing not only blackouts, but also hallucinations, he thought. *What would Susanne be doing in Hawaii at an Elvis concert?*

In spite of where he found himself at that moment, Mason chuckled softly.

"Mr. Anderson," the judged raised his voice.

Feeling a nudge from the attorney his head snapped up.

"Yes sir, sorry sir." Mason stood at attention.

"After giving your situation serious consideration I've decided to give you a choice of two options for your immediate future," the judge stated. "Two years in the Hawaii correctional facility or two years in the service of your country."

Mason looked from the judge to his attorney, who was staring at his shoes.

"For getting into a fight?" Mason asked the judge, a hint of disbelief and sarcasm in his voice.

"Oh. Well, we discovered a few outstanding warrants from the mainland. And it seems you've run up quite a tab in restitution fees," the judge stated.

"So what's it to be?" the judge asked, as he leaned forward on his desk.

Mason had already figured out that jail was not his favorite place to be, and he remembered he'd done fairly well as a kid back in military school. Thinking fast, he decided that eight weeks of training, three squares and a cot, and they'd pay him for allowing them the privilege of his company for two years wasn't the worst that could happen. Looking the judge directly in the eye, he said, "I guess Uncle Sam wants me," and then gave a lopsided grin.

Accompanied by the same police officer that had walked him to the courtroom, Mason entered the local Navy recruiting office just down the street from the court house. Three hours later Mason was on a Military transport being flown out of Hickam Air Force Base en route to San Diego, to settle some of his other legal matters.

The judge in San Diego and Naval officials present deemed it necessary for Mason to do his basic training in San Diego rather than run the risk of Mason performing yet another vanishing act.

"Lord help the Navy," the judge said softly, as he watched Mason being escorted out of the courtroom.

Chapter Fifteen

Tom stood on the beach staring out at the water. He was angry, but he wasn't sure who to be angry with-Aunt Beth, for keeping the secrets, or Uncle for the secrets and the deception. Or Jonathan- *he must be in on this too*, Tom thought.

A gentle voice spoke from behind him. "Can we talk?"

Tom slowly turned to face this man that he had grown to care for so deeply. This man who had taught him to fish with a net, to play the Ukulele, and who he had spent hours with discussing Scripture.

Tom gave a short nod, still too angry to speak. He wasn't a man given to violence, but at that moment he wanted to hit something.

"I wanted to meet you. I was afraid you wouldn't come if you knew I was alive," the old man said softly.

"Why?" was the only word Tom could get out.

"It's a long story," the old man said, as he stepped closer to Tom.

"Yeah, well, I've got time, so let's hear it," Tom responded a bit more gruffly than he would normally speak.

The men talked for several hours. The warm, tropical breeze played across their shoulders and dried tears that occasionally rolled down cheeks.

"Ok, so I guess I understand why you stayed out of my life, and perhaps why Aunt Beth never told me. I can't change the past, but I don't have to like it," Tom commented. "But why did you want me to be married? Not that I mind." For the first time in several hours the hint of a smile slowly appeared on his face. "And why is it necessary for me to stay five years?"

Uncle watched the white foam of a receding wave, and took a moment to answer. "I knew that when you reached Hawaii, and as your inheritance would be increased each year, you would become increasingly wealthy. For that reason, I was afraid that any woman you might became involved with after arriving might only be after your money, and there would be no way for either of us to ever be completely sure she wasn't. So, it made sense to me that you should be encouraged to marry someone who already knew you, and would accept you as you are, without the promise of wealth."

"Can you ever forgive me for the deceit? Truly, this has been the best year I've had in a very long time."

Tom took a step toward the man, glaring at him with something close to hatred in his eyes. But then, seeing, as if for the first time, the man who really was his Uncle, Tom realized this mountain of a man before him was pale and slightly shivering. He also saw hope reflected in the old eyes that stared back at him. Silent moments passed. A long sigh came from deep within Tom's body and then he reached for Uncle, hugging him fiercely and tightly. Tears streamed down his face, and sobs erupted from his throat. The men stood in their embrace for several minutes. Then, as men do, they broke apart, laughed and then hugged again.

After the hug ended, the two men stood and watched the waves gently lap against the shore.

"Tell me about my mother," Tom spoke softly. Uncle smiled and sat down on the warm sand urging Tom to join him. Stars twinkled between gathering clouds as Tom listened to stories about his mother and father, and about many of the adventures of Uncle's life. It wasn't until long after they had parted for the night, as Tom lay in bed listening to the light rain fall, that he realized Uncle never told him about the five year requirement.

As the sun rose the next morning, Tom decided to take a walk in an effort to come to terms with all his Uncle had revealed. Tom walked aimlessly, unaware and unconcerned with time or distance. The roller coaster of emotions that raged through his body was exhausting. Mostly he felt anger.

But who should I be angry at? Uncle, for doing what he thought, at the time, would be the best for me? Or Aunt Beth? True, she took me in and raised me, but why the lies? Why the deception?

Paradise Inherited

The next thought brought with it a deep sadness that caused Tom's stomach to knot. For a brief moment he thought he would be sick. Tom realized he was feeling extreme anger toward his parents for dying. Hot tears began to stream down his face. It was the first time he had ever cried for the parents he had never known. Feeling the need to break something he punched the nearest tree.

"Brilliant, Tyne," he said, cradling his hand, certain he had broken at least two knuckles.

His tears spent, Tom sat down on a large rock beside the road, watching the sun appear at the horizon. He hadn't sat there long before an approaching vehicle caught his attention. He gave a curious glance when the car started slowing down and rolled to a stop next to him. Realizing the driver was Charlie, Tom sighed, stood up and leaned against the car door and stooped down to look inside.

"Wanna ride?" Charlie asked.

Tom nodded, opened the door and got in. "Did he send you after me?" Tom asked.

"Not really," Charlie replied. "He did mention however, that if I just happened to be going out, to keep an eye open for you."

Looking at his watch, Tom chuckled. "So, do you always just *happen* to go for joy rides at dawn?"

Charlie wrinkled his forehead thoughtfully and shrugged his shoulders. "Yeah, well. So, do you want to go back to the house or just ride around for awhile? We can circle the entire island before lunch."

Tom puffed out his cheeks, blew out a lung full of air and replied. "Actually, could you take me to a hospital?"

Charlie sat up straighter and turned to look closer at Tom. "Why?" he asked concern and surprise in his voice.

With the fingers of his good hand Tom pinched his nose between his eyes. "Man, I think I broke my hand."

Charlie wasn't sure if he should be serious or laugh.

Tom saw the expression on Charlie's face and chuckled at the same time wincing at the pain he realized was increasing.

"Had an argument with that rock or a palm tree did ya?" Charlie asked barely able to control the laughter that threatened to let loose.

"Yeah," Tom answered. "The tree won."

***

Back at the house Uncle waited and prayed.

"I took a chance telling him so soon," Uncle told God. "Now it's up to you, Father. I've trusted you all these years and he's turned out to be an outstanding young man. Guess there is no reason to stop trusting you now."

When Tom entered the kitchen later that morning he found his Uncle sitting at the kitchen table reading the paper. Hesitant to speak, Tom walked over and poured himself a cup of coffee.

"Need a refill?" he asked the older man, with no sign of the previous night's anger in his voice.

Uncle looked up from his paper and nodded. Spotting the cast on his nephew's hand, his eyes opened wide, but he decided to say nothing for the moment.

Tom didn't miss his uncle's expression, or his silence. Holding up his cast-covered hand he laughed and said, "You should see the other guy. You can bet that's one tree that will think twice about getting in my way again."

Uncle snickered briefly, then sobered and sighed, "Tom, I want you to know...."

Before he could finish Tom put up his good hand to stop his uncle from continuing to speak. Sitting down next to him, Tom spoke quietly and respectfully. "I can't say I've worked through all of this yet. It will probably take some time," Tom began. "I guess I understand that the decisions you and Aunt Beth made were what each of you felt to be right. I'm not sure I agree, but then I wasn't walking in your shoes at the time."

Uncle nodded, but remained silent.

"I can't ask Aunt Beth, so there is really no point in trying to figure out the reasons. They were hers, and that's all I'll ever know," he added.

Tears filled Tom's eyes as he gazed at his uncle. "We can't go backwards. There are no do-overs in this life. We've got today. Tomorrow is not guaranteed."

Tom stuck out his good hand to his uncle, which the old man grasped and squeezed tightly.

"I'd have preferred that you would have been a part of my life as I was growing up, but, I'll take what I can get. I'm happy you are here now," Tom said. He knew he loved his uncle, but wasn't quite ready to express those feelings.

Uncle took a deep breath and then let it out slowly. "I feel like I've run a very long race and somehow managed to take first place," he said as he smiled at his nephew.

Tom smiled back for a moment and then turned serious again. "Are there any more secrets I need to know about? I think if this new relationship is going to grow it needs to be totally honest."

Tom noticed his Uncle's jaws clinch. "What haven't you told me?" he asked, all humor having left his eyes and voice.

"Tom, don't you think we've had enough emotions for today?" Uncle asked.

Seeing Tom's expression cloud, Uncle sighed again, leaned back in his chair and closed his eyes as he said, "It's my heart. But, you know doctors, always making things out to be worse than they really are," he said in a rush of words.

Tom felt like he had been gut-punched again. For a brief moment the room spun.

"What does the doctor say? The truth," he demanded.

Anger in his voice, Uncle spit out, "He says if I slow down and rest I might live another three or four years-Maybe! He wants to put me in my grave before I'm even dead."

Oh dear God, I've just found my Uncle, please don't take him away now, Tom prayed silently.

"Who else knows about this? Tom finally asked.

"Jonathan, Auntie Lou and Charlie," Uncle replied. "The business trips I've taken recently were to see my doctor. Charlie drives. And I've met with Jonathan several times to make sure all my personal business is tied up neatly. I don't want to leave you with any problems."

Tom nodded his understanding, and then asked, "When were you going to tell us?"

"I can't honestly give you an answer to that question, Tom. Talking about death is never easy. I mean, I know my soul is safe in the hands of Jesus. My eternal destiny is secure. But it's still hard," Uncle answered.

"We have to tell Kate and Susanne," Tom said barely above a whisper.

"I know," was all Uncle could get out.

Then, rallying some spirit he continued, "We can't do it today. So if you feel up to it, how about a tour of the old place? This will be yours after I'm gone, you know."

Tom chuckled, "I'd love a tour. But, if you don't mind, how about not being in a big rush to turn it over to me. I'm just getting used to ya."

"Son, I'm doing everything I can to make sure I'm going to be around for as long as possible. But we have to remember, *'Tomorrow is not guaranteed and no matter what anyone says or does, it's all in God's own time'.*"

Paradise Inherited

The two men stood, gave each other a quick hug, with Tom being careful of his injured hand, and headed out the back door for Tom's first view of 'the farm'.

Chapter Sixteen

Two weeks to the day after Tom had left for Kona, he arrived back at the Lihue Airport. He hailed a taxi for the short ride to his house. There had been no way for him to reach Kate to let her know he was coming. *We are definitely getting a phone,* he thought, as the Taxi pulled away from the airport.

Kate was in the backyard pinning a sheet to the clothes line when she heard the crunch of tires on the gravel driveway. Looking past Susanne, who was holding the other end of the sheet, she was surprised to see a taxi pull away. Her heart began to pound as she walked toward the front of the house.

"Tom!" she squealed with delight.

In a matter of seconds they covered the ground between them. Kate leaped into his waiting outstretched arms. With her arms wrapped around his neck Tom spun Kate around, as she laughed and cried at the same time.

"Oh I've missed you," he whispered lovingly into her ear.

Their kiss was at first tender and then more urgent as they both realized just how long two weeks had been.

"I'm so glad you're home," Kate smiled up at him. "Mele has missed you too."

Susanne stayed back by the clothesline to allow her sister and brother-in-law those first precious moments. It was bittersweet to witness. Seeing that her sister was so much in love and, that the feelings were reciprocated, by Tom, made Susanne very happy. Yet she also felt the heavy loneliness that threatened to engulf her.

As Tom and Kate walked arm in arm toward her, Susanne, with a silly grin on her face, extended her own greeting, "It's about time you showed up, Buster. We were considering breaking your plate!"

"Oh no! Not my plate," Tom teased back, laughing.

Picking up his daughter, Tom was amazed to see how much she had grown in only two weeks.

Mele cooed at her daddy and held tightly to his finger that he had placed in her small palm.

"Have you been a good girl for mommy?" he asked.

"And how is Miss Polly?" he asked looking down at the little girl still sitting in the playpen in the shade of a tree nearby.

Polly rewarded him with a drooling smile.

At the same moment Kate and Susanne spotted the cast on Tom's hand. "What happened to you?"

Tom lifted his arm, and looked at the cast as if it was the first time he'd seen it. With a twinkle in his eye that usually indicated he was about to get silly, he looked over at Kate. Seeing her expression he quickly realized teasing her just then would probably get him into trouble. So, instead of the crack he had started to make, he told her the truth. "I lost my temper and took my emotions out on a palm tree."

"...lost your temper?" Kate gasped in surprise. "Whatever happened to make you so angry? In all the years I've known you, I've never seen you get that mad about anything?"

Susanne, not having to deal with wifely emotions, started to laugh and asked, "Did the tree survive?"

Tom grinned and winked at Susanne's comment, then continued with his tale.

"The business Uncle took me on turned out to be a visit to his home on the Big Island. It's beautiful. I can't wait to show it to you," he said.

"You mean there is more than this place?" Kate asked.

"Oh yes," Tom replied. "Remember I told you that I had inherited a farm? Uncle's home just outside the town of Kona is where the farm is located."

Kate and Susanne both started to ask questions at the same time. Laughing, Tom held up both his hands to silence them, asking, "Hey do you want to hear this story or not?"

Both girls used their fingers to indicate they were zipping their lips. The childlike gesture and mirrored action brought ripples of laughter from all three adults.

"The house is a duplicate of this one, except much larger, more modern, and very clean."

Tom and Kate exchanged a smile as they remembered the condition of their home when they had first arrived in Hawaii. "But the property itself is pretty run down."

Both girls were almost as shocked as Tom had been when he told them about the pictures and how they had come to be there. As he told them about Aunt Beth's involvement, Tom could feel some of the anger building up inside him again.

It's going to take a while to work through these feelings, he thought.

Struggling to remain calm, he went on to describe his reaction to the news. Finally, to Kate's relief, he got to the part of the story where he punched out the tree.

"Bully," was Susanne's immediate response.

This time Kate laughed, as she saw the humor of the event.

"Was it worth it?" she asked, pointing to Tom's hand.

"At the time, it was quite satisfying. I was so angry I didn't feel the pain. However, when it did start to hurt, I knew it was a stupid thing to do," Tom confessed.

Susanne then asked a question without a bit of humor in her voice. "Are you and Uncle all right?"

"Now we are," Tom replied. "It took several long walks and hours of talking, but we are okay now."

Tom considered telling them about Uncle's heart condition, but decided to wait until after he'd told them about the farm.

Paradise Inherited

Knowing her husband well, Kate saw something pass through his eyes and knew without a doubt that there was something he wasn't telling them. She wanted to ask, but decided to hold her tongue. *He'll tell me when he's ready,* she thought.

Taking Tom's pause as an indication to speak, Susanne asked, "What is the farm like?"

Considering her opinion of the farm on the evening their wedding was called off, Tom was surprised to hear this question from her. It was also at that moment that he realized there was something different about Susanne, yet he couldn't quite put his finger on what it was.

At Susanne's request, Kate eagerly nodded, wanting to hear this part of the story.

Tom grinned at both of them. "Uncle owns twelve acres of what was once a twelve hundred acre coffee plantation. Most of the land is undeveloped and some has just grown over from the original plantation. Besides the main house there are five cottages. Only two of them are being used."

"Who lives in them?" Kate asked, as she and her sister finished hanging the laundry.

"Auntie Lou lives in one of the houses. She is a dear sweet old lady. I'm guessing she's about ninety years old. Uncle told me she was born on the plantation. Her family worked there when it was alive and thriving."

"The other house is occupied by a man named Charlie and his wife Ruth," Tom continued. "He acts as caretaker when Uncle is away. They're a nice couple. I'm sure you'll enjoy them."

"Do they actually grow coffee?" Susanne asked.

"Some, but not commercially," Tom answered. "People from the community help with the planting, harvesting and processing of the coffee. For the most part the coffee is grown for the personal use of Uncle and his friends."

"I think the property has great potential," Tom told Kate and Susanne. "Uncle and I talked about some possibilities for the place. We decided it would be important for you both to be involved in the brainstorming, so he sent me to get you."

Susanne looked both shocked and pleased at the same time. Over the last several days she'd been worrying about how to ask to stay instead of returning to California.

"When?" the girls both asked at the same time.

Tom laughed at their enthusiasm. "Two weeks. I need to go over to the hotel and let them know I'll be leaving."

At his words Kate got quiet and sat back to get a better look at his face. "Quitting your job? Why?"

Tom chewed on his bottom lip for a moment. "I had hoped to wait to tell you this, but..."

"What?" Kate and Susanne again spoke at the same time, concern in their voice.

"Uncle is not well. It's his heart," he said.

"Oh no!" Susanne exclaimed.

Kate went to her sister, who had started to cry. Putting her arms around Susanne she looked at Tom, anxiously waiting to hear about Uncle's heart condition.

"The doctor originally gave him five years, but he's getting weaker faster than expected. It's best if Uncle doesn't travel anymore. He needs to rest. I was thinking we should go stay with him until...." Tom couldn't continue, but Kate and Susanne understood his meaning and nodded in agreement.

Everyone was quiet for a moment, lost in their own thoughts. Suddenly Susanne spoke. "We need to pray."

Tom's head snapped up as he looked amazed at Susanne. He'd never heard Susanne speak of prayer. Kate saw his surprised look and smiled.

"Yes, I believe prayer should be the first thing we do."

When the prayer time finished Kate smiled lovingly at her sister and said, "Tom, Susanne has something to share with you."

Tom looked again at Susanne and saw that in spite of her tears, a slight smile had come to her face.

***

Tom was thrilled to hear of Susanne's heeding God's call to salvation.

He hugged her and said, "This is the best news ever! Kate and I have been praying for this for years!"

Susanne returned his hug, and despite the news that Tom had delivered just moments before, smiled broadly at Tom and her sister.

"Are there plans for your baptism?" Tom asked.

"I was waiting for you and Uncle to return," she replied. "I want Uncle to perform the service."

Remembering then that Uncle was not well Susanne anxiously looked from Tom to Kate. "I guess that's out now, isn't it?"

Tom shook his head. "No, actually I think this would be good medicine for him. He's not bedridden, just tires easily. For this I'm sure he'll gather his strength."

Susanne looked relieved.

"So, tell me about it. When? How?" Tom requested with excitement in his voice.

Kate sat by quietly enjoying this moment of sharing, but in the back of her mind thoughts of Uncle and his failing health still lingered. As Susanne told Tom about cleaning Uncle's little house and finding the scripture notes, Kate let her eyes travel around their little home.

I wonder how long we'll be away from here. We've only lived here a little over a year and a half and I've grown to love this island and its people.

The sound of laughter brought her attention back to what was happening before her. "That sneaky old man," Tom said.

"Do you think Uncle placed the notes there specifically for me or . . . Susanne asked still amazed at her discovery.

Tom chuckled, shrugged his shoulders and replied, "God works in mysterious ways. Uncle takes time to listen to God's voice through prayer and the reading of the Bible. I guess you'll have to ask him when we get to Kona."

Finally the day arrived for them to leave Kauai. The two weeks had been busy arranging for someone to water the flowers and vegetable garden, giving away food items from the refrigerator that would spoil if not used, arranging to have their mail forwarded and the utilities turned off, and last but not least, the packing of suitcases and covering the furniture to keep the dust off.

***

Kate gently stroked one of the rockers on the lanai. Remembering the day Uncle had placed them there, a tear slipped down her face. It was hard not knowing when she'd come back to this house, the run-down shack she and Tom had turned into a home.

Tom had watched his wife for several minutes, leaving her to her thoughts. Just as he started walking toward her he heard singing coming from the road in front of the house.

Several of their friends and neighbors came, as they had done when Tom and Kate first arrived. Pastor John prayed for their safety in travel and for Uncle's health. Everyone hugged and kissed Tom, Kate, Susanne and the babies.

"Aloha until we meet again," Alice whispered into Kate's ear as she placed a flower lei around her neck. Tears filled the eyes of both women.

"Aloha to you," Kate replied with a shaky voice. The two women had developed a sweet friendship that both would miss.

"I really don't know how long we'll be away, so please help yourselves to whatever vegetables grow in the garden. No sense letting this food go to waste."

Susanne hadn't made as many friends as Kate, but she was not left out of the hugs, kisses, and wishes for a good journey and a safe return. She had never experienced a sense of belonging like the one she received from those present.

***

Purposely, Tom had not told Kate and Susanne about the Kona airport. He laughed at the expressions on their faces when they first saw the black rock.

Before either could speak he said, "Don't worry, it's not all like this."

Given Tom's history of teasing, Susanne wasn't sure she believed him. As for Kate, her sense of adventure had once again been sparked, but she admitted silently that she was glad their first views of Hawaii had been of Oahu and Kauai.

As they walked through the airport, Tom waved as he spotted Charlie. He laughed again at Kate and Susanne's startled reactions at the sight of the Hawaiian.

"Too much poi," Tom said to Kate, as if that explained Charlie's size.

"Does he play football or is he a club bouncer?" Susanne asked in a whisper.

Laughing softly, Kate asked, "What would you know about club bouncers?" she asked.

Susanne shrugged and replied, "Reno."

Susanne didn't talk about the time she had spent in Reno. It was a subject everyone had an unspoken agreement not to talk about. Kate sometimes wondered if her sister still thought about Mason. She had to admit to herself that thoughts of Mason occasionally crossed her mind, along with thoughts of rat poison, car crashes or sudden death by lightning strike. Kate never told anyone about these thoughts, except, God when she would ask forgiveness for them.

When they reached the parking area, Tom noticed immediately that Charlie was driving a brand new station wagon with plenty of room for everyone.

"Hey, this is beautiful! When did you get this?" Tom asked, as he admired the vehicle.

"Uncle had it shipped in. It arrived yesterday. He said with the family coming we'd need better transportation than old Betsy." Charlie started to laugh as he stated, "We could have loaded the girls and the luggage in the back of my old truck and been just fine. No problem."

Everyone laughed as they piled luggage and themselves into the new car and headed for Uncle's house.

Uncle sat in his rocker on the front porch watching for the car to come around the corner. He loved sitting where the afternoon breeze blew and cooled off the land, and where he had a glorious view of the deep blue ocean. The sunsets off the Kona horizon were the best from this spot.

It was only a short wait before the car pulled to a stop in front of the house. Everyone began to talk at once, excitement filling the air. No one mentioned Uncle's health, but the look in Kate and Susanne's eyes told him that they knew. On one hand he was grateful the secret was out, and yet also concerned that he might be treated differently by his family. It didn't take long, however, for him to realize that even though they were concerned, they were going to respect him and wait for him to approach the subject.

Later, he thought. *I'm not ready to talk about my heart, and definitely not ready to die yet.* Sending up a silent prayer for more time, he gathered his family together to assist them in getting settled and to catch up on what had been happening over the last two weeks.

Auntie Lou and Ruth had prepared a wonderful meal to welcome Tom, Kate, Susanne and the babies. After dinner they all sat out on the lanai to watch the setting sun.

"It's like God Himself was painting the colors on a vast blue canvas, right before your eyes," Susanne stated.

Uncle raised his eyebrows in surprise at Susanne's comment. He had never heard her speak of God in any way except maybe as the 'man upstairs'.

Seeing his expression, Susanne laughed and proceeded to tell him about finding the notes in his house as she had cleaned.

Uncle was delighted with this announcement. "Over several weeks I just felt compelled to write out and post those scripture verse,." he explained. "Sometimes God leads us to do things we don't understand at the time. Sometimes we learn why, sometimes we never know. In this case I see it was God's hand using me as a tool that lead to your salvation. But let me be clear," Uncle continued. "It wasn't me. It was God who softened your heart and opened your eyes and heart to the message he wanted you to receive."

Susanne nodded her understanding, then walked over and bent down putting her arms around Uncle's neck.

"I understand now," she said, "but I thank you for your part in my salvation just the same." She kissed Uncle's cheek as warm tears spilled down her own.

After returning to her chair, Susanne cleared her throat nervously then, a little shyly, asked, "Uncle would you be willing to baptize me? I want to follow Jesus in this way."

"Susie-Q," he replied and smiled broadly, "It would be my pleasure and honor."

Talk then turned to planning the exciting event. When the plans were set, Auntie Lou clapped her fragile old hands and sang in her sweet ancient voice, 'Shall We Gather At the River'. Those who knew the words joined in.

When the song ended, Uncle laughed and said, "In Hawaii, we gather at the beach."

Laughter filled the warm spring evening.

Bright and early the next morning everyone was up and preparing for a tour of the property. Ruth didn't have to go to work and had offered to babysit.

Susanne jumped on the offer. She loved her daughter fiercely, but single parenting was quite exhausting at times. Susanne was grateful for the help she did receive from her sister, but the majority of the responsibility was hers alone to handle. Kate at first hesitated to leave Mele, but with Tom's nod of approval she too felt some relief at a chance for some childless time.

The tour covered only the area of the farm within easy walking distance. This included the barn, coffee mill, overgrown gardens, and a few of the cottages no longer being used. At first everyone kept a slow, easy pace so as not to tire Uncle. After several protests from him to "Hurry up you slowpokes," things became more lively.

At one point Kate tagged Tom on the back, hollered "Beat ya," and took off running. Kate had always been a fast runner, but Tom's long legs easily made quicker strides, and he caught up to her with little effort.

When they reached the barn, Tom let out a whoop when he spotted a '37 Ford pickup in a far corner. It was rusted, needed body work, and could use a new paint job. On closer inspection, he discovered it also needed a new bench seat and an engine. Turning from the truck he called out to his uncle, "Is it okay if I fix up this old truck?"

Uncle laughed as he walked up and threw his arm around Tom's shoulder.

"Sure," he agreed. "I've meant to do that for years. Just never took the time. Mind if I help?"

Tom beamed as thoughts of what he wanted to do to the old truck began to fill his mind.

The project just looked like a lot of dirty work to Kate. Fixing up old vehicles was not her idea of fun, but she was pleased Tom had a new project to work on. She also hoped Uncle would have enough energy to help so the two men could work on it together. *It will be a good memory for Tom when Uncle is gone.*

Tom and the girls agreed that the old coffee mill was the most fascinating part of the outing. The equipment was in excellent condition. Several neighbors who helped with the mill production were busy at work, but stopped what they were doing to be introduced to Tom, Kate, and Susanne. It was while looking over the mill that an idea for the future of the property began to form in Kate's mind.

This place would make an excellent retreat center, complete with an operational coffee mill museum, she thought.

Kate decided to wait to discuss this idea with Tom, but made it a point to listen closely to Uncle's narrative about the mill.

"The original plantation came to be in the early 1800's, shortly after coffee was introduced to the Islands in 1813," Uncle began. "Originally, there were over twelve thousand acres here. For a time it was big business, but in 1849 the coffee market took a dip. Seems everyone wanted to go to the California Gold Fields. By 1860 large coffee plantations had almost vanished. Sugar became the hot commodity. For the most part the only large coffee plantations left were here in Kona and in the Hamakua regions of the Big Island."

Tom, Kate, and Susanne were fascinated with the story and urged Uncle to continue.

"In 1899, the world coffee market crashed. World coffee prices plummeted as a consequence of an oversupply on the world market. It was during this time that 'Haole', or 'non-Hawaiians', investors began to shift their money from coffee to sugar production. At the turn of the 20th century, the era of the large Hawaiian coffee plantation came to an end. The Kona coffee industry was near extinction."

As the group slowly walked toward the flower gardens, Uncle continued his story. "Large plantation owners began to subdivide their property into five to fifteen acre parcels and then to lease, primarily, to first generation Japanese immigrants. The size of the subdivided property was determined by the size of the family who would work the property, to allow them to do so without hired help. Large families of eight to eleven children were very common."

"In the 1930', family farmers continued to produce coffee mostly for their own consumption, as we do today, but they also diversified into macadamia nut cultivation." Uncle pointed out the macadamia nut trees around the property.

"Beginning in 1932, Kona public schools closed for "Coffee Vacation" from August to November rather than June to September like the rest of Hawaii, in order to free the children to help with the coffee harvest."

"The old gent I purchased this property from was the grandson of the original owner. He wasn't interested in maintaining the mill and was eager to sell," Uncle explained.

Susanne, remembering Tom telling them that Auntie Lou had been born here, asked Uncle how it was she remained on the property after he purchased it.

"Ah, well, actually, there were five families living here when I bought the land descendants of the Japanese family that first leased the land. I saw no reason to remove them from their homes, as several had worked the mill and maintained the gardens for years. I offered them the opportunity to work for me. As the younger generations grew up and moved away and the older folks passed on, I just left the houses as they left them."

Susanne nodded at the explanation.

"In order to keep the mill functioning and to help my neighbors with some additional income, I offered to employ some of them to plant, harvest and produce the coffee. As for Auntie Lou, well," Uncle chuckled, "You've met her, she attaches herself to your heart immediately. I hired her to be my housekeeper, allowing her to live in her house rent-free after her husband passed. They never had children of their own so she just sort of adopted every stray that wandered into the yard-Including me," Uncle laughed. Only recently did she tell me she is my mother's youngest sister.

With that said Uncle continued "That's how we got Charlie, too. When he was about twelve years old he walked up to the mill office looking for work. Auntie Lou had just dropped off the lunch basket for the crew working that day and was the first to spot him. To make a long story short, Auntie took Charlie under her protective wing upon learning that he was a orphan trying to survive as best as he could. She eventually adopted him as her son. He's the best overseer I've ever worked with, a good person to have as a friend, and, as well as, a faithful follower of Jesus Christ."

While Tom and Kate explored the Japanese flower gardens, Susanne and Uncle walked arm-in-arm toward one of the old abandoned cabins. Looking around Susanne was thrilled at what she saw.

"This place could stand a new coat of paint, new windows and doors and some upgraded appliances. A few improvements and this would be a lovely home or vacation rental," she said just under her breath.

Uncle smiled at her enthusiasm. "Would you be interested in taking on the responsibility of refurbishing and redecorating it?"

"Who, me?" Susanne responded in surprise.

"Of course you. After hearing about all the work you put into my little cabin on Kauai, which I'm sorry I haven't seen yet," he replied, "I think you are the perfect one for the job. Let me know what you'll need in manpower and supplies and I'll see you have it."

Susanne was beside herself with joy. Any thoughts she had about going back to California immediately vanished. She hadn't realized until just that moment that she had been dreading the idea of leaving the islands and going back to the mainland. Thanks to Uncle's suggestion, she had a bonafide reason to stay-at least for a little while longer.

Taking another look at the area surrounding the little house, she made mental note of what would be needed to start the renovation, both inside and out. Later that evening she shared her excitement with Kate.

"Oh Sus, that's wonderful! I'll be happy to help in any way I can. Just tell me what to do, Boss."

"Haven't I always," Susanne laughed, as she gently pushed her sister and walked past with her head held high.

Kate laughed in return with "Yeah, you always have been pretty bossy."

When the family gathered on the lanai later that evening, Susanne expressed her ideas.

"This is such a peaceful place," she stated. "If we remodeled the cottages and enhanced the gardens with ponds and some man-made waterfalls strategically placed around the property, this would be a wonderful place for people to get away for a few days and relax." Refurbishing the old cottages with modern appliances would allow for individuals or families to come, be on vacation, and yet have some of the conveniences of home. Add to that the historical aspect of turning the working mill into a museum, and we've got a retreat center."

Everyone was very enthusiastic as ideas began to fly.

"How about the outside of the cottages having the style of old Hawaii? Rugged, with a thatched roof. Step inside and it's modern and comfortable." Charlie suggested.

"We could open a gift shop that Ruth could manage," Auntie added.

"Hiking trails and island tours," Tom threw out. "Maybe add a pool."

Uncle had rocked slowly and smiled at the excitement. "You know," he finally added, "these ideas are excellent. We will be able to employ people of the community who haven't been able to find work. Give something back to the island."

***

After putting their daughters to bed, Kate and Susanne sat down to write long-overdue letters to their parents. Susanne also decided, since her salvation, that she needed to be up-front with Mason's parents. They were, after all, Polly's grandparents too, and just because Mason had turned out to be a jerk, she saw no reason to keep them in the dark about Polly, and how wonderfully she was developing.

Both letters contained news about the move from Kauai to Kona, with brief descriptions of the land.

In the short time we've been on the Island of Hawaii, we have discovered that it is always raining somewhere. If you wait a short while the sun will come out and a rainbow will appear. Uncle says to position yourself so that the sun is at your back while you watch the falling water. It's incredibly beautiful.

Stopping to compare their letters the girls laughed to see their twin brains were still operational, as their first written thoughts were almost identical.

"OK, you write this part to mother and father," Susanne suggested, "and I'll write to Mason's parents. Just let me add about Polly at the end of your letter."

Kate agreed and continued her letter.

Uncle told us there are two seasons in Hawaii- summer or 'Kau', from May to October, and winter, or 'Ho'oilo', from November to April. He says you know it is summer if the mango trees are laden with fruit and the white ginger fragrance fills the air.

Neither girl mentioned Uncle's health. He didn't seem too bad just then, and they didn't see the point in worrying their parents unnecessarily. Glowing reports of the babies' development filled several paragraphs. Kate told her parents of Susanne's redecorating project, leaving the exciting news of her salvation for Susanne to add to the letter. At the end of the letter both girls invited their parents to fly over to spend Christmas with them in their new home on the Big Island.

Susanne's letter to the Andersons went into less detail about the island or the new project. She wrote as gently as possible about Mason's abandonment and was careful not to say anything ugly about their son, a task that was not easily accomplished. She failed to mention that they were not married.

In her letter she explained that Mason didn't know about Polly, as she had not seen or heard from him since five days after they had run away to Reno. She also assured them that Polly was healthy and happy, and that living in Hawaii suited them both quite well. Before closing the letter, she wished them well and promised to stay in touch, and then added some recent photos of Polly before sealing the envelope.

California

The postman delivered two letters from Hawaii. The first on his route went to the Hampton home, the second to the Anderson home.

"Big day for mail for you folks," the Postman told the Andersons, as he dug into his bag and pulled out another letter for them. This one was from the Navel Training Center, San Diego, California.

Chapter Seventeen

Mrs. Anderson was surprised and delighted when she opened her mailbox and discovered Susanne's letter. Still believing Susanne and Mason were together in Reno, she was confused by the Hawaiian postmark. Instead of opening the letter immediately, she hurried down to the bank to share the letter with her husband.

Mr. Anderson was surprised to see his wife walk into the bank. She rarely if ever made an appearance anywhere in town except perhaps the beauty parlor every week. Noting that she waved an envelope in her hand, he stood and greeted her just as she reached his desk.

"This is a pleasant surprise. What brings you to town?" He asked, genuinely happy to see her.

Not being accustomed to walking so far, she was breathing hard from her quick walk. It took her several seconds to catch her breath before she spoke.

We've received a letter from Susanne and Mason."

"Really?" Mr. Anderson said, rather amazed, as this was the first written correspondence they had received from the couple.

He offered a chair to his wife and then took the letter she held out to him. Opening the envelope he first spotted and removed the pictures Susanne had enclosed of his granddaughter. Tears came to his eyes and a smile to his lips as he handed the pictures to his wife. Within seconds of starting to read the letter a frown appeared making deep groves in his forehead.

Seeing the stormy look on his face, Mrs. Anderson quietly asked, "What's wrong, Dear?"

Taking several deep breaths to bring his emotions under control, he set the letter down on his desk and practically growled as he replied. "My son abandoned that poor girl in Reno a week after he married her. He hasn't been seen or heard from since, and knows nothing about his own daughter."

Mrs. Anderson clutched her pearl necklace and gasped. "But...But he was here and told us. . ." The look in her husband's eyes stopped her in mid-sentence.

A thought crossed Mr. Anderson's mind as he remembered the lunch date he had scheduled with Samuel Hampton, Susanne's father, for later that day. *I wonder how much Samuel knows?*

Looking at his distraught wife he also couldn't help but wonder how much of her concern was genuine. He hadn't been blind to her behavior toward Mason over the years. He had just chosen to ignore it.

He took her hand and helped her up then handed her some money, suggesting she go get her hair or nails done. This approach had always worked before when he wanted to avoid talking about something with her, so he wasn't surprised when it worked again.

Samuel was waiting at the diner when Mr. Anderson entered. One look at the banker's scowling face and Samuel knew something was wrong.

Once the had been seated and had placed their orders, Mr. Anderson came right to the point.

"We received a letter from Susanne today. She's told a very interesting story." He said then handed Samuel the letter.

Quickly scanning the letter, Samuel let out a deep sigh, then set the letter aside and admitted, "She asked us not to tell you. She wanted to give Mason some time to work things out."

"Oh, he's worked things out alright," Mason's father said, through clinched teeth.

Samuel cleared his throat and then admitted that he had hired a detective to locate Mason, and had been receiving reports up to and including the recent jail stay in Honolulu.

"My daughter does not know about the detective," he finished.

Samuel took a letter out of his jacket pocket and handed it to Mr. Anderson.

Opening the letter from the Los Angeles Detective Agency he read to himself. *Subject has enlisted in the U.S. Navy. Currently stationed at the Navy Training Center, San Diego, California.*

Slowly putting the letter down, Mason's father stared out the window for several minutes, not speaking.

Seeing a break in the conversation, a waitress came to their table and delivered coffee. Samuel sipped his and waited. Each father remained silent, deep in thought. When the meal was served, Mr. Anderson picked up his hamburger, took a bite, and between chews looked at Samuel and said, "I received a letter from my son also. According to his letter, Susanne is being the perfect little wife keeping house in Reno while he's in training."

"Up for a road trip?" Samuel suggested, as he picked up his own hamburger and bit down hard.

One phone call confirmed the date of Mason's graduation from basic training. Two fathers with an agenda would be sitting front row center, in the viewing stands, with carefully made plans to insure that Mason would see them as he marched by in formation. Even more carefully planned was a meeting scheduled with Mason's commanding officer. It insured that Mason would not be able to leave the base until the four of them had had a nice long chat.

"Sometimes having old friends in the right places opens all kinds of doors," Anderson stated after getting off the phone. When he had called asking to speak to the Chaplain at the base, he'd had no idea the man who answered would be a fraternity brother from long-gone college days.

Kona, Hawaii

The farm became a busy place. Uncle had made an offer to anyone in the community who was out of work or could use some extra cash to bring their tools and help put the old place back into working order. Gardens were tended, and in some cases even torn out and replanted. Pathways, to each of the outer buildings and cottages, were cleared and edged with lava rock.

Uncle suggested tiki torch lamps along each pathway to provide a festive atmosphere and give a bit of light in the dark. For fun, Charlie took it upon himself to light them each evening at sunset as he'd once seen done at the hotel in Waikiki. This ceremony included the blowing of the conch shell before he took off at a run, swinging a lit torch at each lamp to ignite it as he passed.

"You know, for a big guy, he runs pretty fast," Susanne teased Ruth.

"When we get the retreat cottages and living museum with a working coffee farm up and running, our guests will love this," Kate told Tom, as each lamp came to life.

Tom saw how excited Uncle was about the project and didn't want to dampen his enthusiasm, but couldn't help keeping a close eye on the older man, watching for fatigue or any other stress that might cause him harm.

One afternoon as Tom and Kate took a stroll after lunch, Kate asked a question that had been on her mind for some time.

"Tom, do you know how Uncle is paying for all this? I mean everything since we arrived in Hawaii. Where is the money coming from?"

Tom stopped in mid-step and turned to face his wife. "To be honest, I haven't given it much thought. I guess I've been too caught up enjoying the ride. But you are right, as usual," he grinned at her. "All I know for sure is that he and Aunt Beth were financial partners for many years, and between them they invested very wisely, so he told me. He didn't tell me what the investments are, but he did say that when I'm twenty-five I'll be a very rich man."

Kate was shocked to hear this. Not that Tom would be rich, but that he hadn't given their situation much thought. Tom had always been a planner, making lists and schedules. He'd had a five-year plan before the telegram came announcing a different five-year plan. *Should I be concerned about this?* She silently asked herself.

Tom felt like he'd just been struck by lightning. A mixture of emotions raced through his body. Mostly he was amazed at how easily he had allowed his every move to be dictated by his Uncle and the idea of money, not to mention the generous allowance that had been doubled after the first year. Feeling ashamed, Tom realized that he and Kate had more money in their bank account than most people earned in ten years. They'd done nothing to deserve it. They hadn't earned it.

Kate stood and watched Tom's face as thoughts raced through his head. She could tell he was struggling with something. Deciding to wait for him to speak rather than interrupt him until he'd worked his thoughts out, she just stood still and looked out at the blue ocean in the distance.

After several silent moments Tom pulled Kate into his arms and kissed the top of her head. "What would I do without you?" He asked softly.

A wisecrack came to Kate's mind, but she caught herself before speaking and instead hugged him tightly.

"You've always had a way of helping me face reality, get my feet back on the ground and my head out of the clouds," he whispered into her ear.

Turning them both around to head back to the house, Tom spoke with a new determination in his voice. "It's time for a family meeting. If this new business adventure is going to work, we all have to be on the same page on all issues of its development, including financial."

As they walked back to the house, Tom silently prayed, seeking God's forgiveness for his leaving Him out of the plans, and for so easily being drawn to the materialism that having money can lead to. He knew they had started out with a budget and careful spending, but realized over the last few months, he'd begun to spend without a single thought about anything except satisfying his own wants and pleasures.

Stricken by his unquestioning acceptance of it, he also suddenly realized that he hadn't even been grateful, or said thank you to Uncle for providing the income to allow these things into his and Kate's life. Another flash of insight gripped his conscious as he also realized Uncle could have left everything to

Kimo or Charlie or anyone other than him. He gripped Kate's hand harder and quickened their steps.

After supper Tom told everyone that he wanted to have a family meeting, only hinting at the topic.

I wondered how long it would take before the question came up, Uncle chucked to himself as he went along with the others to settle on the lanai.

Uncle and his attorney had discussed the subject of when to tell Tom about the finances. Jonathan had wanted everything up front from the beginning. Uncle had been determined to get to know his nephew first. Now a year and a half since his nephew's arrival, the old man had come to the conclusion that Tom was a man of good character, but still a bit immature when it came to finances. He hoped this meeting was a sign that Tom was beginning to take this part of his inheritance seriously.

Waiting for Tom to start the meeting, Uncle gently rocked in his chair, enjoying the evening breeze and watching the ocean and the sun, as it slid toward the horizon.

Finally Tom cleared his throat nervously and asked, "Uncle, I don't mean to be rude, but well, we'd all like to know how you are paying for this reconstruction." Then more boldly, he asked, "For everything actually. Where is the money coming from?"

For just a moment Uncle remained silent, rather enjoying Tom's discomfort at posing the question. Looking around the lanai, he noted that everyone seemed to have the same quizzical expression on their

Paradise Inherited

faces, and each one had a hard time maintaining eye contact with him. That made him laugh out loud.

"Ah, is that what's on your minds?" he grinned. "I wondered what all the whispering has been about all afternoon." Uncle laughed again, and everyone visibly relaxed.

"It's pretty simple really. I'm seventy years old. I collect Social Security." Uncle stated. "It came with statehood," he chuckled.

Groans came from all corners of the lanai.

"Okay, Okay," he laughed. "As a young man I worked hard and saved my money. I didn't have a wife or children to support, and living with my parents I had few expenses. Papa always taught his children to be thrifty, and purchase only what was actually a need."

Tom squirmed a bit in his chair at that comment.

"When my parents passed on I received a small inheritance, which I used to buy and then sell some land. As I've told Tom, his Aunt Beth was way ahead of her time when it came to finances. Based on her suggestions, I have investments in oil in Texas and Alaska, hotels and land in Waikiki, Kona, Maui, Kauai and Mexico, and even some nice stock in the shipping and airline industries." He paused, then added, as if it was an afterthought, "Oh, yes and some healthy stocks in a diamond mine in Africa."

He laughed as everyone around him sat with their mouths hanging open. "Better close those before the geckos around here begin to think they've found a new home."

He then continued.

"Since learning of Beth's death, I have engaged a new financial advisor who has his eye on some up-and-coming industries. Of course I can't tell you what he hasn't told me yet, but the guy is good and very excited. So you see, our monthly income is well established, with an even healthier amount being reinvested."

This subject concluded and the talk then turned to the ongoing renovations taking place and the hopes and dreams for the retreat center.

San Diego, California

Standing in formation after marching into the stadium, Mason casually scanned the crowd of visitors in attendance for the graduation ceremony. His eyes passed over the front row, when it registered that he'd just seen a very familiar face. Keeping his face forward he was amazed, and secretly pleased, to see his father sitting there. He gave only a passing notice to the fact that his stepmother was nowhere to be seen, partly because he didn't care, but mostly because the greater part of his attention was on the vaguely familiar-looking man sitting next to his father. Suddenly, realization hit him like a punch in the gut. The man with his father was Susanne's father. A string of curse words slipped quietly out of his mouth.

Immediately following the ceremony, Mason became instantly aware of the two military MP's that had seemingly materialized out of nowhere.

"Come with us," was all that was said.

Mason nodded and followed quietly. He could only guess at what would come next, and he wasn't thrilled about it.

Escorted to the commanding officer's office, Mason knocked once and was admitted immediately. As he had feared, his father and Mr. Hampton sat in chairs in front of the C.O.'s desk. To Mason's surprise his C.O. remained silent, and just nodded toward Mason's father.

"Sir." Mason greeted each man individually.

Mr. Anderson stood slowly, and then looked his son in the eye. "Mason, I want the truth, and I want it now."

Mason's first thought was to lie and stall while he thought up quick answers, but he realized he'd told so many lies he couldn't remember what he'd already told his father on his last short visit. Sighing deeply, he proceeded to tell the story of his failure to marry Susanne, and of his abandonment of her in Reno.

As Mason talked, Samuel Hampton had to draw on every ounce of willpower he possessed not to get up and deck the kid that stood before him. The one thing that he did give the boy credit for was that so far, his story matched Susanne's, so at least he knew he was getting the truth.

When Mason finished speaking, his father handed him a picture of Polly. Mason looked at the picture of the infant and at first was confused as to why his father would hand him a picture of himself. Looking at the expression on his father and Mr. Hampton's faces it suddenly dawned on him what he was looking at. Visibly shaken and a little pale, Mason looked at his C.O., but quickly realized that no help would come from there.

"This is your daughter, Mason," his father spoke softly. "Her name is Polly. Susanne named her for your mother." Mason flinched. "She was born September 8, 1960."

Calculating quickly in his head, Mason knew immediately when his daughter had been conceived.

"I didn't know," was the only thing he could think to say.

Susanne's father stood, then, and walked to the window that overlooked the parade grounds. Without turning around he spoke calmly but firmly, "Mason, I don't know why you did what you did to Susanne, and frankly, I don't believe you could ever come up with an excuse that would satisfy me or anyone else in this room for that matter. What I want to know now is, what are you going to do about it?"

Mason said nothing for a several long moments, while his thoughts swirled through his head. Even if Susanne would be willing to take him back, he knew he wasn't husband or father material. Yet for all of his failures, somewhere deep inside him he felt a degree of guilt and the need to do something for his daughter, his mother's namesake.

About to lose his patience, Mason's father spoke, "Well, son, the man asked you a question."

Mason looked at all three men in the room individually and then again at the picture of Polly. He came to attention, eyes forward. "Sir, I admit my lack of responsibility and disrespect toward your daughter. I cannot take back what I did. Susanne is free to go on with her life."

At this point the C.O. spoke up. "Seaman, what are you going to do about the child?"

"Well I. . ." But before Mason could finish what he started to say, his C.O. continued.

If it were my daughter you trifled with you'd be taking a long walk off a short peer, wearing cement boots. But as you've confessed this abandonment to your father and Mr. Hampton," he said with emphasis, "They have come up with an alternate solution."

Mason looked at both men, prepared to take whatever they had in mind just to get this meeting over with.

"First, you will fill out this pay allotment paperwork that will ensure that the mother of your daughter receives forty percent of each pay check for the duration of your enlistment, for childcare expenses."

"Secondly, you will list your daughter as your sole beneficiary on your life insurance policy. And, lastly, you will sit here and write Miss Hampton a letter.

"Sir I don't even know where Sus. . . I mean Miss Hampton is living at this time." Immediately realizing he's just made a stupid comment with her father standing right there, Mason glanced at Samuel Hampton and quickly said, "Sorry, Sir. Will you see that she gets the letter?"

Samuel nodded his head but did not speak,

All the details completed, Mason was escorted to the ship he had been assigned to. It wouldn't be leaving port for several days, so Mason was confined to the ship for his own protection-or so he was told.

As he lay on his bunk, he thought about the letter he had written to Susanne. He had apologized, and decided that he did mean it. He had also told her how beautiful Polly was, and again apologized for his lack of responsibility toward their child. Because his father and Mr. Hampton had been reading the letter over his shoulder, he had ended with his disclosure to their fathers about the lack of a wedding. Inside the envelope he also enclosed a copy of the allotment paperwork, so she'd know about the forthcoming support for Polly.

Rolling over, Mason closed his eyes and sighed. Just before drifting off to sleep something that Mr. Hampton said hit home. "Hawaii," he'd said, something about taking the letter to her in Hawaii. Mason sat up quickly, banging his head on the bunk above.

"It *was* Susanne I saw at that concert! I wasn't having alcohol induced hallucinations!" he said, as he rubbed his head. He laughed with relief that he wasn't losing his mind, and then quickly checked himself. *What the heck was she doing in Hawaii?*

Chapter Eighteen

The weeks flew by as the work of remodeling and planning took place on the farm. Uncle had hired Ku and Sons, a local construction crew, to manage the project. Mr. Ku generally supervised, leaving the actual work to his three big strapping Hawaiian sons. Each had a specialty, but each one knew how to do the work of the entire process. Sam Ku was in charge of building construction, Edward Ku did the plumbing work, and the youngest brother, James, took care of the electrical requirements.

News travels fast in small communities, and it wasn't surprising to see people from the neighborhood casually stroll up the road to get a peek at all the activity. Nor did it take long for the enthusiasm of those working to spread to those who watched. Several asked if they could help, and Susanne, who had become the unofficial foreman, jumped at the offers. Within days the grounds began to take shape, and the old, forgotten cottages came to life.

"Don't you just wish these building could talk?" Susanne asked one afternoon while she and two of the neighborhood women were working.

"They'd have quite a story to tell," a deep male voice said from behind her.

Susanne spun around to find James Ku standing in the doorway of the cottage she was working in.

"Sorry." James laughed. "I didn't mean to startle you. I do agree with you. The history this place has lived would be fascinating. There are many historic sites all over the islands. I'd be glad to show you some of my favorite places if you are interested," he offered shyly.

"I'd love to go," she said, excitement in her voice "We haven't taken time to see any of the sights since we arrived."

"How about this Saturday? I could pick you up at ten o'clock and we could make a day of it," James said, matching her excitement.

Susanne nodded, smiling. Feeling the depression that had plagued her for months begin to lift, she went back to work, humming a tune as she hung curtains and arranged furniture.

Later that evening she shared her news with Kate.

"Should I go?" she asked.

"Of course you should go," Kate replied. "James seems to be a nice guy. Uncle speaks highly of the entire family."

Susanne didn't respond, just rocked Polly and watched the setting sun.

The sound of the phone ringing inside the house broke the silence.

"Susie Q, it's for you," Uncle called out.

Responding as she had as a teenager, Susanne almost overturned her chair as she leaped out of the rocker and ran into the house. She nearly knocked Tom down when he passed between her and the phone on his way to the couch with the evening paper. As she reached for the phone Uncle mouthed the word *James,* and winked at her. She blushed when she saw the twinkle in Uncle's eyes.

After talking quietly for a few moments she said, "Let me ask."

Looking at her sister who had just walked into the room, she said, "James wants to know if you and Tom would like join us?

Looking up from the paper he was reading, Tom spoke up, "I think that's a great idea. We could use a break, and some sightseeing could be just the ticket."

He looked to Kate for confirmation and laughed when he saw her bouncing on her toes.

Kate eagerly said, "Tell James we'd be happy to join you."

Susanne repeated this information to James and then hung up the phone.

"Oh!" she exclaimed. "What will we do with the girls?"

Ruth, who was sitting on the lanai steps pretending not to eavesdrop, jumped up and did a little jig. "Auntie Ruth to the rescue," she sang, bringing laughter to the entire family.

Saturday morning at ten o'clock on the nose, James drove up to the house and gave two toots of the horn to announce his arrival.

Taking a quick look in the mirror to check her hair, Susanne sang out, "He's here!"

Kate grabbed the camera and called out to Tom, "Honey, don't forget the picnic basket."

And then linking arms with her sister, the girls walked out into the beautiful sunny morning.

When Tom appeared at the door he whistled and said, "Nice car!"

James grinned and rubbed the steering wheel of the black '57 Cadillac convertible. "Got it for a steal at an auction awhile back. It's a bit rusty in places, but it rides like a dream."

Tom opened the car door for the girls. A slightly nervous Susanne slid onto the front seat, and Kate and Tom got in the back. After Tom reached over and closed the door Susanne slid over as close to the door as she could get.

"Hey I don't bite," James said as he patted the place in the seat next to him.

Susanne blushed and scooted over. They all laughed and turned to wave at Uncle, who now stood on the lanai.

Uncle returned the wave and hollered, "Have fun!" as the car smoothly eased out onto the roadway.

Neither of the girls had thought to bring a scarf, which allowed their long hair to billow and swirl as they cruised along in the convertible with the top down. Kate enjoyed the experience, and laughed at

Susanne who struggled to contain her blond mass of hair.

After several minutes of this struggle, Susanne threw her hands in the air and proclaimed, "I give up!"

Turning in her seat she glared at Kate for just a moment, and then added, "I hope you brought a brush."

The first stop on the day's agenda was *Pu'uhonua o Honaunau*, also known as 'The Place of Refuge'.

As the foursome walked the trails, Kate stated, "Oh, it's so quiet here, and all the swaying coconut trees are so calming."

Everyone agreed and then James told stories, which he announced as, "Time to 'talk story' about some of the history of this place."

"In ancient times the culture was governed by chiefs, called *Ali'i,* who established a long list of taboos called *Kapu*. My Tutu told me there were hundreds of these *Kapu*."

"Like what?" Kate asked.

James smiled, took a deep breath, let it out slowly for emphasis, and began.

"It was *kapu* to look at or walk on the same trails as royalty. One did not dare allow your shadow to cross paths with a chief. It was *kapu* to prepare men's food in the same container used for women's food. It was *kapu* for women and men to eat together. It was *kapu* for women to eat pork or bananas."

"I'm seeing a pattern here," Susanne interrupted. "What about *kapus* for men?"

"Well, most of the same as I've already told you. Men and women also had to be sure to observe the days dedicated to the gods. They also had to be aware that certain areas were *kapu* for fishing if the fish ponds became depleted, allowing the area to replenish themselves. And that is only a speck of the *kapus*."

"So what happened if these *kapus* were broken?" Tom asked.

Solemnly James replied, "The penalty for breaking a *kapu* was death by club, strangulation, fire, or spear. And if the broken *kapu* was considered serious enough, the entire family of the offender would be put to death, as well."

Speaking softly, Susanne asked, "If the offender was killed, why is this place called a 'Place of Refuge'?"

Slowly turning to look at her, James spoke with a sense of reverence in his voice.

"If the offender was able to elude his or her pursuers and get to this place, which offered asylum, a *Kahuna Pule* or priest could mandate specific rituals to be performed and then the offender was considered clean and could return to his or her village without fear of punishment."

"Tutu's stories of my ancestors included tales of those who reached this place safely and of those who tried to swim here from one of the other islands and were drowned or eaten by sharks right here in this bay."

Kate and Susanne turned to look at the peaceful bay, where children now splashed in the shallow water and adults snorkeled a bit further out.

"Is it safe to be out there?" Kate asked.

Nodding, James answered, as he too watched the children play.

"Legend has it that the sharks only came into these waters if the gods deemed the offender not worthy of asylum or forgiveness."

Seeing Kate shudder, Tom put his arm around her shoulder and drew her close to his side.

"I am so grateful that our God is a God of love and forgiveness freely offered to anyone, he said softly into her ear.

It was several minutes before anyone spoke. They were all lost in their own thoughts about the beauty of the place and what had happened here in times long past.

Breaking the silence, Susanne spoke to no one in particular. "This is where I want to be baptized, right there in the bay," she said as she pointed to the area where waves gently rolled in and out.

As an afterthought, she looked at James and asked, "Is that allowed?"

"Sure, this place is open to the public. Many locals and tourists come here to enjoy the water, and even to picnic," he replied.

"I think a baptism here would be perfect, considering the significance of the history," Tom added.

Susanne smiled and nodded in agreement.

James took her hand and said, "Great idea."

Paradise Inherited

As they continued to walk the trail around the property, James continued his story.

"The trail we now walk on is called the 1871 Trail. It was named this because area residents paid their taxes in 1871 by fixing up the formerly dilapidated trail."

The trail circled back to the main ground where a thatched- roof structure stood.

"This building is a reconstruction of a building that would have been here in the early days of the Place of Refuge. It is called a *Hale-o-Keawe,* and was originally a mausoleum, containing the bones of twenty-three chiefs."

Kate and Susanne grimaced and said, "Yuck," taking two steps back.

James and Tom laughed at the girls, and then James continued.

"No, no, the bones were thought to contain supernatural power or *mana*. This ensured that the Place of Refuge would remain sacred."

Susanne looked at her sister for support then stated, "Well, that may be a good thing, I suppose, but bones . . . gross."

This brought laughter to other tourists who had stopped to listen to James as he talked.

When the laughter subsided, James stated, "Ok, tourists, there is more to see before this day is through. But I'm hungry. How about we have our picnic lunch down in Kailua-Kona Town?"

"Sounds great," Tom answered, for himself and the girls.

They returned to the car to continue their sightseeing journey.

Finding a place on the lava rock sea wall to sit, they ate their lunch of cold chicken, apple salad and macadamia nut cream pie. Auntie had also included two jars of passion fruit iced tea.

Once again they were all lost in thought as they sat quietly for several minutes.

Susannne was first to break the silence. Pointing at a building just a short distance from them she asked, "Who lives there? That is a beautiful building."

Following the direction her finger pointed, James replied. "Ah, that is the *Hulihe'e Palace*. It was built in 1838 by Governor Kuakini, and quickly became the vacation home for Hawaiian royalty, up until 1914. It is currently being renovated into a museum."

"And across the street," James pointed, "is the Mokuaikaua Church, the first Christian Church in the islands, built in 1820. The original structure was a thatched hut. This building was erected in 1837, is built of lava rock and crushed coral."

"The church is generally always open," he continued. "We can go there after lunch."

"It's stunning," Kate spoke softly as they entered the cool interior of the church.

The tall interior was graced with koa wood. Tom noticed the joints and asked James what the pins were made of.

"Oh those pins, yeah, they come from gnarly *'ohi'a* trees.

Back on the road, James headed to the north shore of Kohala. At the town of Kapa'au, on the *mauka* or mountain side of the highway, he pulled over at a statue of King Kamehameha the Great.

"Hey, this looks just like the one in Honolulu," Tom observed.

"It is . . . sort of," James replied.

"When the Hawaiian legislature commissioned the statue in 1878, it was cast in Paris and put on a ship."

"Oh! And the ship went down and was lost at sea near the Falkland Islands," Kate jumped in. "I remember Kimo telling this story."

"Hush," Susanne teased. "I wasn't there and I want to hear the story."

Kate crossed her eyes at her sister and stuck out her tongue.

"Oh, that's mature," Susanne laughed. "I'm glad Polly wasn't here to see that."

Everyone chuckled then James continued.

"The money from the shipping insurance was used to order another one. Meanwhile the captain of the lost ship later spotted the 'lost' statue, with a broken arm, standing in Port Stanley. Someone had salvaged it. He bought it back for five hundred dollars, and this time successfully shipped it to Hawaii. The broken arm was repaired and it was erected where you see it now."

Once again on the road Susanne started to laugh and pointed at a sign as they drove by.

"Donkey Crossings," she read aloud. "I don't see any donkeys."

"Ah." James laughed. "The 'Kona Nightingales,' as the donkeys are called, come down from the mountains, crossing here over the older lava beds at night and early morning. They come to lick the salt off the rocks on the shore and drink water from springs that flow nearby."

"Who do they belong to?" Susanne asked.

"No one. They are wild and free, descendants of coffee hauling pack animals, which escaped."

***

In what seemed like moments they arrived at Parker Ranch.

"My, it is so different here," Kate said, as she looked at the scenery around them.

There was mile after mile of rolling, grassy hills and wide open plains with rows of trees at different locations used as wind breaks.

"Look! Cowboys!" She added.

"We call them *Paniolo*," James explained.

"Captain George Vancouver brought long-horned cattle to Kamehameha as a gift in 1793. The King made the area *kapu,* or off limits, for ten years, to build up numbers. And build up in number they did, causing all kinds of mischief and destruction. Eventually the king ordered that the herds be thinned out, and asked John Palmer Parker to kill some."

"Why this guy Parker?' Tom asked.

James laughed. "He was the only one around who possessed a musket and knew how to shoot."

As payment he was given 225,000 acres of land and his choice of one animal for each one killed. Realizing the Hawaiians did not know how to handle the cattle, he brought three Mexican cowboys to Hawaii. And, as they say, the rest is history."

As they stood watching the, Kate gently nudged Tom's side and bobbed her head in the direction of where James and Susanne stood with arms casually wrapped around each other's waist.

"She looks happy for the first time in a long time," Kate whispered to her husband.

Once the sun went below the horizon, Kate spoke up. "You know, I have an idea."

"Oh, no." Tom moaned. "The last idea you had has taken months of hard work."

He laughed when Kate stopped in mid-sentence and punched him in the arm.

"May I continue now?" She asked, with a joking tone to her voice.

"Sure," Tom, said smiling at her as he stood next to her rubbing, his arm.

"Okay, well, after listening to James tell his stories, I've realized there is a wealth of information we haven't even heard yet. We should interview the older citizens of our community and get their stories. When we open for business we could have a bonfire on Saturday nights and Uncle could tell the stories. Although, you did a pretty good job with the *Talk Story*," Kate complimented James.

"That is a great idea," Susanne agreed, and squeezed James hand.

Uncomfortable with all the praise, James spoke up, quickly changing the subject.

"I have an idea, too. I'm hungry, and there is a great steakhouse just down the road."

***

The weeks passed quickly and the work was shaping up nicely. Gardens were perfectly groomed and tags were placed near the plants so that tourist could identify the tropical flowers and bushes.

As construction was coming to an end, the fun part started for the young women. Shopping! It was time to purchase the appliances and furnishings.

With Ruth, Charles, Tom and Uncle watching the children, the sisters flew to Honolulu and spent a week shopping and ordering from catalogs. Kate's experience with inventory and keeping the books at her father's hardware store came in quite handy. The girls worked off of a list they had prepared before leaving Kona, and Kate made sure every purchase was well-documented.

At the end of their shopping week, Kate suggested they take a quick detour and go to Kauai. "We have collected so many marvelous treasures on our garage sale hunts. I can think of several items that would enhance the cottages."

"Great idea," Susanne agreed. "And we could take the quilt you made for Uncle, as a surprise."

After a moment of silence Susanne added, "The curtains we made for his house in Kauai would go great in the house in Kona. What do you think?"

"Oh yes, we have plenty of that fabric left. Let's leave the curtains in Kauai and make new ones for the main house in Kona," Kate responded enthusiastically.

After a quick call to Kona to explain their delay, and another quick call to the General Store asking Mrs. Wong to get a message to Alice, the girls packed and headed for Kauai.

Alice, as faithful as ever sat at the airport, in the jeep, Tom had loaned her while the Tyne's were away. As a joke she had taped a sign to the side door that read: "Alice's Taxi Service." Several people stopped, asking for a ride, which Alice thought was quite funny. Some saw the humor when the reason for the signs were explained, others tired from their travel were not amused. Kate and Susanne thought the story was a hoot.

As the jeep came to a stop in front of the house both Kate and Susanne sighed at the same time. They looked at each other and laughed.

"We've been so busy I didn't realize how much I've missed this place." Kate commented.

Susanne sat down on the top step of the porch and nodded in agreement. "It's funny, in a strange way I feel like I've come home."

Kate looked at her sister for several minutes without speaking. Picking up her luggage she noticed that her sister looked at peace here. "Have you considered staying in Kauai, Sus?"

Susanne slowly turned to face her sister. "Not really. But I don't have anywhere else to go besides back to California, and that doesn't appeal to me at all. I also don't want to burden you and Tom. I want my own life. Do you understand?" she asked with tears forming in her eyes.

Kate put down the case she was holding and sat down on the step next to her sister. Putting her arm around Susanne's shoulder she spoke softly. "First of all, you and Polly are not a burden." Trying to lighten the mood for her sister, she then said, "A royal pain in the neck sometimes" ... to which both girls laughed before Kate assured, "No seriously, it's been wonderful having you here. I can't imagine what it would have been like without you."

"My guess," Kate continued, "is that Tom, Mele, and I will be permanently moving to Kona. And I doubt Uncle will be coming back here, due to his health. So, you are more than welcome to come with us. Or ... how about this idea, you and Polly could live here in this house and turn Uncle's place over there into an antique store or a rental for tourists. Or ... the other way around," Kate's eyes began to sparkle as she spoke of these ideas.

Susanne sat in amazement, watching her sister's mind work.

"Do you think Tom and Uncle will go along with idea?" she asked.

"Does that mean you would be interested?" Kate excitedly asked.

"Of course. I love it here. I'd have my own home, and a job." Susanne replied. Looking at her sister she teased, "How much does this job pay, running the antique store or managing a rental?"

Kate pushed her sister gently. "Why? You got a better offer?"

Both girls laughed and stood, taking the luggage with them into the house.

As they prepared a light meal Susanne was deep in thought when Kate suddenly asked, "What about James?"

"James and I are good friends. It's wonderful that we share the same belief in Jesus as our Savior. He makes me laugh, and he's very good with Polly."

Kate took her sister's hand. "But . . ."

"But, I haven't told him about Mason and my situation." Susanne, as she started to cry. "James is a good man, and I think I'm beginning to have feelings for him, stronger than friendship. I'm afraid of what he'll think or do when he finds out I was not married to Mason."

Kate took her sister into her arms and let her cry against her shoulder. Silently she prayed for God to comfort Susanne and give her peace as only He can, until such time as He'd show her what to do.

***

Within a few days the sisters had sorted through the treasures of their garage sale collection. Boxes of fabric and decorating items were packed and shipped off to Kona. Kate realized she would miss their home in Kauai, but was anxious to get back to Tom and Mele.

Being at the farm and helping with the reconstruction efforts had been exciting and stretching for her. She smiled as she recalled Tom's last words before she and Susanne left home two weeks earlier.

Don't be gone too long. Without you two here to crack the whip these boys are likely to get lazy and we will never be finished.

The crew, within hearing range, had laughed and started to playfully yawn and talk about it being almost nap time.

***

Arriving back at the farm, Susanne hopped out of the truck put her hands up to her mouth and yelled, "Nap time is over! Back to work!"

Cheers and whistles greeted Kate and Susanne, who waved and stood in awe at how much more had been accomplished in their absence.

Both babies were delighted to see their mommies. Polly ran to her mother and squealed as she was spun in the air. Uncle held Mele, who reached for Kate when she came close. This little act of recognition made Kate's heart skip and brought tears to her eyes.

Charlie came in, having just returned from the post office. He welcomed the women home with a warm hug and a letter for each of them.

"Well, this is a first," Susanne said in surprise, as she looked at the envelope. "Father actually wrote a letter."

"Apparently he wrote two of them," Kate said, indicating that her letter was also from their father.

As Kate silently read her letter a large smile spread across her face. Looking to her sister to share the contents of her letter, the smile disappeared when she saw the look on Susanne's face.

"What's wrong?" she cried out, rushing to her sister's side.

Susanne had turned pale and started to tremble. "It's from Mason," she said just above a whisper.

Everyone in the room stopped talking and turned to face her. Tom walked over and put an arm around Kate. Uncle moved to stand by Susanne and then led her to a chair.

Tears streamed down her cheeks. Too emotional to read the letter aloud, Susanne handed the letter and some other documents to Kate, who read them quickly. Tom read over her shoulder.

Anger filled Susanne's brain. "He's sorry," she hissed, speaking to no one in particular.

Uncle looked to Tom and Kate for explanation. Tom took the documents from Kate and handed them to Uncle.

After a quick scan of the contents, Uncle spoke. "Well, regardless of the reason, at least he's going to take some responsibility for Polly."

Putting his hand on Susanne's shoulder he gently squeezed it and said, "Susie Q, whatever you decide to do, your family and friends are here for you. You've always got a home, and we're here to help you with Polly."

Susanne made efforts to calm herself. She knew she didn't want Mason back. It was an unsettling feeling and yet a relief that he had finally appeared, if only in letter form.

Susanne snatched the letter back and waved it in the air.

"This letter came through father, which means father must have found Mason. I don't know how and I don't care how. Considering how angry father was when he found out that Mason had abandoned me and Polly, I'll just bet *that* was an interesting reunion."

No one else laughed, but they did smile, relieved that she seemed to be through the worst of the shock.

No one noticed as James, who had been standing just outside the front screened door, quietly turned and walked back to the worksite, a mixture of anger and relief on his face.

Turning to Kate, Susanne asked, "What did father say in your letter."

Kate recognized Susanne's efforts to take the spotlight off of herself.

This is a new creation in Christ, she thought, as she lovingly gazed at her sister for a moment. *The sister I grew up with would do anything to keep the attention of any who would listen. God, you are amazing.* She silently spoke words of thanksgiving and praise to Him.

"Christmas," Kate said. "Mother and father have agreed to come for Christmas. They will be the first guests of the new *Paradise Retreat Center*."

Breaking from the earlier mood, everyone cheered and went back to work. Tom put the finishing touches on the newly carved and stained sign.

Uncle sat quietly with Susanne and explained about the allotment money she'd be receiving each month from Mason's pay.

Chapter Nineteen

By Thanksgiving all five of the cottages had been restored. The official opening of the retreat center was scheduled for January 15. Uncle had been persuaded, without much effort, to have a special opening for friends. Letters and phone calls had been exchanged, and Jonathon, Kimo, Lani, and the children, and even Stafford and Ellen were coming to Kona for a two week holiday visit. Kate and Susanne's parents would arrive the day before Thanksgiving and stay through the New Year. The high energy that comes with such excitement electrified the air.

Several young people from the surrounding communities had been hired as maids, lifeguards for the newly finished swimming pool and bellhops. Susanne and Kate would share the responsibility of greeting and checking-in their guests. Tom would head up the maintenance crews, with calls to the Ku brothers when he couldn't fix a problem himself. This decision had thrilled Susanne, when she realized there would be more opportunities to see James. At least she hoped so.

There wasn't an official office yet, just a section of the living room changed to look more like a lobby with a check-in counter. The bright red and yellow Hawaiian flower print fabric the girls had brought back from Kauai had indeed brightened the room when the new curtains and pillow covers were added.

Ruth had designed and purchased the items needed to open the gift shop next to the coffee mill. Her experience working in Kailua-Kona was proving to be most valuable. Her beloved Charlie decked out in new Hawaiian shirts and putting on his best Aloha smile became the perfect driver for those needing to be picked up or dropped off at the airport. When the retreat was full, he would become a wonderfully funny tour guide.

Kate had paid close attention when she had visited other coffee farms, and had asked questions about the operation of a coffee mill. She would be the official coffee mill guide. For days she practiced her presentation before the bathroom mirror, or to anyone who would stop and listen.

One afternoon Tom found her walking slowing through the mill speaking to an imaginary audience. He stayed in the shadows and followed her, but not too closely, just close enough so he could hear what she was saying.

"Coffee is grown on small trees, which usually reach just 10 to 20 feet in height. Coffee is a hardy plant, but cannot be grown successfully in areas

where temperatures dip below 32 degrees for any length of time. An optimum temperature range falls between 65 to 80 degrees. Did you know coffee is extremely easy to grow as a house plant?"

She paused for a moment as if thinking of possible questions or comments from a tour participant. Continuing, she pointed out some small tree starts.

"Coffee prefers medium amounts of rainfall and will not stand droughts or flooding. Here in Hawaii, coffee plantations are found only in drier zones."

Leading her imaginary group outside through the wide double doors of the mill, she walked over to a small grove of trees next to the building. She pointed out the small flowers on the trees.

"Coffee is a short-day plant, blooming most profusely when sunlight lasts for eight to ten hours a day. However, coffee may bloom year-round depending on temperature and rainfall conditions."

"Excellent question," she responded, as if one had just been asked.

Slowly walking back inside the mill, Kate continued.

"The highest quality coffee is generally hand-picked. Coffee beans do not become ripe at the same time, even if they are on the same tree. After picking, the coffee beans are pulped, usually using a mechanical pulper. This machine removes the thick skin of the coffee cherry exposing the coffee bean. The beans are then fermented, most often in water, for 10 to 36 hours."

Kate pointed to some beans currently in that process and stepped back as if to let someone get a closer look.

"After this, the beans are washed with pure Kona rainwater to remove the last of the sticky mucilage not removed by fermentation, and dried, usually in the sun for about fourteen days."

She walked over to a table with a screened bottom covered with drying beans. *"This process is time-consuming and expensive. Coffee at this stage is known as milled beans."*

From this point the bigger growers ship the raw, or green coffee beans to their destination country, where they are roasted. This darkens their color and alters the internal chemistry of the beans and therefore their flavor and aroma. Once the beans have dried they are roasted again, and become much more perishable.

The coffee grown here is primarily used by the retreat center, and for those who work the mill. We don't roast the beans until we receive an order. The closer to the roast, the more flavorful the coffee.

Kate stopped talking at this point, and nearly jumped out of her shoes when Tom began to whistle and clap.

"That was wonderful," he excitedly told her. "You sound like you've been growing coffee all of your life."

Kate blushed with pleasure at Tom's compliment. She then threw her arms around his neck and tilted her head up for a kiss.

"I love it here, Tom," she said, after the kiss ended. "This will be a wonderful place to raise Mele."

The words were barely out of Kate's mouth when the sound of a woman's pained scream filled the air. Tom grabbed Kate's hand and ran with her toward Ruth, who was standing in the doorway of Auntie's cottage. Tears streamed down Ruth's face and she was trembling violently. Kate put her arm around Ruth's shoulder as Tom entered the cottage, and Kate heard him softly say, "Bless her heart."

Slowly walking out the door just as Uncle and Charlie arrived, Tom faced them and quietly told them that Auntie was gone. "She apparently died in her sleep sometime during the night"

"I didn't wake her this morning because I thought she was just extra tired," Ruth sobbed.

Charlie held her close and assured her there was nothing she could have done.

"Auntie lived a long full life. She died the way she always hoped she would. Look at how peaceful her face is." He let out a single sob, but regained control of his emotions for his wife's sake.

Uncle did not speak for several minutes. "She was the finest woman I've ever known," he finally said, as tears rolled unchecked down his cheeks. Turning back toward the house he spoke over his shoulder, "I'll go make the necessary phone calls."

Nearly everyone from the community knew and had loved Auntie. She was surrounded by those who held her in their heart as family.

Flower leis representing every family present were tossed one by one on top of the coffin, and then the large group joined hands and bowed their heads and prayed. The Pastor from the community church first prayed in Hawaiian, and then Uncle prayed in English. This was followed with singing praises to God.

At sundown the coffin was lowered into the ground up on the hill behind the coffee mill. Uncle stood over the grave, opened his old worn Bible and read from the book of I Thessalonians 4:16-18.

For the Lord Himself will descend from heaven with a loud cry of summons, with the shout of the archangel, and with the blast of the trumpet of God. And those who have departed this life in Christ will rise first. Then we, the living ones who remain on the earth, shall simultaneously be caught up along with the resurrected dead in the clouds to meet the Lord in the air; and so always through the eternity of eternities we shall be with the Lord. Therefore comfort and encourage one another with these words.

Closing his Bible, Uncle looked at the group before him, smiled and said, "Auntie will rest in peace beside her husband, until that day when Jesus comes to awaken them and raise them in new glorified bodies to live with him eternally."

Everyone answered with a heartfelt, "Amen."

Uncle had seen to it that all of Auntie's affairs were in order. Charlie, as her adopted son, inherited all of her earthly possessions. He was surprised to discover that Auntie's cottage and the cottage he and Ruth lived in and five acres directly behind the cottages were owned outright by Auntie. Uncle had given this land to her for her 90th birthday, without ever telling anyone except Auntie and Jonathan.

Jonathan told Charlie later, "She suggested that you move into her cottage as it is bigger and perhaps rent out the other cottage for extra income. There is a nice amount of money in her savings account, some of which you can use to upgrade the appliances and furnishings in both cottages and work with Kate in renting it out as part of the retreat center."

Despite the sadness of their loss, everyone cheered considerably upon the arrival of all the expected guests for the holidays. At Thanksgiving, there was much that all those around the table could share that they were thankful for. At Christmas, Ruth announced she was pregnant, surprising Charlie. On New Year's morning, Kate woke Tom and whispered in his ear causing him to sit bolt upright.

"Are you sure?" He grinned from ear to ear.

"Pretty sure," Kate giggled. "The doctor says so."

"How long have you known?" Tom asked, dumbfounded that he hadn't noticed.

Kate laughed harder this time. "I've known since Thanksgiving. I had planned to tell you at Christmas, but when Ruth shared her joyous news, I didn't want to take away her moment of glory.

Taking her hand, he gently pulled her from the bed and wrapped her in her robe. "Come on, let's go tell the family."

New Years Day 1962 turned out to be a day full of blessings. First was the shared news about the baby. Susanne and her mother squealed at the same time and then laughed and hugged each other and then Kate. Tom and Charlie patted each other on the back, as if the accomplishment was something they alone had brought about. Ruth and Kate hugged and smiled at their husbands. Uncle and Samuel Hampton laughed at the sight of their excited family.

Secondly, everyone packed up the lunch boxes and beach gear and spent the day in the sun, playing in the ocean waves after Uncle performed Susanne's baptism at the Place of Refuge. It had been several months since she'd asked him to do it, but they had decided to wait until her parents could be there to witness her public testimony of her decision to follow Jesus Christ.

Kimo, Lani, and the children came back to Kona for the celebration.

Moments before the baptism, Susanne was tingling all over with joy that she was finally obeying Jesus with this symbolic act of being lowered into the grave and raising out of the grave a new creation in Christ. Uncle held one arm, Tom the other as they lowered her into water. Charlie stood at Uncle's side in the event a bigger wave rolled through and Uncle lost his balance.

Susanne couldn't help but smile as she wiped her eyes. Her smile grew even wider when she saw James standing beside her father. She was delighted to know that James had arrived just in time to see her baptism.

Her father had met James at Thanksgiving and by the end of the day, had decided he liked the lad. Now, standing next to James, and after witnessing him and

Susanne and Polly together over that last two months, he hoped and prayed his daughter would not let this one get away.

As Susanne walked out of the water toward them, she was thinking exactly the same thing.

***

After the holidays, the retreat center opened for business. A full week of celebrations was held for the grand opening. Prayers and Hawaiian chants of blessings were offered. Musicians played and dancers danced. Tours of every building on the property were given to anyone who asked. On Friday night a luau was held for family and friends and the owners of tour booking agencies and car rentals. Ruth had placed a call to the local paper and a reporter took notes for a spread in the next day's paper.

By Saturday night the reservations started coming in with bookings all the way up to the next holiday season.

Word spread quickly to the mainland and outer Islands with the help of some advertisements that Kimo and Jonathan had taken back to Oahu and distributed to local tourist agencies and gift shops on that island.

By Uncle's directive, any church group wishing to use the center for weekend retreats were welcomed at no charge. Generally these groups insisted on leaving a "love offering" just the same. Uncle and Tom made sure these gifts were passed on to local charities.

With the parties over and the staff hired to take care of the guests, Tom and Kate planned to make a trip back to Kauai to check on the house, but with Kate's pregnancy the decision was made for Susanne to go instead.

"I've never been completely on my own," Susanne confided to James one evening when he'd stopped by to visit.

"Will you be alright?" he asked, with a hint of concern in his voice.

"Oh sure, we have neighbors who keep an eye on us, and our Pastor and his wife are just up the road," Susanne replied. "We also have a telephone in the house now, so I'm not completely cut off from help if I need it."

James just nodded, not at all sure he liked the idea of Susanne and Polly leaving and their being alone. He also knew that his feelings for Susanne were growing stronger, but, unsure if she returned those feelings, he had decided being a supportive friend was all he could be, and that didn't hold much weight in speaking his opinion.

Susanne, although slightly nervous, was also excited to have been given the responsibility of being the caretaker for the property on Kauai. Uncle had given her permission to turn his little house into a vacation rental, and had already advertised its availability.

"Now I'm really glad we cleaned the place up and redecorated before we left," she told Kate as they waited at the airport for Susanne's flight back to Kauai.

Kate was proud of her sister. *It's a miracle how much she has changed,* Kate thought. *I never imagined I'd see the day when Susanne would willingly take care of other's needs before her own.* She smiled as she watched Susanne play pat-a-cake with Polly.

Susanne suddenly turned to Kate and asked, "Are you sure you'll be alright?" "I'm sure Alice could handle the rental just fine."

Kate gave her sister an affectionate squeeze and smile. "I'll be fine. The morning sickness is almost gone and the doctor says the baby's heartbeat is strong and steady. And don't forget, Tom has promised he'll get you back over here in plenty of time for delivery."

Just then Susanne's flight was called, not giving her a chance to argue. "Alright, but I want you to call me if anything changes."

Kate kissed her sister's cheek and gave Polly a squeeze, which sent the little girl to giggling.

"Go, you'll miss your plane," She said giving Susanne a gentle push.

Kate stayed to watch Susanne's plane lift off, waving nonstop until it was just a small speck in the sky.

Now who is having an adventure? she said to herself, and smiled with a slight blush when she realized there were people walking through the airport near enough to have heard her speak.

Kate took a slow, leisurely drive back to the house. Charlie had taught her to drive shortly after they had arrived on the Big Island. She had been a fast learner, and loved the independence and freedom driving the car gave her.

When Kate had an opportunity to get away for a drive alone, she used the time to pray, sing along with the radio, or just have a time of peace and quiet.

"I love all the excitement our guests bring," she had told Tom, "but sometimes it does get a bit overwhelming, and I miss the peace and quiet of our house on Kauai."

On this drive her thoughts were with her sister as she reflected on the last two years.

Tom and I married because Susanne wouldn't come to Hawaii with him. Now she's living with only her child in my house in Kauai. Chewing on her bottom lip, Kate realized she felt some resentment toward Susanne.

Later that evening when Tom and Kate went for their evening stroll through the flower gardens, Kate brought up what had troubled her earlier in the day.

"Tom, do you see our life as adventurous? Remember on the ship all the things we talked about? We were so excited not knowing what to expect."

Tom put his arm around her shoulder and stopped their strolling. One look at Kate's face told him there was something on her mind.

"Go on," he encouraged.

Sighing, Kate looked up into the dark chocolate colored eyes that searched her face.

"Think about what we've experienced during the last two years. Sure, we had to clean up the old house, and remodel this place, but we've also not suffered for anything financially. We've traveled first class on ships and airplanes. Where is the adventure in that?" She asked with a near sob escaping her throat.

Tom wasn't sure where she was going with this, and hesitated to speak too quickly.

This could be one of those pregnancy things. She does get a little odd when she's pregnant, he reminded himself.

Speaking carefully, hoping he would answer in a manner not to upset her further, he replied, "Yeah it hasn't been too rough, has it!"

Looking away from him, Kate set her focus on the setting sun. After a brief silence she continued. "When I think about what Susanne has experienced over the last two years, well, I'm not sure if I'm jealous or ... oh I don't know what I'm trying to say." She blew out a breath, exasperated with herself.

Tom waited a moment to make sure Kate was finished, then kissed her forehead, took her hand, and started to stroll again.

Speaking quietly, Tom asked, "What experiences are you referring to?"

"Well," Kate started, "She ran off with Mason, and then because he abandoned her, she lived in a strange town for an entire year. Then she went through a pregnancy and the delivery of her baby without any support from those who love her. My sister never lifted a finger to help at home, yet she was a companion and caretaker for Mrs. Lawson. Now look at her, she's taken her daughter to Kauai, to manage a vacation rental property for us. Alone, Tom. Do you realize I've never done anything alone in my entire life?"

Tom suspected now was not the time to speak, and was thankful a moment later when Kate continued her speech, which was gaining in volume and causing her to speed up the pace of the walk.

"And what have *I* accomplished in the last two years?" she asked, stopping dead in her tracks. She planted her hands on her hips and glared in his direction, but not necessarily at him.

Tom had a feeling what he was about to say was probably not the answer she was looking for, but he sensed he was supposed to say something.

"Sweetheart, you've been instrumental in refurbishing a home and you've given birth to Mele." And, Tom stammered, wracking his brain for words to encourage his wife, "The coffee museum is a total success because of the time you took to learn the history, and um, oh! You've learned to drive a car," he added brightly.

However, his smiled slowly vanished when he saw Kate's usually sparkling eyes darken like thunder clouds.

"Okay, look, this hasn't been the adventure we thought it might be," Tom backpedaled. "But honey, we have to remember God has each of us on a path. We have the free will to choose for ourselves the steps we will take in this life, and then the consequences of those decisions. Your sister made some choices, and she's learning to trust God in spite of some very difficult consequences. We've made some choices, and the same applies for us. So far we've been blessed over and over, but that doesn't mean we will always have good things in our life."

The anger that had been on Kate's face slowly gave way to a calmer expression.

"I'm sorry," she spoke softly as a warm tear trickled down her cheek. "I'm really happy for Susanne. The changes in her have been so exciting to see. And I wouldn't have really wanted things to have turned out any differently for us. I guess I'm just tired of being sick and tired, and I let my emotions get the better of me."

"Thanks for listening," she whispered.

"Anytime," Tom answered, thankful he hadn't said the wrong thing as he pulled her into his arms and kissed her tenderly

"Let's go put this baby to bed," he said, as he gently patted her expanding tummy.

Kate laughed for the first time all evening and followed him into the house.

Uncle grinned as he watched from the shadows of the lanai and then as he did every evening he had his conversation with God. His prayer this time was for himself.

"Give me more time Lord, please, just a bit more time."

Chapter Twenty

The months passed quickly as everyone settled into a regular routine of daily living. The retreat center was so well-organized it practically ran itself. General upkeep and maintenance kept Tom and his crew of employees busy, as did the daily tours of the island that Charlie conducted.

With Kate's advancing pregnancy, her feet began to swell, making it difficult for her to give tours of the coffee mill, which also resulted in her mood and emotions being up and down like a roller coaster ride. Usually sweet tempered and agreeable, in the final months before delivery, Kate often exploded into fits of anger at things she normally would not have even noticed or would let slide. Or she would burst into tears at something as small as a flower floating in the pool.

"I don't know what's wrong with me," she said to Uncle one afternoon just after giving Tom an especially harsh tongue lashing. All he wanted was a pitcher of iced tea sent out to the crew working on the luau pit."

"I wouldn't worry about it, Katie girl. Tom understands . . ."

"Tom understands nothing!" Kate screeched, before Uncle could finish his sentence. "He's not walking around with an extra large watermelon attached to his body. His feet aren't swollen to the point that he can't wear shoes. No one has told him he shouldn't drive a car. He can sleep in any position without having his insides beaten with kicks and punches. He doesn't wet his pants when he sneezes or laughs too hard." Taking a deep breath she glared at Uncle as she completed her ranting. "No, don't tell me Tom understands. He hasn't got a clue!"

When she was done, Kate stomped out of the room, waddling as fast as she could, great sobs erupting from her throat as she went.

Uncle chuckled softly and said to the cat curled up on his favorite chair, "That baby better come soon!" The cat meowed back as if to agree.

Later that night Tom held Kate in his arms as she cried, "I want to go home. I want to see my mother. I miss my sister. Mele is becoming impossible. And I'm sick of having no place to go but around and around this stupid island."

Tom had heard about Uncle's experience with Kate earlier in the day, so he decided to keep quiet. Unfortunately, this time it was the wrong thing to do.

Say something!" Kate yelled. "Do something. Anything. Oh, never mind," she cried as she wrenched herself out of Tom's arms and with much effort rolled to her side and went to sleep.

Tom lay awake for a long time that night. Over the years he'd observed what he thought was every emotion Kate had ever expressed. But this was something he'd never experienced, and had no idea how to handle it. Before drifting off to sleep, Tom silently prayed.

Ease her burden Lord, and help me stay out of firing range of her temper. Oh, and bring this baby soon, he finished with a soft chuckle.

The next morning, both Tom and Uncle were surprised to find Kate up before them, and amazed that she was smiling and singing softly as she prepared breakfast. From the doorway, the two men watched in puzzlement for a few moments then looked at each other and shrugged. It was a silent agreement that neither had any idea how or why Kate had changed from a sobbing shrew back to her normal sweet self over night, nor did they care. Anything was better than what they'd been experiencing from her recently.

"I just hope it lasts," Tom whispered to Uncle when Kate left the room to go retrieve the paper from the mailbox outside.

Even Kate was amazed at how good she felt. "Thank you, Lord," she whispered. With her emotions in check, she also realized she had energy she'd been lacking in recent weeks. Despite her slightly swollen ankles, Kate set about cleaning and even sat down to sew new curtains for the kitchen.

She had just finished when Charlie ran up the back porch steps and yelled for Kate to come quickly.

"What's wrong?" she asked with alarm in her voice.

"Ruth is having the baby," he said.

"Go get the car!" Kate ordered.

"No Kate, she's having the baby right now!" he cried out, as he grabbed her hand and pulled her along behind him as fast as she could waddle.

From a perch high on a ladder where Tom was trimming a palm tree, he spotted Charlie and Kate crossing the grounds. Quickly, he slid down the ladder like it was a fire pole and hit the ground running.

Tom reached the cabin to find Charlie pacing in the middle of the floor, but didn't see Kate anywhere. Tom had barely stepped over the threshold when the sound of Ruth's scream came from the bedroom. Before he could ask what was going on, Kate, looking pale as a sheet, flung open the bedroom door.

Both men rushed forward. Charlie pushed past Kate and went in to be with Ruth, as Kate with voice and hands shaking instructed Tom. "Quickly, go call an ambulance! Ruth's baby wants to hit the world running. It's presently feet first and I don't know what to do!"

Tom raced toward the house, yelling for Uncle, who was just coming down the porch steps to call the ambulance for Ruth. Within minutes the wail of sirens could be heard in the distance. The wait felt like hours as they paced helplessly.

Tom was on the phone to Susanna when the ambulance arrived. He quickly told her of Ruth's situation and then said, "I'll have a ticket waiting for you at the airport. I think it best you come back. I suspect Kate will need you now more than ever."

By dinnertime that evening, Ruth was resting in a hospital bed with her son in her arms. Meanwhile Susanne held and consoled her sister as Kate cried with joy and relief that Ruth's baby had been delivered safely.

Kate couldn't remember ever being so glad to see her older sister. At that moment the six minutes difference in their ages could have been six years. Susanne had again risen to the occasion and shown maturity Kate had never seen in her before. And Kate suddenly realized just how much she dearly loved and admired her sister.

A week later Ruth returned home with her son, and settled happily into motherhood. Susanna took over the cleaning and cooking while Kate was put in charge of sitting on the lanai and watching over Polly and Mele while they played in the yard each day

Since her sister's arrival, Kate's emotions seemed to have settled back to normal, with only occasional times of crying due to her discomfort. She still had eight weeks to go and dreaded every moment of it, but tried to focus her thoughts on the day when she'd hold her sweet babe in her arms.

Kate was enjoying the warmth of the early summer sun and had just drifted off to a light sleep as she rocked, when suddenly a pain like a knife cutting across her belly jolted her into an upright position.

"Oh!" she exclaimed and called out for Tom, Susanne, or anyone who might be close by. Susanne was the first to reach Kate and at first could only stare at her sister as she watched water run down Kate's legs forming a pool beneath the rocker.

Paradise Inherited

"It's too soon," Kate said in a terrified whisper.

Once again the siren of the ambulance screamed up the mountain road. Tom instructed them to be extra cautious as the paramedics were loading precious cargo. Uncle pulled up in the station wagon just as the ambulance pulled away. Calling out a quick thank you to Ruth and Charlie for watching the girls, Tom and Susanna jumped into the car with Uncle to follow the flashing lights

After what seemed like hours of pacing in the waiting room, Tom broke into a huge grin as he watched a nurse come through the door carrying a tiny blue bundle and announce, "Mr. Tyne."

However, just before the door closed, the grin immediately disappeared as he heard a doctor say, "Get her to surgery."

The nurse had immediately turned and reentered the labor and delivery room completely forgetting to show the new born babe to his father. Uncle, Susanne and Tom stood for a moment, bewildered and not sure what to do next.

Forty-five minutes later the doctor walked into the waiting room to find Tom pacing, Uncle with his head bowed in prayer, and Susanne starring out the window. All heads turned as the doctor entered.

"How's my wife?" Tom's asked.

The doctor smiled which drew a hopeful sigh of relief from Susanne, and said, "Mr. Tyne, your wife is in recovery, she came through the cesarean delivery just fine. And your sons are doing as well as can be expected, given their small size.

"Thank you, God," Tom said with a sigh of relief.

Suddenly the words the doctor had spoken registered in Tom's brain.

"Did you say 'sons'?" Tom asked with amazement and confusion clearly expressed on his face.

The doctor laughed and said, "Yep, there were two of them."

"Sons! Two of them!" Tom shouted with joy, as he hugged first Uncle and then his sister-in-law.

Everyone, including other waiting fathers laughed.

After the laughter subsided the doctor grew more serious. "The boys are very tiny. The first one born weighed in at four pounds. His brother is just less than three pounds. I'd strongly suggest we fly the boys to the hospital in Honolulu. They are better prepared to handle babies this tiny."

Tom slowly sank into the chair behind him. Uncle wrapped his arms around Susanne who was weeping softly. Unable to speak Tom looked to his Uncle for support.

"We should do what the doctor suggests, Tom. Spare no expense for those boys."

Tom nodded in agreement then drew in a strengthening breath and told the doctor to do whatever was needed for his sons.

"When can I see my wife?" he then asked.

About forty-five minutes later Tom sat beside Kate's bed and gently spoke to her about the boys. She cried when told that the babies were to be sent to Honolulu without her and begged Tom to take Susanne with him to stand in her place.

"I'll come as quickly as the doctors allow me to travel," she assured him.

Uncle stayed with Kate and gently cranked her bed into a sitting position so she could see the helicopter that carried her sons away. Tears slid down her cheeks, but she made no sound. When they could no longer see or hear the helicopter he gently lay her back down on the bed, then knelt at her bedside and prayed for his niece and the two tiny great-nephews.

***

Susanne was concerned about Kate traveling immediately after leaving the hospital but she was also relieved. She was exhausted from the near round-the-clock watch she and Tom had kept at the Honolulu Hospital where the premature babies were being treated.

She had spoken to her sister on the phone just before Kate had boarded the plane and was pleased to report that both of the boys were doing well and gaining in strength and weight. It had been rough the first couple of days, but the littlest one had rallied and was almost equal in weight to his older brother.

As he watched his sons sleep, Tom recalled how hard it had been to leave Kate in the hospital after the emergency delivery of the second twin. She had barely come out of the anesthesia when the decision had been made to fly the boys to Honolulu.

Uncle had stayed with Kate while Tom and Susanne traveled to Honolulu with the twins. He left her side only for needed bathroom breaks and to get something to eat. The nurses tried to get him to go home and get some rest, but he insisted on sleeping in the chair next to her bed.

"There really isn't much I can do for Kate, but she seems to rest easier when I'm here," he'd told them.

Kate had slept most of the first few days after the surgical delivery of Sam. The doctor had kept her heavily medicated more to help with the stress of having her babies flown off to another island rather than from the pain her body was experiencing. Tom had faithfully called everyday to give them updates about the twins. Thankfully it was always a good report.

"Wait until you see them," Tom had told Kate the last time he called. "Both of the boys are gaining weight, they've got the bluest eyes and 'Little Man,'" as he called the smaller twin, "Well, that boy has got a grip."

Kate had laughed at the enthusiasm in Tom's voice. "He was beside himself when Mele was born, but he's over the top for those boys," she said to the nurse who was taking her last set of vital signs before her release.

It had been a long week and even though Kate was supposed to go home and rest, she was determined to get to Honolulu and hold her sons. There had been several heavy discussions between Kate and Tom, Kate and Uncle, and Tom and Uncle. Each one as determined as the other to do the best thing for Kate. Uncle and Tom wanted her to go home and rest. They had tried to convince her that the twins would be allowed to go home in two weeks and the rest would do her good.

Eventually Kate had won the discussion, simple by announcing "I am a grown women with three children and no one is going to prevent me from going to my babies. I'm perfectly capable of calling a cab. I have my own money with which to buy a plane ticket at the airport and get myself to Honolulu. Not only that, but if Kimo can't pick me up at the airport, Lani will. I've already spoken to her about it."

Both men knew it was useless to continue to argue with Kate, especially after they'd been flat turned down by Susanne to join their way of thinking.

"Those babies need their mother and I need Polly!" she told them emphatically

Tom and Kate had spoken on the phone several times over the last week. After details of the boy's condition were given they would argue in a teasing manner as they discussed a name for the second-born.

"I suppose calling him Angela is out," Tom had teased. This had been the name they had chosen should their unborn have been a girl, and unaware there would be two.

Eventually they had agreed to name the first born Tony, for Tom's father, Anthony, and the second-born Sam, for Kate's father, Samuel. Little colored beaded name bracelets had been put on their tiny wrists declaring their names to the world.

"It's a miracle," Tom had told his wife. "We are seeing answers to the prayers of many." He said softly then kissed the tiny head of his oldest son who slept peacefully, snuggled against his father's chest.

***

Kate was anxious for the flight to be over. Not only did she desperately need to hold her babies, and missed her husband, but she was *also* still sore and in a bit of pain from the surgery. It had happened so fast she sometimes thought it had been a dream. That is until she moved and the stitches that secured her belly reminded her of the reality of the procedure. The doctor had wanted her to go home and rest, but Kate was determined to get to her babies.

"What the doctor doesn't know won't hurt him," she told herself firmly.

People were beginning to assemble for the arrival of the plane. Four sailors approached the magazine counter, having spotted a shapely blond who was engrossed in a fashion magazine. One of them walked up behind Susanne and scared her half to death when he boldly flung an arm around her should and said, "Where have you been all my life?"

Reacting on instinct, Susanne bent her arm and elbowed the sailor in the gut with all her strength. Spinning around and away from his reach, she glared at the doubled over young man demanding, "How dare you!"

The momentum of her turn caused her to go slightly off balance, and as she started to fall, the hand of another sailor caught her.

"Sorry miss, my friend. . ." The sailor suddenly stopped talking as Susanne flung her hair out of her face.

Looking up she gasped. "Mason?"

Mason let go of her arm as if it were on fire and snatched his hat from his head.

"Susanne," he spoke softly. For several seconds neither of them spoke. They could only stare at each other.

All of the people who had stopped to watch after Susanne had elbowed the sailor were now watching the couple who stood like statues.

Without taking his eyes off of her face Mason spoke to the sailor who had been gut punched.

"Apologize to the lady."

"Why? I didn't hurt her," said the sailor who stood rubbing his stomach.

Turning piercing sapphire blue eyes toward his buddy, Mason glared at him for just a second and then returning to look at Susanne, "Because I said so, and because she's ... my wife."

At those words Susanne began to tremble.

Whether from the scare and adrenaline rush of moments ago or from seeing Mason after nearly three years she didn't have the presence of mind to respond to his last words. Nor could she find her voice to speak.

Tom pushed his way through the crowd. Coming to stand protectively next to Susanne he asked if she was okay and in the next instant recognized Mason. Instinctively his hands curled into tight fists ready to do some serious business if needed.

Mason looked from Susanne to Tom and back to Susanne again. He was surprised that he felt a wave a jealousy seeing the two of them together. Several questions rushed through his brain, but he quickly decided not to voice any of them at that moment. He knew Kate had gone off to marry Tom, so why was Susanne in Honolulu with him? He wanted answers but knew now was not the time to ask, and probably not even his business to ask, all things being as they were.

Turning back to Susanne, Tom asked, "Are you sure you're all right?"

She assured him she was fine as she continued to stare at the man she knew she had never married, despite what he'd just said, and to top it off, had abandoned her. Emotions of rage, fear, and sorrow were fighting each other for control of her body.

Father God, help me, she prayed silently.

Finally finding her voice, Susanne asked. "May I speak to you privately Mason?"

"Yeah, sure," Mason replied, as he secured his cap back on his head, straightened his shoulders and gestured with his hand for her to lead the way. The few who remained stepped out of their way.

"I'll be right over here if you need me," Tom told Susanne as she stepped away from the counter.

Mason directed Susanne to some empty chairs in an empty waiting area. He suddenly realized he was nervous. Not because of what he'd done to Susanne, but rather because he realized she was more beautiful than he remembered, and there was a softness to her expression than gave a light to her face that he had never seen before.

At the same time, Susanne was desperately trying to recall all of the rehearsed speeches she practiced should a meeting between them ever occur. She was surprised to realize they were completely gone from her memory. The odd thing was that the longer Mason remained silent the more peace she felt flowing through her spirit.

She smiled gently as she realized that the Holy Spirit was allowing her to feel God's grace and mercy and even though she still had times of feeling angry toward Mason, she also realized as she looked back at his face, that through her faith in Jesus she would be able to forgive Mason.

He's a lost sinner, just like I was. Jesus, he needs you, she prayed silently.

Mason started to speak twice before actually getting any words to come out of his mouth. "Susanne," he spoke softly, and then hung his head like a school boy who was about to be punished. "I'm sorry." Was all he could get out before his words were again choked back in his throat.

Susanne didn't immediately reply, and wasn't sure exactly what she wanted to say. Mason slowly raised his head, and in doing so, noticed her left hand clutching the collar of her blouse. It was then his eyes shot open with surprise when he noticed she wore a cheap wedding band on her finger.

He slowly reached up and took her hand. She watched as he gently spun the ring, and then with a question in his eyes and a quick glance over at Tom who stood like a bodyguard watching the exchange, returned to search her face.

"But I thought . . . You and Tom . . . ?" He spoke totally confused.

Susanne let a small smile play across her lips, and then grew serious. "Mason, I would have married you. I would have taken the words seriously, you know the ones about sickness and health, richer or poorer, till death do us part," she spoke softly and calmly.

"I have a child Mason, your child. Just imagine how tongues would wag about her if they knew I wasn't married!"

Before either of them could say anything else the arrival of Kate's plane was announced and Susanne stood up and turned to leave.

"I now live on the Island of Kauai, just outside of Kapaa. I hope one day you'll take the time to come visit your child. She's a treasure, Mason. Of everything that has happened between us and the stupid decisions we've made, she is truly the most perfect thing either of us has ever done. I'll pray for you Mason." With that she reached up, brushed some lint off his uniform, turned and walked away.

Mason stood stunned, watching her as she walked up to greet Kate, who had just gotten off the plane. He watched as they embraced and then let out a breath he'd not realized he'd been holding when he saw Tom enfold Kate in his arms and kiss her soundly. As the trio started to walk down the corridor, Susanne and Kate both looked over their shoulders in his direction. Kate's expression was that of someone who'd been surprised, and wasn't happy about the surprise. But Susanne's expression was calm and she gave him a small smile and a quick wave as they walked on.

When he could no longer see Susanne, Mason turned and walked back to where his friends were waiting for their flight to the mainland. The look on his face told them not to ask questions. They were pretty sure if they waited until he was good and drunk they'd get the story out of him. What they didn't plan on was Mason remaining stone cold sober the entire flight to California.

He'd originally planned to spend his thirty day leave between his father's house and Vegas, but something had happened to Mason upon seeing and talking with Susanne. He couldn't explain it, but he just knew deep inside that he needed to meet his daughter, and he wanted to know what Susanne had meant when she said she'd pray for him. Both of them had been raised in church going families, but announcing that you'd pray for someone had never been a part of his experience. Something was different about her, and he wanted to find out what.

Cutting his visit short with his family he headed back to Hawaii.

Susanne flew back to Kauai just after Kate's arrival. Alice had been taking care of the rentals just fine, but Susanne was anxious to get back and settle into the routine of life she was beginning to enjoy.

For several days Polly would not let her mother out of her sight, which thrilled Susanne.

The next renter wasn't due for two more days so Susanne used some of this time to play on the beach with her daughter and begin the child's swimming lessons. It was while playing in the gentle surf that Susanne spotted Mason sitting on the sand next to Polly's bucket and shovel. Her heart began to pound and for just a moment her vision blurred. Shaking her head to clear it, she turned her attention back to her daughter, who was kicking her tiny feet with abandon.

"Me swim, mama, me swim!" Polly said laughing as foam from the waves crawled up her back.

"Yes baby, you are swimming," she replied holding fast to Polly's swimsuit.

She chewed her bottom lip trying to decide what to do. She hadn't really expected Mason to come to Kauai to find her. He's been out of her life for almost three years, and only three weeks since they had parted at the airport.

"Why now?" She whispered.

The next thing Susanne knew, Mason, shirtless and with his pant legs rolled up, was walking toward her through the shallow water.

Her reaction to seeing him shirtless surprised and annoyed her. His time in the Navy had certainly helped to improve his already well-developed shoulders and chest muscles. Quickly turning back to her daughter she splashed water on her own face with the hope of masking any blush that was sure to be on her cheeks.

I can blame it on the sun, she said to herself just as he stopped at her side and squatted down to say hello to Polly.

The little girl, who had never known a stranger, looked at him curiously for a moment and then shocked Mason when she pointed at him, smiled broadly and said gleefully, "My daddy."

Susanne's mouth snapped open in surprise, then shut quickly. Mason was so shocked that he fell over backward, soaking his uniform and causing Polly to giggle and clap her hands.

***

Chapter Twenty-One

Upon arrival at the Honolulu airport Kate had been engulfed in Tom's arms. They had clung to each other for several minutes, not saying a word, then had laughed together as each tried to talk at the same time.

A moment later a stewardess stepped up, and to Tom's surprise, he saw that his daughter was in her arms. "Mele," Tom whispered in happy surprise as he reached out to take her in his arms.

"I couldn't leave her behind. I wanted my entire family to be together," she told him, looking lovingly at each member of the family.

This is what it's all about, Uncle thought. *Family.*

Tony and Sam were released from the hospital a few days after Kate's arrival. Tom insisted they stay in Honolulu so she could rest.

At the hotel Kate lounged by the pool while the twins slept peacefully beside her on blankets in the shade of a palm tree that gently swayed in the breeze. Tom and Mele played in the shallow end of the pool, where her bubbles of laughter brought smiles to the faces of several other hotel guests who enjoyed the warm Hawaiian sunshine.

Our time in Hawaii has certainly not been the adventure I thought we'd have when we left California, Kate chuckled softly as she realized that she originally had expected to be living like Tarzan and Jane from the movies, swinging from vines and eating tons of bananas.

"We've certainly got the monkeys," she spoke softly to the twins. As her eyes turned to again watch Tom and Mele, Kate gasped with surprise as she saw Susanne and Polly walking toward her. The smile that had sprang to her face upon seeing her sister vanished when she noticed the black eye Susanne had done a poor job trying to cover. Jumping out of her chair she quickly rushed to Susanne. "Sus, what happened?"

Tom, hearing his wife's cry of alarm, quickly gathered Mele and her water floats and came out of the pool. When he reached them, he too spotted Susanne's eye and swollen lip. Tom hadn't been comfortable with the idea of Mason knowing where Susanne was, and now he could only hope that his sister-in-law's battered appearance had nothing to do with Mason. But his gut was telling him otherwise.

"Let's go back to the room so we can talk privately," Kate said softly to Susanne.

The boys were quickly moved to their double stroller and Tom escorted them all back inside. In minutes Polly and Mele were playing happily on the floor, delighted to be reunited. Susanne had started to cry and it took her several minutes to calm down enough to get the story out.

Susanne struggled at first as she reminded Kate about seeing Mason at the airport. Glancing quickly at Tom, Kate noticed he didn't seem at all surprised at the news and wanted to ask him about it but decided to talk to him later so her sister could continue with the story.

I told him we lived on Kauai, not really believing he'd ever show up given his history the past three years."

"He showed up?" Kate questioned.

Susanne gave a slight shudder and nodded her head. "Yesterday. Just out of the blue he was standing there watching as Polly and I played in the shallows on the beach." Susanne's eyes took on a faraway look as she recalled the last forty-eight hours. "He was pleasant for most of the day. Played with Polly. Posed for pictures with her and even rocked her to sleep for her nap."

Susanne stopped talking then and tears again slipped down her cheeks. She collected herself after a moment and continued. After putting Polly to bed, Mason changed. He got mean."

Kate put her arms around her sister and let her cry. Tom began to pace and Kate noticed he was clinching and unclinching his fists.

"Tom, please sit down," Kate directed firmly.

"Alright, you are safe now; can you tell us what happened? Kate gently asked her sister.

Susanne nodded and took a deep shuddering breath. Looking quickly at Polly and Mele she was glad to note the girls were still caught up with their toys and grateful the boys still slept peacefully. It was hard to enough to tell the next part without having to take care of the children as well.

"At first we talked about how I'd come to live in Hawaii and about how he'd joined the Navy. He asked about the money I received from his paychecks. I could tell he wasn't happy about being forced to give me money, but he didn't say it directly. Then he tried pressuring me into picking up where we left off before he abandoned me. I laughed at him and quite firmly told him it wasn't going to happen. I'd barely gotten the word no out when he...."

"He what?" Tom yelled as he jumped out of his chair.

This caused Polly and Mele to stop their play and for a moment both girls looked as if they would start to cry. Both mothers rushed to their daughters and used the strength that only a mother can possess at a moment like that and willed themselves to be strong to soothe their children.

Tom had sat back down and massaged the back of his neck with his hand. The pulse-beat at his temples was visible and it was all he could do to keep his mouth shut.

After the girls were again playing, Kate and Susanne settled back onto their chairs, and Susanne continued speaking so softly that Tom and Kate had to listen very closely to hear what she said.

"Mason said awful things. He even said Polly was probably not even his." She gave a small tortured laugh. "He actually said that after spending all afternoon talking about how much she looked like him. Then he ranted about being cheated out of his money. I assumed he meant the allotment money I receive. He grabbed my purse and threw everything out on the floor. I asked him what he was looking for and he told me to shut up or he'd shut me up."

As Susanne talked, her speech got even softer; making it harder to understand the words and several times Kate had to ask her to repeat what she'd just said.

"Mason opened my wallet and saw the picture of us taken the first night we ran away. The one I've shown Polly many times. He took it out and began to laugh. It was a weird, crazy, horrible, laugh. He tore the picture into pieces and dropped them on my head."

With glazed eyes that didn't appear to be seeing anything but the story being played in her head, Susanne continued. "He just stared at me, saying nothing, for a minute then grabbed my arm and dragged me to the floor.

"Oh dear God," was all Kate could say.

"I'll kill him," Tom growled.

Suddenly calm Susanne said, "You won't have to.

Tom and Kate both sat up straighter and said at the same time, "Why?"

A gentle smile slowly formed on Susanne's face. "Well for one he was so angry he couldn't manage all the buttons on his pants quickly enough and because a big beautiful Hawaiian Angel came to my rescue."

Seeing the look of confusion on Tom and Kate's faces, she giggled and continued.

"Who?" they both exclaimed.

"James." She smiled brightly.

"He was on Kauai working on a project and had decided he's pay a surprise visit to Miss Polly and me. He had just parked in the driveway and gotten out of his truck when he heard me scream. He practically broke the door down getting into the house."

"Oh, praise the Lord!" Kate sighed and slumped with relief.

"Everything sort of went into slow motion for me from the time Mason grabbed me until he suddenly went flying through the open screen door. Yet it happened so quickly," Susanne said.

"James roared and followed Mason outside. Before Mason could get up off the ground James had him pinned, yelling for me to call the police, and at the same time getting in a few solid punches of his own."

"It only took a few minutes until we heard sirens. Dust flew as two patrol cars raced down the road and stopped out front. I can tell you I was never more happy to see Alice's brother, our favorite police officer, Timmy. The surprise was the occupants of the other patrol car-two mean and nasty looking Naval MP's."

"MP's? Why?" asked Tom

"It seems Mason has been up to his old tricks. He deserted his ship to hunt me down. Apparently he'd bragged about it to some of his buddies. Even told them where he was going. Thankfully someone couldn't keep a secret.

"Timmy told me the MP's were at the station when the call came in," Susanne finished, and let out a big sigh."

Uncle had quietly entered the room during Susanne's tale. He was very excited to tell the family about his visit with the doctor, but quickly realized it was much more important for the family to give all their attention to her and Polly just then.

Noting that Susanne seemed finished speaking, he coughed twice, getting everyone's attention

"I do believe that boy has finally done one honest thing," Uncle said, and laughed at the expressions of shock on their faces. "Yes indeed, Mason has honestly earned a Court martial and long long prison stay."

Later after the family had turned in for the night Uncle went outside and sat down at the lanai table, put his head in his hands, and prayed.

Dear Father God, thank you for the blessing that will come from today. As your Word says in Psalm 27:14, Wait and hope for and expect the Lord; be brave and of a good courage and let your heart be stout and enduring. Yes wait for and hope for and expect the Lord. Father, your word tells us that each person on earth is given free will to choose between your ways and the ways of the evil one. Those who choose your way are not promised a perfect life on earth, but one of pure peace and harmony in the eternal life to come through Jesus Christ your Son. And yet you also promise good things. Help us to remember your promise from Psalm 27:13, What would have become of me had I not believed that I would see the Lord's goodness in the land of the living.

Those who choose the way of evil, may for a time seem to get off easy in life, yet one day they too will stand before your judgment throne and will be cast into the eternal lake of fire for their refusal of your Son's free gift of salvation.

Father, thank you for being my strength and my shield; my heart trusts in, relies on, and confidently leans on you and I am helped. And thank you for the time you are giving me to shepherd my family. I praise you for the unexpected good news from the doctors. In Jesus Name. Amen!

Chapter Twenty-Two

During breakfast the next morning, Uncle shared with the family the doctor's words that still rang clear through his memory.

"Tom, I don't know what you are doing, but keep it up. Your blood pressure is the best I've seen in years. And don't ask me how, but your heart is beating almost normally. Keep this up and your may live to be a hundred!"

Everyone sitting at the table, except Susanne, cheered and with glasses of juice toasted Uncle's good news.

Laughing Kate teased, "Whew, now we won't need to find a new babysitter."

Without saying a word, Susanne rose from the table and went to her room, leaving Kate to take care of Polly.

The lighthearted mood of a moment ago quickly changed to one of concern.

"She seems to be getting worse," Tom said.

Taking his coffee out to the lanai, Uncle sat down on his favorite rocking chair, and slowing rocked and sipped his coffee. Reflecting, he remembered how Susanne had been subjected to several interviews by military personnel and local law enforcement.

The Navy inquiries had ruled that for his actions Mason would be dishonorably discharged and spend twenty-five years in prison. The general opinion of those who had known Mason agreed it couldn't have happened to a nicer guy.

"That guy was like a ticking bomb just waiting to explode," One of his shipmates commented to Tom and Uncle at the close of the legal proceedings.

The months involved in the investigation had taken a heavy toll on Susanne emotionally. When asked if she wanted to go back to Kauai, she had responded with one word. "No!"

***

Shut away in her room with the blinds closed, Susanne had laid on the bed for days and watched the ceiling fan slowing spin. She knew she should get up and get back to the business of living. But nothing had motivated her to move, not even Polly. In her depressed state she couldn't even find the energy to eat much or the words to pray.

It was James who finally broke through the hard emotional wall Susanne had built around herself.

He had stood at the closed bedroom door talking to Susanne, telling her he'd be there whenever she needed him. And faithfully every day he came and read poetry or various verses from the Bible to her. Sometimes he just talked about his day.

Kate was the only person Susanne would allow in the room. Not talking, Kate had watched her sister hoping for some reaction. All she saw was tears that welled up in her sister's eyes.

"I've ruined my life and if it hadn't been for me Mason wouldn't be in prison," she finally told Kate.

"That not true and you know it," Kate firmly replied. "Mason is responsible for his own actions. And he has to live with the consequences."

Susanne didn't reply, Kate noted, as she watched her sister simply roll over and face the wall.

This behavior went on for three weeks. It had taken a few days, but slowly after each time James had faithfully made his daily visit, Susanne had begun to pull herself together. Finally, one morning Susanne bounced out of bed, threw open the curtains and hugged herself. Polly lay in her bed watching her mother and after a moment her tiny voice said. "You happy Mama?"

Susanne picked up Polly and twirled her around the room, causing the little girl to giggle with glee. "Yes precious, Mama is happy and hungry. Maybe I should eat you," she said as she nibbled Polly's tummy.

Hearing the giggles and voices coming from her sister's room, Kate softly knocked on the door and walked in to see the dance Susanne and Polly were having.

Almost afraid to say anything, Kate kissed the forehead of baby Sam who was curled in her arms and whispered. "Sam, I do believe your Auntie has rejoined the living."

Susanne stopped dancing with Polly and gave her sister a beautiful smile. Then a small chuckle erupted from Susanne when she saw the puzzled expression on Kate's face. "It's alright Kate. Everything is going to be alright."

Kate nodded and then cautiously asked, "What's changed? I mean, I'm delighted to see you feeling better. What's happened?"

"James stood outside my window and sang to me last night." She smiled brightly.

"When he finished his song, he crawled through my window, and we had a long talk."

Kate laughed. "He told me that he had something planned, but I thought he was going to knock the door down and drag you out of this room."

Susanne laughed at the thought of James doing something like that, and then threw her arm around her sister's shoulder and announced, "I'm starving. Got anything to eat in this place?"

As they sat and ate breakfast, Kate hesitantly brought up the subject of Mason. "Have you worked through your grieving for all that happened with Mason?"

A dark look crossed Susanne's face but passed quickly. "Grieving for Mason? I wasn't grieving for him. I've just been having a royal pity party. I saw James leaving an interview with the MP's but we didn't have a chance to talk, and I decided he couldn't possibly be interested in me any longer after the truth came out about my not being married when Polly was born. I made myself believe I'd totally blown it with a perfectly wonderful guy."

"But last night he told me he'd known the truth about Mason and I long before the court hearings. He doesn't care about my past. He said he loves me and Polly and wants to marry us," she finished with a giggle.

It took awhile but I've finally realized that I got myself into that situation and I didn't do anything to deserve what Mason did to me or tried to do to me. I'm worthy of love and respect and that is what James is offering me."

"Oh Sus, I'm so happy for you," Kate said as she hugged her sister

After eating, as the sisters stood side by side doing the breakfast dishes Susanne softly said, "Thanks for taking care of Polly while I've been so. . ."

Kate gently put her fingers on Susanne's lips like their mother would have done.

"That's what sisters are there for."

***

Two months later Kate and Susanne hugged, laughed and gathered their bouquets of gardenias and tuberose.

"Well let's get this show on the road before James gets cold feet," Kate teased her sister as they walked out of the house and down the path to the chapel Uncle had had built at the retreat center.

One half hour later Susanne beamed, as she and her groom walked out of the chapel, as man and wife. Neighbors from all over the island and friends from Kauai and Honolulu attended a reception that provided good food, dancing, singing, laughter and love, late into the Kona night.

Christmas Eve
1964

Kate took a few minutes before the evening festivities began to write in the new diary she'd recently purchased.

It's really been five years since we were married on a ship out in the middle of the Pacific Ocean? We arrived on the islands so filled with thoughts of adventure and dreams for our future. There have been so many wonderful changes over the years.

The retreat center has been a huge success. Most of the time we have reservations we can handle.

We have been blessed with three, soon to be four, beautiful children, she wrote as she patted her enlarged tummy. *After their worrisome start, the boys have grown to be normal, healthy, ornery toddlers. And, Mele is a blossoming beauty.*

Susanne and James got married and live in the house on Kauai, mother and father retired and moved here last summer and with Uncle's improved health, I couldn't ask for more.

She had just set down her pen and closed the journal when Tom entered the bedroom.

"Happy Anniversary Sweetheart," Tom announced as he walked up behind her.

"We made it. Or maybe I should say you put up with me for five years." He teased.

Paradise Inherited

Taking her hand Tom helped Kate to her feet. Using her current nickname he lovingly said, "Come on Waddles, it's Christmas Eve and the family is waiting for you so the party can begin.

With glasses of hot apple cider, everyone, guests and children included, toasted the anniversary couple, then settled in to listen to Uncle 'Talk Story' about the birth of the Christ child.

Later as the family gathered outside to watch the setting sun, Tom looked at each person sitting in chairs or on the steps of the lanai, and smiled as he realized it wasn't the money, or property, or investments that were his inheritance. Although very nice to have, he also knew it could vanish as quickly as it came.

"And you can't take it with you," he spoke aloud.

Uncle and Kate, sitting on either side of him, had looked at him when he spoke.

"It isn't about money, is it Uncle?" Tom said. "What we get in this life is like the cake, but the best part is the icing on the cake. A family who shares the same faith in Jesus Christ as Savior, total forgiveness of our life's mistakes or sins, and eternity with God on the New Earth He will create, that is our real inheritance."

Uncle smiled at his nephew and replied, "Hawaii is called paradise by many. And it truly is a beautiful place." He lifted his arms and spread them wide. "You are correct. All of this is just wood, hay, and stubble. It's basically worthless."

As adults left carrying sleeping children, and guests strolled down tiki lit paths, Uncle slowly rocked in his chair, and sighed contentedly, as he gazed at the star filled night sky, and silently prayed.

Father, thank you for answering my prayers in ways I could never have imagined. You have given me more days to my life and a loving family to share it with. And you have taught not only the young, but also this old lazy Hawaiian what it really means to inherit paradise.

***

Tom and Kate were also saying their nightly prayers before turning in, when suddenly Kate's hand flew to her belly.

"Oh!" she gasped, as water began to puddle at her feet. Giggling she looked from the floor to Tom and said, "Merry Christmas. Looks like I'll have another gift for you on Christmas morning."

Tom laughed as he calmly reached for the car keys hanging on a hook next to the bedroom door and said, "Yep, it's just another day in paradise!"

LaVergne, TN USA
20 August 2010
193909LV00006B/1/P